W9-CPY-027

HEATHER GRAHAM

New York Times bestselling author Heather Graham has written more than one hundred novels. An avid scuba diver, ballroom dancer and a mother of five, she still enjoys her south Florida home, but loves to travel, as well. Check out her website, theoriginalheathergraham.com.

DEBORAH LEBLANC

This award-winning author is the creator of the LeBlanc Literacy Challenge, an annual campaign designed to encourage people to read, and Literacy Inc., a nonprofit organization that fights illiteracy in America's teens. For more information go to www.deborahleblanc.com and www.literacyinc.com.

KATHLEEN PICKERING

Believing that stories are excellent tools for teaching life lessons while entertaining, Kathleen wants her characters to overcome their life challenges with dignity, grace and a good dose of humor to deserve that special "happily-ever-after" ending.

BETH CIOTTA

Dubbed "fun and sexy" by *Publisher's Weekly,* Beth specializes in writing romantic comedy with a twist of suspense. She lives in New Jersey with her husband, two zany dogs and a crazy cat. To learn more about her colorful life, visit her website at www.bethciotta.com.

THE KEEPERS:
CHRISTMAS IN SALEM

HEATHER GRAHAM,
DEBORAH LEBLANC,
KATHLEEN PICKERING
AND BETH CIOTTA

H HARLEQUIN® NOCTURNE™

Recycling programs for this product may not exist in your area.

ISBN-13: 978-0-373-88581-7

DO YOU FEAR WHAT I FEAR?
Copyright © 2013 by Slush Pile Productions, LLC

THE FRIGHT BEFORE CHRISTMAS
Copyright © 2013 by Deborah LeBlanc

UNHOLY NIGHT
Copyright © 2013 by Kathleen Pickering

STALKING IN A WINTER WONDERLAND
Copyright © 2013 by Beth Ciotta

HARLEQUIN®

www.Harlequin.com

Printed in U.S.A.

CONTENTS

DO YOU FEAR WHAT I FEAR?

HEATHER GRAHAM

Dear Reader,

People come in all shapes and sizes. They have different backgrounds, different homes and different beliefs. But the message of the holiday season transcends all those differences. The season speaks to us in the language of peace and love.

No matter what we believe, this is inherently true; our time on earth is short, and the greatest gifts we can focus on are health, peace and happiness. Our Keepers are certainly different. Their charges are extremely different. But in all ways, we hope that they'll bring the same message: may you have a wonderful holiday season; may all remember those who need our help; and to whomever we pray, may we pray for peace to all men and find it within ourselves.

Not, of course, that our Keepers won't have a little trouble getting there.... Then again, sometimes, don't we all?

We hope you enjoy, that your trials and tribulations will be small, and that you'll have the best holiday season ever!

Best,

Heather Graham

For families everywhere, in every sense of the word *family*. Sometimes we're bonded by blood, and sometimes by friendship and caring.

Prologue

Winters came with a vengeance to Salem, Massachusetts. When settlers had first come to the shores of the
then colony, many had not survived. Those who had settled Salem and her environs had been devout Puritans,
and they had seen the Devil in the darkness, in the forests
that surrounded the land they worked so hard to cultivate.
They were, in fact, so convinced that the Devil was in the
forest that they believed he also somehow entered their
homes—and from this belief came the terror of the witch
trials. But people learned the bitter lesson of the cruelty
they had perpetuated. Salem's name became famous in
history, the city itself a place dedicated to the awareness
of man's inhumanity to man, where people could learn
from the past so that they never again allowed such cruelty and injustice to occur.

By the twenty-first century, the city welcomed any and
all, embracing those of different ethnicities and becoming
a place where every religion was welcome, from Wicca
to Buddhism to the more traditional forms of worship.

Even now, it was easy to understand how people without electric lights, without communication, could play on

old grievances, look around the woods where natives they didn't understand were lurking, where God only knew what might emerge from the never-ending forests and the land beyond, and fear what they didn't comprehend. When winter came, the wind howled and ice formed on houses. They sat huddled before their fires and feared what lay beyond.

When winter was at its height, darkness came by late afternoon, and they shivered in their homes and prayed for dawn. Then.

But this was now.

And the darkness had never been anything like this.

At first the darkness had seemed to come normally. October arrived, and with it Halloween, Salem's favorite holiday. November followed, and daylight savings time was gone. Then winter came, and with it, shorter days.

And that was when the darkness began to extend its reign.

People would get to work, stare at the sky and say, "Wow. It's not light yet."

Children would get out of school in the afternoon and say, "Wow. It's dark already."

The mayor called the governor; the governor called the president.

The president called the experts at NASA.

But they were all completely stymied. Because the darkness had settled only over Salem, Massachusetts.

For the most part, the citizens of that fair and historic city lived with it. But each day they grew a little more concerned, a little edgier. They became prone to rudeness, to attacking one another. They behaved the way people had a way of behaving whenever they were…

Afraid.

With winter came the holiday season. For the city's

Wiccan community, the winter solstice was the day of highest importance, and while they tried to make it a time of celebration, many were short-tempered, their moods as dark as the sky. Hanukkah was not much better. Now as the community moved to welcome Christmas, their shared but unspoken fear was that Christmas Day would dawn with complete darkness, and rather than being the celebration of rebirth it was meant to be, Christmas would bring something evil leaking from the stygian darkness that enveloped the city.

And even in this enlightened day, they began to wonder.

Was the Devil more than a myth, and was he running loose in the world?

Was he back wreaking havoc in the Salem woods—this time for real?

Chapter 1

The bulb Samantha Mycroft was trying to replace was just above her reach. She swore softly—and then felt guilty.

It was Christmas Eve. One was not supposed to swear on Christmas Eve. In the front yard, next to the tall and beautiful pine she was trying to decorate, the motion-activated Santa was singing in Bing Crosby's voice, cheerfully telling the story of the Little Drummer Boy.

She should not be cursing on Christmas Eve, she thought again.

But, she thought, pausing to look at the sky, this was a most unusual Christmas Eve.

It was dark. Darkness was to be expected at night, of course.

But the darkness had started coming earlier and earlier. At first it had been natural, as fall had come to Salem. But four in the afternoon had become two. And where at first the sun had come out at six in the morning, six had become seven. Then eight. Then nine.

Finally there had been just an hour of light at midafternoon, and today, Christmas Eve, she wondered if even that hour would come, because it had gone from being one hour to fifty minutes, then forty, then thirty....

They kept the Christmas lights on 24/7, which, Samantha was convinced, was why her Never Burn Out! Christmas lights were burning out.

She managed to reach the offending bulb and change it, and then, from her perch atop the ladder, looked up at the sky again.

The news, of course, was filled with the phenomenon. It was centered on Salem, but it had begun spreading— though to a lesser degree—south toward Boston and north toward the Gloucester area. None of the rest of the country was any darker than it normally was at this time of year. Naturally, scientists and meteorologists were having a field day with the situation. They all had theories that explained what was going on, from the extremely esoteric to a strange type of sun flare. How a flare could cause such darkness, Sam didn't know.

It didn't matter.

Their theories were all wrong; she knew that much. Whatever was going on in Salem was being caused by a miscreant in the Otherworld.

"Hey! Pretty lights!"

She heard the deep voice and for a moment, she froze. She knew that voice, though she hadn't heard it in years. It was rich and fluid; it had made her laugh.

And its absence from her life had, once upon a time, made her cry.

She turned quickly, then remembered that she was on a ladder and grasped hold of it, absolutely determined that she wouldn't humiliate herself by falling off and landing at his feet.

With all the control she could muster, she turned regally to look down.

Maybe she was imagining that it was him.... He had disappeared on a Christmas Eve, exactly two years ago now.

She'd imagined nothing.

There he was. Daniel Riverton in the flesh.

As if on cue, the stupid Santa began singing "I'll Be Home for Christmas."

Daniel was tall and appeared lean, but she knew from experience that his shoulders were broad, his chest and arms muscled and honed, and he could move with incredible grace, speed and agility. He was the epitome of "tall, dark and handsome."

Naturally.

Because Daniel was a vampire. And an exceptional one.

He was striking as only a vampire could be; his hair was coal dark and his eyes were that burning, intense hazel often seen among his kind. When he was passionate or angry, the hazel burned with a golden light that seemed more intense than the sun. He looked up at her now, those eyes of his enigmatic, a slight smile curving his lips.

Leave it to Daniel to come back smiling. She wanted to smack him—smack that smile from his face.

And she also wanted to touch him, feel his arms around her again, look up at him and smile and laugh because they were a duo, soul mates.

Yeah, so much for that.

"How are you, Sam?" he asked softly.

"Fine. What are you doing back in Salem?" she demanded curtly.

It would have been nice if he'd said something like *I tried to survive without you but I couldn't. I had to come back to Salem. I don't care about rules or regulations or if we're damned for all time. I can't live without you.*

He didn't.

"I was called back," he told her.

"Oh?" she demanded. She was the Salem Keeper of the Vampires. If anyone had been called back, she should have known about it.

"My father," he explained.

His father. Great. His father, who hadn't approved of a vampire dating a vampire Keeper. Her parents hadn't approved, either, of course. But they had kept their disapproval fairly quiet, telling her that she had to make her own decisions about life.

She shouldn't have had to take on the Keeper role for years, but the International Council had been formed and her parents—having managed the area exceptionally well since their arrival in response to the insanity of the witch trials—had been called to be part of that council. That left her generation, the younger generation, to take on their responsibilities far too soon.

Justin Riverton, Daniel's father, was a pillar of the community. Or had been. Like her parents, he was now serving on the International Council. Everything, all those departures, had happened at around the same time. Daniel, fresh out of law school, had been swept up in the whole council thing, and now, while he didn't sit on the council, he worked for it, going from place to place to settle vampire affairs whenever trouble arose and no local Keeper was at hand.

But the real issue was the age-old taboo against Keepers having relationships with their charges.

That was changing now in many places—newer places than Salem, where the old ways died very slowly.

She knew that everyone had considered what she and

Daniel shared to be nothing but a fling—a silly school thing that would end. They were both excellent students, bright and responsible from an early age. When it was time for them to end it, they would end it.

Despite that prevailing belief, Sam was pretty sure that both her parents and Daniel's had conspired to keep them apart. And, she was forced to admit, her attitude might have had something to do with it. Maybe she'd pushed too hard in her desire for some kind of passionate declaration from him. She'd wanted him to tell her that what they had was too unique, too incredible…too passionate…for him to turn his back on her and leave.

Hadn't happened.

So the fact that he was here now was doubly galling. Not only was she embarrassed not to know he was on the way, his presence meant that the council believed she couldn't keep her affairs, her responsibilities as a Keeper—her charges—in order. That what was happening here was somehow her fault.

Which was ridiculous. Vampires might be exceptionally fond of darkness, but they were not known to have any special powers to create it.

"Well. Nice to see you," she said. There was no reason for her to remain on the ladder—she'd changed the bulb. If she didn't come down, she would look like a coward.

Sam was the oldest of the new generation of Keepers now in charge of Salem's Otherworld. It wasn't an actual title or position, but with all the changes that had taken place, she was more or less the "Keeper of the Keepers." She was supposed to be calm, cool, stoic—wise at all times. Looking like a coward—or appearing unable to handle Daniel's sudden reappearance in Salem on Christmas Eve—just wouldn't do.

She willed her hands not to shake as she started to descend. Maybe that wasn't such a great plan. She was tall, nearly six feet. But Daniel, though only about six-three, seemed to tower over her. And he was standing way too close to the foot of the ladder. He might have moved to give her a little more personal space, but he didn't.

"Uh, good to see you, but I have things to do, so…?" she said.

He smiled—well aware that he was blocking her path back to the house. "It's nice to see you, too. I wanted you to know that, and that I was back in town. I guess we both have things to do."

"Thanks. Now if you don't mind, you're blocking my way into my house," she told him.

Ignoring her, he asked, "Still the best tour guide in the city?"

"You know I love my heritage," she told him.

He grinned and said in a very proper tour guide voice, "In the winter of 1623, a fishing village was established by the Dorchester Company on the shores of Cape Ann. The settlers struggled with the windy, stormy, rock-strewn area, and then a man named Roger Conant led a group to this fertile spot at the mouth of the Naumkeag River. At first they called it Naumkeag, the native word for 'fishing place.' And then they chose Salem, for *shalom,* meaning 'peace.'" He shrugged. "Well, after so many years of peace—years of infamy, too—now we have…this. This darkness."

"Is it dark?" Sam asked, her voice dripping sarcasm. "I hadn't noticed."

He stared at her. "I know that you've noticed."

"Good. Then you don't need to be concerned."

"It's most likely not a vampire matter," he said.

"Which is great—you'll be even less necessary."

"I never wanted us to be hateful toward each other," he said quietly.

Good old Daniel. Always controlled. She wanted him to be hateful—to rage against the powers and circumstances that had separated them. Apparently she wasn't going to get her wish.

"I'm not being hateful," she said with a shrug. "That would require me to actually feel something about you. Please, don't be concerned on that account—I do not hate you. Frankly, and not to be rude, I really don't think about you at all."

What a lie! She missed him every day of her life. Every single day she hurt, trying to figure out exactly what happened, how it had happened...

"Actually," he said. "That was...a smidgen rude."

"I'm sorry. I'm just busy. Seriously, if you don't mind, I have things to do."

He stepped aside. "I'm staying down the street," he said.

The Riverton house had sat empty now for some time, ever since Daniel's parents had joined the council and he had followed, leaving her behind.

"How nice that you still have the house," she said.

He smiled, looking down at her. It was that slow, easy, somehow rakish smile that he had always given her. There was something in that smile that seemed to speak of a unique, sensual relationship, of things shared that were incredibly special and wonderful. She saw all that and more in the smile that he gave her....

Her—and probably dozens of others.

"Happy Christmas Eve," he told her.

"Thanks. You, too."

"I'll see you soon."

"Soon?"

"At your party, of course. I got the invitation. I remember your family's Christmas parties—I've missed them."

How the hell had he gotten an invitation?

Because he was on the damned mailing list. The e-vites had gone out automatically.

Great—just great. He'd not only walked back in on her today—she would see him again tonight.

Oh, joy.

Sam managed to escape him and hurried along the path to the house, willing herself not to trip. It was a cold winter. Plenty of snow had fallen already, snow too easily turned to ice. She would not embarrass herself in front of him by slipping on the ice and landing flat on her backside.

As he walked away, the stupid Santa began singing again: "I'm dreaming of a white Christmas."

She somehow managed to refrain from yelling at it.

Forget Daniel Riverton, she told herself. She would do exactly that.

She *had* to.

Okay, just take a minute, she told herself. *Take a minute; take a deep breath. Stop shaking.* They had been so crazily, ridiculously in love. They'd spent all their time together. And once they'd gone away to college, they'd managed to slip away on regular "excursions," once just to Boston, once to New York City and one glorious time to England, Ireland, Scotland and Wales. There was nothing she hadn't loved about them together, sleeping together, waking together, shivering through horror movies, traveling and meeting interesting people along the way.

Even then, though, there were Others who had lifted their brows in disapproval.

What did they know? Mixed marriages were springing up everywhere.

She gave herself a firm mental shake; she was doing just fine. She was respected—she knew that most in the Other community gave her a thumbs-up. People still kept a wary eye on her less experienced cousins, but she loved them and knew that they would be fine, too—even June, who tried hard to appear strong, though she still felt overwhelmed by her Keeper role.

Sam made a note in her mind to make sure that the walkway was free of ice by this evening. She couldn't have any eighty-year-olds—human or Other—crashing down and breaking a hip.

Tonight was traditionally a huge night for the Mycroft family and for the local Other community—and for those who knew about it and embraced it.

Salem was, in Sam's opinion, an exceptionally fine community, and she felt privileged to be a Keeper here. Yes, at one time the Puritans had persecuted and executed poor human beings who were no more witches than they were angels. But that dark past had ultimately enlightened future generations. Now the city was filled with people of every religion, including the Wiccans—popularly if inaccurately identified as witches—whose presence had done so much to enhance the commercial value of what was now a tourist mecca. Salem was also home to many different Others, from vampires and werewolves to leprechauns, gnomes, selkies and more.

Every Christmas Eve—for centuries now—the Mycroft family had hosted a party celebrating faith, life, belief and love. The guests were of many faiths and many species—the requirement for the human guests, of course, was that they were among the few who knew about the Other community and respected its code of silence.

The world had come a long way from the days of the

Salem witch trials—but not far enough. Knowing that your next-door neighbor was a vampire wouldn't sit well with those who pictured vampires only as vicious bloodsuckers. They could never comprehend that the average, modern-day vampire was an upstanding member of the community—just one who had to survive on a great deal of slaughterhouse blood. Thankfully, due to the council and the widespread alliances that had been formed over the years, that commodity was readily available as long as you knew where to shop.

The minute she got inside, Sam leaned against the door and exhaled.

It was going to be a trying day and an even more difficult night, and she resented the hell out of that. Ever since she had been a small child, she had loved the Christmas season. But this year...

There was the darkness. And the suggestion that it might be caused by a vampire, and that she was failing in her duties as Keeper of the Vampires.

And now...

Daniel was back.

"Think of him as no more than a pesky fly that needs to be swatted," she said aloud.

But even so, there were other problems. Her cousins were distracted, the cousins who should have been helping her.

This was the year Katie Sue was waiting for the love of her life, a selkie who could only return to land once every seven years. Talk about your long-distance relationships, Sam thought. But in truth, she was slightly jealous. Katie Sue was the selkie Keeper and she didn't give a damn. She was in love with a selkie, and the hell with anyone who objected.

Her cousin June was just back from Europe; as Keeper

of the Witches—the real witches, not the city's many practicing Wiccans—she had been studying Celtic ways. She'd also, Sam thought, run away. She'd been madly in love, as well—only to find out the entire relationship had been the result of a spell.

And then, of course, there was her other cousin Rebekah whose greatest rival was also the man she loved, rendering any attempt at romance pointless.

None of them seemed to be lucky in love. Well, Katie Sue thought she was lucky—if seeing the one you loved once every seven years counted as luck.

She straightened. She was being too hard on herself and her cousins. They were good Keepers—especially considering the way they'd expected to have many more years to prepare and had simply been thrown into the fray when the International Council had been formed. They were just… Well, they had their own secret demons living in their souls, but they were able to step up to the plate when they needed.

And so what if Daniel was back? She still had matters to attend to. Mycroft House, first of all. There was a party tonight, darkness or no darkness, and she intended to be ready.

She looked around. The house was beautiful, and she allowed herself a moment's pride.

It was an old house, of course. One of the oldest in Salem. The ceilings were low, and there were no closets in the upstairs bedrooms—the original settlers had used wardrobes and trunks. Back then, bedrooms were not elegant places of repose as they were now. They were where you slept when you weren't working. The original house had consisted of a central hallway running front to back, a left room and a right room downstairs, and two bedrooms upstairs, along with a cellar and an attic.

An addition in the early 1800s had given it a back wing and an upstairs apartment. Right now a gorgeous pine tree sparkled with lights to her right, while a menorah flickered from the mantel. Hard to know when to light the candles when you had a day without sundown. Both religious and secular adornments filled the house, which was colorful and festive—and demonstrated a respect for just about every belief out there.

She'd baked cookies and cakes, so the air was filled with the wonderful aromas of sugar and cinnamon and all things good.

She was ready.

Except, of course, for the last errand she had to run before welcoming her guests for the evening.

She was still leaning against the door when it began to open. She moved away quickly, startled for a moment, even a bit frightened, and then belatedly aware that it had to be her cousin June.

"Hey!" Sam said, jumping back and throwing the door open.

"Oh, good," June said. "You're still here. I was afraid I'd get here and you'd be gone already and I wouldn't know what to do."

"I was about to head out, but thank you for coming over. I really do have to run out for a bit. You're a doll for helping out, and I really need you. This group… You never know how soon people will start showing up. Give Johnny Fields a call. I pay him to keep the ice and snow off the walk. You don't need to do anything, really, except verify that he'll be here and do it. There's a ridiculous amount of food in the kitchen. Everything's ready to go—juice, eggnog, 'special' Bloody Mary mix and regular Bloody Mary mix. I should be back in plenty of time, but in case I'm not, you can go ahead and start serving."

June was as pretty as a picture; she looked like a gorgeous gamin. Of all the cousins, she was the tiniest. She was also…

Eyes wide, June interrupted Sam's thoughts. "Okay, but please hurry. I'm not the hostess you are."

June was just a little overwhelmed, Sam told herself again. She tried so hard to appear refreshed and happy to be home, but coming back had been hard for her.

She loved her craft and her witches. Despite popular belief, even the real ones tended to love the earth, nature and being kind to their fellow man.

Sam offered her a smile. "You're friendly, beautiful and a sweetheart. You're the perfect hostess. The older ladies from the Baptist church sometimes show up early, but they're sweethearts and easy to talk to. The Catholic crew tends to come late, and it's hard to figure exactly when the Protestant groups will arrive. Rabbi Solomon comes really early sometimes, too. I don't expect any of the Others to arrive too early, but every once in a while the leprechauns are feeling feisty. Don't let them goad the Baptists. Okay, I'm off. I'll be back quickly, I promise. I just have to pick up that Christmas mix CD from Mica and the cold-cut platter from the grocery store."

"I'm sure I'll be fine," June assured her, though she didn't sound terribly convinced.

Sam turned and fled the house—and her too-vivid memories of Daniel's return.

She was already in the historic district—Mycroft House was a federal landmark property. All she had to do was hurry down Essex Street to reach Ye Olde Tyme Shoppe, the establishment owned by her friend, Mica Templeton. Mica was a witch—a real witch, not a Wiccan. There was a world of difference. One was a state of being, while the other was a religious choice.

"Hey there," Mica said. She had just been locking one of the cases where she kept beautiful locally crafted jewelry. "I was starting to worry that you weren't going to show up."

"Sorry. I've been running late all day. I forgot I'd promised to do a speech this morning for the Brattle Corporation board—they're looking to open an office in Salem. They're an internet company, and they'll bring us a lot of great jobs, so… Well, yeah, I know, it's Christmas Eve, but I gave the speech anyway."

"Did you take them through the cemetery and do one of your dramatic scenes, then tell them that the poor condemned during the trials weren't even allowed Christian burials?" Mica asked, and grinned. "Then tell them all to take care, because you never know who from history might be wandering the streets?"

"Of course not. I only do that at Halloween," Sam told her.

"And I'm getting ready to close up for your party— where you should be already. This is pretty much it for the holiday season, but I did a lot of business."

Mica usually did a lot of business. She carried gorgeous handmade capes and cloaks, a truly artistic line of shirts and spells, potions, herbs and other paraphernalia for the local Wiccans and tourists alike. Plus the jewelry. At Christmas she added beautiful one-of-a-kind ornaments, along with candles and garlands—and, for the local Jewish community, elegant menorahs.

"I need that CD you were making for me."

"Oh, yes, of course. I'm sorry I couldn't get it to you sooner."

"It doesn't matter. I have to stop at the grocery store on Essex, too," Sam assured her, studying Mica as she went to get the CD.

Her friend was a very pretty woman, with bright blue eyes and pitch-black hair. She turned half of the shop into a haunted house at Halloween. Creatures came out to "attack" the shoppers, who were saved by the "witches who guarded the woods."

Mica returned, holding on to the CD a little too tightly as she studied Sam.

"You've seen *him,* right? You know he's back in town?"

"You mean Daniel, right?" Sam said. "Yes, I've seen him."

Mica nodded. "He's even better looking than I remembered."

"He looks the same. He's good-looking. So what? So are a lot of men."

"Oh, yeah? Then why haven't you dated any other men in the past two years?"

"Looks aren't everything," Sam said.

That caused Mica to laugh. "No, of course not. But Daniel is also intelligent, funny, concerned for humanity, charming…."

"And he left me."

"Hmm. If I remember correctly, you *told* him to go."

"Look, Mica, the International Council was forming and everything was changing. His parents were against the relationship and so were mine. *Everyone* frowned on Keepers seeing their charges."

"*Sleeping* with their charges, you mean," Mica corrected.

Sam glared at her.

"You were totally in love with him. You're *still* in love with him."

"Mica…"

"And *he's* still madly in love with *you.* I can see it.

The two of you really need to cut out the noble crap. I can burn the right incense for the two of you, you know, and say all the right prayers."

"They'd better be prayers and not love spells," Sam warned her.

"Never," Mica promised her. "You two don't need a love spell."

"And *I* don't need *him*. We're dealing with far more serious matters," Sam said.

"The darkness," Mica murmured. "Sam, there's no reason to think a vampire is behind it. I know Dracula is referred to as the 'Prince of Darkness,' but that doesn't mean anything. We both know how much novelists love to go crazy making up legends so they can sell more books. I mean, the vamps—especially the ones here in Salem—have practically been angels for years now, other than an isolated incident here or there. And those are always handled perfectly by the Keepers, of course. But—" Mica suddenly stopped speaking, looking at Sam with wide eyes.

"But what?" Sam demanded.

"Nothing."

"Don't you dare look at me like that and then say nothing's wrong!"

"Well…" Mica said.

"Well, what?" Sam demanded.

"There *is* August Avery," Mica said.

"What about August?" Sam asked, her eyes narrowing. August was a young vampire, a senior in college. Like many his age, he'd taken a bit of a twisted path, experimenting with drugs and causing his share of trouble around town. But none of it had been more than mischief, really, and Sam was sure he was just struggling to find himself the way kids often did.

"He was probably just being August," Mica said.

"By?"

"Well, he was in here muttering about the fact that only vampires know what eternal darkness really means," Mica said.

Sam stiffened. "I'm going to have to talk with him," she said. "And, Mica—" she said, pointing a finger at her friend "—you have to tell me when someone says something like that. This darkness is real, and whatever's causing it, it's nothing to play around with."

As she spoke, the little bell above the shop door tinkled. She swung around to see who'd entered.

Daniel Riverton.

"Daniel!" Mica cried happily. "I'd heard that you were back in town."

Leave it to Mica.

"Great, just great," Sam muttered.

And while Mica rushed forward to give Daniel a welcoming hug, Sam took the opportunity to hurriedly escape the shop.

And another encounter with the love of her life.

The love of her life who had deserted her—even if she *had* told him to go.

Chapter 2

Samantha Mycroft, head high, nodded Daniel's way as Mica rushed forward to greet him.

Sam left the shop; he heard the little bell tinkling—a toll in his heart—as she went past.

"Daniel, so good to see you. What a lovely Christmas Eve gift you are for our community," Mica told him.

If only Sam saw it that way, he thought.

While he was here—had been sent here—because of the darkness, there had been little on his mind except for Sam.

But then, there had been little on his mind besides Sam in all the years he'd been gone.

He knew there were people who believed that love at first sight wasn't real, that everyone had any number of potential matches in the world.

But from the moment he had seen Sam, when they had both been little children, he'd known that she was meant to be in his life. And as he'd grown, he'd known that she was the girl—and then the woman—who was what romantics called a soul mate, the one person he was meant to be with for his entire lifetime.

Life, however, had gotten in the way.

"Mica, it's wonderful to see you," he told her.

She drew back and looked around. "Well, um, sorry. I guess Sam moved on. She's in a hurry today—big party at Mycroft House, of course. And it's left to her now to make sure the tradition continues and all goes well."

"She hates me, Mica," he said flatly.

"No! No, of course not. She's just hurt, and, okay, maybe a little bit mad."

Be that as it may, he was here on a mission. He wished that Sam could understand that the council hadn't sent him to usurp her territory, just to help in whatever way he could. In truth, the council members didn't believe that a vampire was guilty of causing the constant darkness. But, he wondered, was that only because they didn't want to believe? Possibly. In any case, he'd been sent to help, and the logical place to start was with Sam, because she wasn't just the Keeper for the vampires, she was the backbone for the new young community of Keepers.

"She refuses to talk to me," he said.

"Well, you didn't come back to talk to her, did you?" she asked, staring at him. "You're here because of the darkness."

He shrugged. "I'm here with a different perspective on life, too. But yes, I'm here because of the darkness. The council sent me."

"Ouch. Sorry, but that has to make her resent your being here right from the get-go."

"I know, but she's got to get past that. The darkness is out there," he said. "We all, as a community, have to find a way to stop it. It can only be a harbinger of something far more sinister. The whole world could be at risk."

"But it's only in our area," she said.

"For now," he told her. "So I'm no fool and I'm sure

the two of you were talking about me and why I'm back, so what were you and Sam saying?"

"Daniel, I'm friends with both of you—that isn't fair."

"Spill, Mica."

"I can't. Really."

He held her eyes, his gaze steely, and finally she sighed and spoke again.

"Oh, all right," she said. "There's a kid who's been walking around saying stuff, behaving as if he might have something to do with what's going on—even though I'm sure he doesn't. August Avery. Do you remember him?"

"He's really not a kid anymore, Mica. We're only about five years older."

"I think he's just being rebellious. We've all said wild things now and then."

"Thanks, Mica," Daniel said.

"Wait! What are you doing?" she demanded as he walked to the door.

"Going out to support my Keeper," he told her softly.

"Oh, no! She'll know I told you."

"See you at the party," he said, and hurried out of the store. He stopped on the sidewalk and looked up at the sky. Christmas Eve, middle of the day—and the darkness was nearly complete.

Christmas Eve, yes. And he'd seen Sam. His heart ached.

Essex Street was busy with last-minute shoppers—both Others and humans—and even with the ominous darkness, people were stopping to hug and wish each other a happy holiday.

Because Christmas was about love, he thought. Forgiveness, love, family, sharing…

A beautiful season, no matter what religion one believed in.

A beautiful season in which...

He paused in the middle of Essex Street. Salem had witnessed laughter and tears, love and prejudice. Now bright, colorful lights were ablaze in the street at noon.

He looked up to the sky. "Christmas is about another chance, too, isn't it?" he said aloud. He thought about Sam and her sleek auburn hair, her brilliant green eyes. He thought about the way they had been together, both of them opinionated but able to argue and laugh, debate and fall into one another's arms until...

Until the end.

And then they had both just walked away.

"All I want for Christmas..." he said softly as he started walking, "...is Sam." Because he knew now that they weren't responsible for solving every problem in the world.

They were only responsible for doing their part, and then—he prayed it was not too late—for living as if it were Christmas every day of their lives.

Sam needed to find August Avery before the evening festivities began. Because if he didn't show up at the party, she would spend the whole time wondering what he was doing.

Afraid of what he was doing.

Christmas music seemed to be playing from everywhere. Speakers above the open pedestrian mall rang out with "Have Yourself a Merry Little Christmas." One of the "haunted" houses was playing "Santa Baby," and the giant werewolf in the window was dressed in a Santa suit.

That reminded her that she needed to check in with Victor Alden—the werewolf who played Santa for the party every year—and make sure he was ready to go.

She was actually reaching into her bag for her cell

phone when she realized that she was standing right in front of Father Mulroney.

"Samantha!" he said cheerfully, greeting her with a kiss on the cheek. "Merry, merry Christmas Eve."

She offered him a weak smile. She loved Father Mulroney. Everyone did. She had never met anyone as open to different beliefs and convinced of the all-encompassing nature of God's love as Father Mulroney. His heart had room for everyone and he looked for the good in every situation.

"Hi, Father, wonderful to see you. You *will* be at the party this evening, right?"

"I would never miss an occasion where so many hearts come together in good cheer to celebrate the joy of the season," he replied.

Her smile faded. "Oh, Father, I'm not so sure about this year," she said.

He looked at her quizzically. He was a lean man with snow-white hair and bright blue eyes, and he reminded her of Father Time.

"You mean the darkness?" he asked her.

"Yes. It's frightening and disturbing—and I don't know what it means," she admitted. "Father, everyone is worried about the darkness," she added.

"Well, it would be wonderful to find out exactly what is going on," he admitted. "But I'm not worried about the darkness, Samantha. Someone will get to the bottom of it."

"Yes, soon, I hope," she murmured.

He set his hands on her shoulders. "True darkness can only exist in the heart, Samantha. Let your heart be light, and that will do away with the darkness."

For a moment she thought that the day actually became a little brighter.

"You do what you need to do, young lady," he told her. "But remember—light burns from within. It's in the heart and soul of all of us."

Impulsively, she kissed his cheek. "Thank you," she told him. She refrained from saying, *Oh, Father Mulroney, I'm just not feeling that light.*

And she had to go, because time was running short. She had the CD, so now all she needed was the cold-cut platter—and to find August Avery.

"See you in a bit," she said, trying to sound cheerful— as if a light were shining deep in her heart.

She hurried by him.

Ten minutes later she'd picked up the cold cuts, and though she was only a matter of blocks from her house, she wished she'd brought her car. The platter seemed to weigh a thousand pounds.

Like the darkness.

Her cell phone started ringing when she was still a block away from home. She couldn't possibly reach it and had to figure that whoever it was would leave a message, so she could just call back once she'd dropped off the food and headed back out to find August.

When she reached the house, arms straining, June was ready to greet her at the door. She passed the singing Santa—who was using Peggy Lee's voice and singing "Santa Baby"—and made it up the steps to the porch.

"Thank heaven you're here. What are you going to do about the problem?" June asked.

"Problem? What problem?" Sam asked worriedly.

"There's—there's been a bite!" June said in horror.

"Where? Who?"

"Some tourist was watching a band play on Salem Common when all of a sudden she started screaming.

She was rushed to the hospital about ten minutes ago," June said. "I was trying to reach you."

"Ten minutes—how do you know all this?"

"No, no," June said. "It's already on YouTube and Twitter. And the local news is all over it, too."

"Over a bite? Calm down, June. Tell me slowly. Maybe it was a dog bite, or a crazy squirrel, or a bird swooped down and—"

"No, it wasn't a dog, a bird or a crazy squirrel," June said, staring at her evenly. "Come on. I'll show you."

She set the platter on the table next to the turkey Sam had cooked and the two women rushed past the Christmas tree in the formal parlor, the menorah on the mantel and the Nativity scene to one side of the archway and into the family room. The flat-screen TV was on; June had obviously been watching. There was Salem Common, white with snow and filled with people. The Believers, a local group, had been playing Christmas music, but according to the reporter on scene the show had stopped abruptly when a young woman had suddenly begun to scream loudly, leading to chaos. She had received what was by all accounts a human bite; the young man sitting next to her had suddenly lunged closer and bitten her.

"Did you record any of this?" Sam asked June tensely.

"Of course," June assured her.

Sam glanced at her. "Thank you. You're thinking like a Keeper," she said.

June hit the remote. The local station had been airing live from the concert even before all hell broke loose, and they'd done a good job panning the crowd, allowing Sam to slow the recording and search faces.

She gasped. There was August Avery. A handsome man in his early twenties, he was in a wool coat, watching the concert, hands in his pockets. The girl next to him smiled at him, and he gave her a smile back. August bent as if he was about to whisper in her ear, his eyes light, his fingers moving back a lock of tawny hair.

And then the screaming began.

Sam swore. "All right, June, I have to leave the rest of the party prep to you—I'm off to find August," she said, then turned to rush back out of the house.

She opened the door and crashed right into Mrs. Livia Peabody, a local scion of the Baptist church.

"Sam, dear, the house looks beautiful! Am I the first to arrive? I'm always the first—and let me say, perhaps I will also be the first in heaven."

"It's lovely that you arrive so early," Sam said quickly. "June will take your coat. I'm afraid I forgot something, so I need to run out. I'm so sorry."

She sped past Livia before the older woman could stop her.

The plastic Santa began to sing "Grandma Got Run Over by a Reindeer."

Sam raced out to the road, wondering who on earth had thought it was a good idea to put that song onto the playlist of a smiling plastic Santa—and realized that she didn't know where she was going.

Stop, think, she told herself.

The house wasn't far from Salem Common, so she hurried in that direction.

Would August have stayed around?

Perhaps. He might have been eager to see the chaos his actions had caused.

She passed crowds of people on the streets, both locals and tourists. While Salem's main tourist season was summer through to Halloween, people poured in for the holidays as well, because the town and its inhabitants knew how to do Christmas.

Bright lights were shining everywhere, and at least half the people she saw were wearing red and green. But when she listened as she passed them, they were all talking about the tourist who'd claimed she was bitten during the concert.

"At least the poor girl is going to live," one woman said to her male companion, shaking her head as she read the latest news on her smartphone. "Apparently she didn't lose much blood. But the doctor says it was definitely a human bite, which is ridiculous. Humans don't bite."

"Are you sure of that?" the man said with a smile. Remember how James bit the dog when he was two?"

"That's different," she said. "James was teething at the time."

Sam hurried past them, glad to hear that the woman was going to live. As long as she didn't bleed to death, the damage could be repaired.

She reached Salem Common, bright under the lights that had been set up for the concert. People were still standing around in little groups. The live music had stopped; now the music came from a sound box up on the stage.

She saw a couple of local college students talking to Nils Westerly, a young vampire. His friends obviously had no idea what he was or they would have run away shrieking, considering the earlier events.

Sam headed toward him with long strides. He saw her and went pale.

"Nils!" she called, then asked, "Did you see August Avery here earlier?"

"Um, hey, Samantha," he said, his expression uneasy. "Meet my friends Charlie Sizemore and David Hough."

She nodded curtly to both men.

"Wow, Nils, you should introduce us to all your

friends," the man named David said. "Nice to meet you, Samantha." He offered her a hand, his smile obviously flirtatious.

She smiled back briefly but ignored his hand. "Nils, where's August?"

"I don't know. I swear I don't know, Samantha," Nils said. There was a pleading tone in his voice. "He was here earlier, but then I lost sight of him. He's been depressed lately."

"Depressed? Why? What has he been saying?" she demanded.

"His girlfriend left him," Charlie offered. "He was madly in love with her—and she just up and left him."

"When?" Sam asked.

They all looked surprised by her interest, but they answered her anyway.

"Uh, I'm not sure," David said. "Recently. He was crushed—went on and on about Christmas being a sham, that there was no love in the world and when love did exist, the world conspired to make it end badly. He says he hates what he is… Though, you know, I didn't get that, 'cause honestly? His grades are great, and he's on the football team—a starter."

"Do you have any idea where he hangs out?" Sam asked.

"He likes to walk around the Old Burying Ground," Nils said.

"Or Dead Horse Beach," Charlie said. "Crazy—middle of winter, the guy likes to hang around at the beach."

Sam inhaled a deep breath. From the Common she could see the Gothic edifice of the Salem Witch Museum. It was one of the best venues in the city if you were looking for a concise history of the witch trials, she thought.

She just hoped August Avery's stupidity wasn't going to plunge them into another dark era worthy of a museum.

"Thank you," she told the boys, then turned and hurried away from the Common, passing last-minute shoppers and carolers.

It wasn't late; it wasn't even evening yet—it just felt like it because of the darkness.

She passed the Hawthorne Hotel and raced back down Essex Street, turning to head toward the Old Burying Ground.

A sign announced that it closed at dusk. As if that word meant anything anymore!

Despite the holiday, a few people were visiting the memorial connected to the cemetery, sitting on the benches provided for visitors paying homage to the innocents who had been executed. She'd always thought the place was beautifully done and that there was something extremely special and poignant there, especially in winter, when the tree limbs were skeletal and the old gravestones rose beyond the memorial in the cemetery itself.

She hurried through the memorial area and entered the cemetery.

Gravestones broke through the snow that covered the ground. She hurried through them, thinking of what it had been like growing up in Salem—knowing the town's history, learning the lessons of tolerance born of hate.

"Samantha!"

Startled at the sound of her name, she turned quickly. For a moment she didn't see anyone. Then old Ogden Taylor—a benevolent ghost who often chose to haunt the cemetery—materialized.

Ogden had been arrested during the witch craze, but when the governor disbanded the first court and refused to allow spectral evidence, he had been judged innocent.

Luckily he'd had the money to pay for his time in jail and his chains, and he had lived another forty years.

"Ogden," she said, smiling.

"Merry Christmas Eve," he told her, and smiled back. She felt the cold touch of his fingers on her cheeks. "Dear girl, what are you doing running around in the cemetery? You should be getting ready for your annual gala."

"Ogden...I have to find one of my charges. August Avery. He bit someone, and I'm worried that he... The darkness... Oh, never mind."

"Oh, dear! That's certainly a shock. And on Christmas Eve." Ogden had long, curling gray hair that gave him a dignified look beneath his hat. He wore a handsome frockcoat and carried a cane. He looked at her curiously. "Were you saying you think this fellow has something to do with the darkness? Doesn't seem like something a vampire could manage."

"I don't know, Ogden. I know we all have to worry about it, though. And I know that I have to find him before he bites someone else."

"He was here," Ogden said.

"He was? But he's gone now?"

Ogden nodded somberly. "He came through, sat on a grave, cried like a baby—then hopped up and jumped the fence down to the street. I tried to talk to him, but you know how it is. People don't hear me or see me unless they choose to."

"Thank you, Ogden. Thank you so much."

"I'll see you later—I love to slip into your house during the party. And don't worry—I won't materialize and scare anyone, I promise. I just love all the love that fills the house when you have everyone over."

"You're always welcome," Sam assured him.

She went into vampire mode to give herself added

strength and speed, grateful for her Keeper ability to take on the characteristics of her charges, then leaped over the fence and raced down the street. Dead Horse Beach was a fair way off; she had to hurry if she was going to get there in time to prevent further trouble.

She ran past the crowds still thronging the streets, past the brewery where the Christmas celebrations seemed to be in full swing. She raced by one of her favorite tourist attractions: a popular museum housing an array of movie monsters.

But she couldn't pause to think about the things she loved about Salem. She couldn't even pause to think about the words that Ogden had spoken: that he loved the love that filled her house on Christmas Eve.

Those words made her think about Father Mulroney, too.

Light burns from within.

Well, her light didn't seem to be shining very brightly anymore.

She realized she probably should have taken her car if she didn't want to be noticed because a woman racing down the street as if the hounds of hell were at her heels didn't really blend into the crowd. Once she made it out of the busy tourist area, she slipped behind a tree and emerged as a bat, which would certainly raise a lot less notice than her other available option: a wolf.

At one time, Dead Horse Beach had been well beyond the residential area and, legend had it, people would therefore use it to bury their dead horses. Eventually it became known as Dead Horse Beach—a strange name for a beautiful little spot of land. It offered a view to the northwest, making it a popular place to watch sunsets in the summer.

In winter…

In winter it was a cold stretch of sand near Willows Park, fringed by the skeletal brush and trees of winter, frigidly cold when the night wind blew.

Sam gauged her abilities as she flew. She didn't change often, and her sonar wasn't good. Near the House of the Seven Gables, she swooped low. Something was going on at the property—something that created a burst of light against the darkness.

A holiday bonfire surrounded by laughing partygoers.

Salem residents were a resilient lot. They would have their holiday parties no matter what.

She was glad of that. Concentrating, she lifted herself higher into the sky. She passed over residential streets and out where the houses thinned out, and soon she was soaring above Willows Park and wishing that she could smile as she heard the laughter of children. There was snow on the ground, and the air was crisp and cool, but it wasn't a bad night for winter. This year they even had the 1866 carousel up and running, and the children loved it.

She got to the beach at last and made an awkward pitched landing on the frosty sand as she shifted back into human form and stumbled to her feet. She saw someone standing in about a foot of ice-cold water.

"August! August Avery, what in the world are you doing?" she called to him.

He looked back at her.

It was a day with no sun, and the moon had yet to rise in the sky over the gray clouds of winter. From a distance, Christmas lights twinkled as if they were colorful little rays of hope.

"Sam!" he said. "Sam, I'm sorry."

Then he turned and continued walking into the icy sea.

Sam rushed into the water. It hit her flesh like a wave

of knives, it was so icy cold. "August!" she shouted again as the salty spray shot up over her face and onto her lips.

She struggled to keep her footing. The waves were vicious. She was still in the shallows, but the swells threatened to bring her down.

She wondered how long it would take for hypothermia to set in.

"August!" Despite the spray of frigid salt water that stung her lips, she kept calling him. She couldn't see him. He must have gone into the water. Then, twenty feet away, a head popped up.

August Avery was dead set on drowning himself. She allowed herself a small grim smile at the pun.

She plunged after him, her heart thundering. She couldn't let him die.

She could have sworn she heard the distant sound of her plastic Santa singing.

"Oh, holy night..."

Chapter 3

Nearly too late!

Daniel Riverton had seen the news and recognized August, and he'd done some investigating among the kid's friends and found out about the breakup. He'd even found the girl who had ditched August, and frankly, he hadn't been impressed.

Her name was Ciara Mullins, and she'd been sulky and rather full of herself when he found her hanging out with a group of her friends. A pretty thing, yes, but vacant and empty, and not in the least concerned with anyone else. The great thing about being a vampire was that he could look at her, capture her gaze with his own and get anything out of her that he wanted, silently compelling her to tell the truth.

She was convinced that she was just passing time in college, getting a degree only to mollify her parents. When she graduated she was going to head to New York City, where she would walk around in Times Square until she was discovered. Agents and directors would flock to her, of course. She was beautiful.

If the situation hadn't been so serious, he would have

found it all a bit amusing, because she was speaking honestly, compelled by his will and demand for the truth. When she finally finished speaking about herself, she went on to August Avery.

He was very cute, she admitted. He had *something*. Some kind of mystique. But she was above a relationship with anyone in Salem. The world was waiting for her. And he was such a silly boy. He loved to go on long walks at Dead Horse Beach—even in the middle of winter.

Daniel left Ciara in the midst of her friends, who were all staring at her, stunned and appalled.

He didn't feel guilty that he'd forced her to bare her soul. Her soul could use some help, which just might come her way now in the form of a serious wakeup call from her friends.

But when he reached Dead Horse Beach, following up on what she had said about August's fondness for the place, he was afraid he was too late. Looking out, he saw nothing at first.

And then…something, a leap of motion in the depths of a wave. He narrowed his vision and focused, and he felt as if his heart leaped into his throat.

August Avery was out there, all right—struggling like crazy with Sam.

Daniel was good at everything vampires were supposed to be good at—he'd been forced to be, enduring hours of training with the council. Vampires were like everyone else, really. Some people had a talent for music, some for art and some with numbers and gadgets and electronics. He had never been fond of turning into a bat or a wolf. He'd grown up being taught that all creatures had a right to walk the earth, and that a man—any man—owed compassion and aid to every creature on the earth. Becoming a wolf or a bat did nothing to further any of those ends. However, he'd learned to use his speed, his tremendous strength and the power of his mind to compensate for his unwillingness to shift. And so, in the blink of an eye, he was out there in the water, wresting the struggling August away from Samantha, who had to be growing exhausted.

After all, she was only using borrowed powers—the gift every Keeper received.

But those powers could never equal his. On the other hand, she had what he never could: humanity. The ability to really see and appreciate the sunlight, to function as effectively in the light as she did in the dark.

None of that mattered now, though. The water was close to freezing and while August Avery was a fool, he wouldn't die, only turn into a popsicle.

Samantha, on the other hand…

"My God!" Sam gasped, head just above the water. "He really is intent on this!"

"I've got him—I've got him. Get yourself out of the water," he told her.

She nodded. He'd always respected her for being realistic about her own abilities and limitations, as well as those of everyone around her, both human and Other. She could be stubborn, but not when it came to getting something done.

She made it to the shore, although once she crawled up on the sand she started shivering so violently that she almost seemed to be engaged in some form of St. Vitus dance.

Daniel tossed August, who was gasping and choking, down on the sand by her side. Then Daniel used his enhanced ability for speed to burst into a nearby convenience store and rush back with a huge thermal blanket that he wrapped around her—making a mental note to find a way to pay the owner later.

August shivered and sputtered, but not for long.

"What are you trying to do, August?" Samantha demanded. "Don't you know it's impossible for you to drown?"

"But not Samantha," Daniel said harshly.

"I bit someone," August said, his voice filled with self-disgust and loathing. "I bit someone. I don't know what happened to me. I was upset…hurt. I don't know. I wanted to feel…better. No, strong. As if I couldn't be hurt. I was horrible. I deserve to die."

"You didn't kill her, August. She's going to be all right. She'll have some nightmares, and she'll be sick for a few days, but she'll be fine. Yes, you behaved badly—horribly. What you did threatens our very existence. But you're lucky. We're all lucky. She didn't die, and what happened can be explained as a college prank, someone going a little loopy. And you stopped, that's the point. The good in you won out. You hurt her, yes—but you stopped. You're not a killer. You did know better," Daniel said. "That doesn't demand a death sentence."

August looked at them both. "Oh, yeah? I betrayed us all. I was evil at heart. I brought on the darkness!"

Daniel was startled when Sam laughed at that.

August appeared to be indignant. "What? You think I couldn't have caused this?" he demanded.

"August, I don't think any vampire could have caused this," Samantha said. "I wish I could believe that it was a vampire—because then I could do something about it. But I think it's a different form of Other who brought this about. It's just not in our realm. Not to mention that the darkness began before you bit that girl—the darkness has been coming on for a while now."

"So what? Is it going to last forever?" August asked. "I can't bear it!"

"Hey," Daniel said, hunkering down by him. "Vampires love the dark. We shouldn't be suffering the way so many other people and Others are. Fairies—they must be struggling. And the leprechauns—when it's dark too long, they get ridiculously grumpy. And human beings—they get seasonal depression, cabin fever. Come on, August. It can't be that bad."

August looked at Samantha. "I am so sorry. I really didn't want to hurt that woman. I just—I just want to stop the hurt in *me*."

"As your Keeper, and since you did stop before really hurting that poor woman at the concert, I am willing to think about probation," Samantha told him. "What you did is wrong, but you know that. Come on, August—it can't be that bad."

"I think—I think I was caught on video. People will know what I did," August said.

"I can get in and get rid of the video," Daniel said.

Samantha nodded. "And one of us can go see the victim. A little hypnotism will get rid of her memories." She smiled. "You might deserve a little jail time, but I don't want attention focused on the vampires. You don't need to learn remorse—you know remorse. Except that you know damned well that you can't drown, so what were you trying to do?"

"I thought if I froze, perhaps my head would break off," August said.

"August! That's terrible. You have a family—people who love you."

"You think? My father is always furious with me."

"Fathers are always furious with their sons," Daniel assured him.

"I don't want to live," August said bleakly.

"August—all this over a girl?" Samantha demanded. "Come on. Life is like that for all of us—sometimes we fall in love with someone who just doesn't love us in return. But we get over the hurt and move on. And if *you* can do that, then the right person can find you—the person who appreciates you for all the incredible things you are."

"It's not just Ciara," he said wistfully, meeting Samantha's eyes. "It's the world. Love has left the world. That's why it's dark. No one loves anyone anymore." He waved a hand in the air. "No one stays together. Nothing means anything. Why bother?"

"Of course people stay together," Samantha said.

"My parents are talking about splitting up," August said. "Love is all a lie, a joke. Christmas cheer, the spirit of the season—hah!"

"You're wrong," Samantha said passionately. "There's a *lot* of love and goodness out there. All the time. The point of the holiday season is that it's a good time for all of us to stop and think about what we have, about all the wonderful things in our lives."

"Yeah? Well, what are they?" August demanded.

"Come on, August," Daniel said, shaking his head. "Life may be tough right now, but you have a lot to be grateful for—you had it good growing up. And you're special."

"Yeah, *special.*"

"Privileged," Sam said, her patience growing thin. "You're a vampire. You have strength that others couldn't begin to possess. You can literally soar, and you can run like the wind. Yes, you have responsibilities, too, because you're part of a special breed. But you have people who love you, an entire community that cares fiercely for you, and if one love affair goes wrong, you can move on and look for the next."

"What are you talking about?" August asked. "Look at the two of you. Yes, I know about the two of you." He stared at Samantha, then Daniel, and finally returned his attention back to Samantha. "Everyone knows about the two of you. You were the perfect couple. But the world threw a monkey wrench into things, so you two just caved in and threw everything away."

Samantha was obviously taken by surprise. She turned bright red and gaped at August for a moment, and strained *not* to glance in Daniel's direction. Her jaw seemed to be locked hard.

"August—" she began, but he cut her off.

"Yeah, right, it's Christmas Eve. I have to be cheerful, look on the bright side of things. Except it's dark as pitch out here."

"Yes, and I think you enjoyed pretending that you were causing the darkness," Samantha said.

"Because I *am* dark," August said.

"Drama queen, more like," Daniel commented.

"You're being an immature brat, if you ask me," Samantha said.

Daniel almost laughed. She'd been trying so hard to be gentle with August, but when she finally lost her temper, it seemed to affect him more than anything else she had said.

It was his turn to grow flustered. "I—I— Uh, yeah. I'm sorry."

"You're hurt and you're lashing out," Samantha said. "And I'm freezing. Could we move this conversation back to my house? The party has started by now, and we're going to go in looking like drowned rats—not to mention I think I have icicles dripping off my nose."

"I'm so sorry," August said. "I really didn't want to hurt you, Samantha."

"August, you don't really want to hurt anyone," Sam said. "I can see that. We can both see that."

"Let's go," Daniel said. "Sam is freezing." As much as he disliked it, sometimes there were no other options, so he transformed himself into a bat, assuming the other two would quickly follow.

August flew with him, but he realized that Samantha was missing and looked back down toward the beach.

She was struggling, wet and soggy, on the sand, one wing dragging.

Swearing softly, he swooped down beside her, transforming back into a man. August quickly followed suit, as did Samantha, though she changed more slowly.

"Okay, so this isn't going to work for me when I'm this soaked," she said. "You two go ahead and get back and—"

"Not in this lifetime," Daniel said. "We head back together. We'll just go on foot."

"That will take us forever," she said.

"Then we'll call a taxi." Daniel reached into his pocket for his cell. He began to key in a number, then realized his phone was soaked.

"I threw mine in the bushes," August said. "I'll find it." He emerged a moment later. "I was going to call Ciara and tell her I was killing myself because of her," he admitted.

"Did you?" Daniel asked him.

"No, I chickened out," August admitted.

"No, you were smart," Daniel told him.

"Really?" August asked.

"You don't want her having that power over you," Daniel said. "Trust me—you're going to get over her. And when you're over her, you're going to be glad that she never knew you wanted to call it quits because of her."

August looked at Samantha, waiting for her opinion. "I don't know your girlfriend, but—"

"Ex-girlfriend. She dumped me, remember?"

"I don't know her, but I do know you. Yes, you've made some trouble, you've let her lead you around a little bit. So let me be blunt. Use this occasion to grow some balls. You can be whatever you want to be. Get over this and move forward. Decide on a dream and go for it."

"She *was* my dream!" August said.

"Don't be an idiot!" Sam said, growing impatient. She was really freezing now, and she needed to get home. "I told you to grow some balls."

Somehow, Daniel managed not to laugh at the stunned expression on August's face as he said, "All right, let's get going." He knew Sam wasn't going to manage the trip on her own, so he swept his arm up to transform and enwrapped her in his hold before she could protest. She realized his intent.

She didn't protest. She had to have been really cold. At his side, August Avery transformed, as well.

A moment later they were flying. The night air was cold, but he kept her within his hold and protected her from the force of the wind, keeping her as warm as possible while managing a decent level and speed.

He tried not to tremble at having her so near after so much time apart, but it was impossible.

He'd learned a lot in the past two years. They'd both been way too young when the council was formed, dutiful children who had behaved in a way they had considered responsible, by virtue of their birth.

What they had lacked was wisdom and a sense of perspective.

And the knowledge of just how rare it was to find the kind of love they had shared.

And now that he knew those things…

It was too late.

Samantha had taken on not only the vampires but all of Salem as her responsibility. She was there to guide her cousins, to watch out for everyone. She had grown up and grown strong, and she had closed her heart to him.

He'd dreamed of a chance to come home for Christmas and get her alone, leading to a passionate declaration. In two years, he hadn't forgotten a thing. They'd both been swept up in the nobility of serving, when there had been no need. They could serve and still be together. Others had feared for them. That was understandable. But those Others had been wrong. He had never stopped loving her; he had never strayed from her. All he wanted was a chance.

And now the darkness might give it to him.

Because while he didn't believe it was a vampire matter, he knew that Samantha's feeling that the whole town was hers to protect meant it was still her responsibility.

They could stand strong together, he thought.

If only she would let that happen….

Chapter 4

When they neared the center of town, Daniel slowed down to a less noticeable pace and August fell into step beside him.

"We can't exactly walk into your party looking like this," Daniel said to Samantha. "But my house is nearby, so let's get over there and dry off."

"Have you suddenly started carrying a supply of women's clothing?" Samantha asked him.

"No, but I can get you in front of a fire while you figure out what to do next."

She nodded, and they hurried down the street toward his house.

Like Samantha's home, it was old, with low ceilings and exposed beams throughout. Sam had to admit the Rivertons had done a beautiful job, sticking with the old but bringing in the new. There was something that spoke of a long-ago gentility in the parlor: the drapes were heavy damask, and the hand-hewn furniture was covered in shades of royal blue and crimson. But they rushed by the formal parlor and back to the family room, where the double fireplace—which opened to the parlor on the other side—was framed by a mantel that held family pictures going back generations. The furniture was comfortable, soft leather, and a wide-screen TV hung on one wall, while another held a stereo system and shelves of games, DVDs and hundreds of books.

They had barely entered the room when Daniel lifted then extended one hand toward the fireplace.

A blaze immediately rose up.

She stared at him, astonished. Fire starting wasn't a known vampire talent. In fact, on the whole, vampires weren't terribly fond of fire. It was the one element that could destroy them.

"Where did you learn that?" she asked him.

"Cool!" August said.

"Not so cool, really," Daniel told August, then turned to Samantha and grinned at her ruefully. "Sorry—that's not a vampire talent, as you know. Motion detector. My father met an elf in Stockholm who's quite the inventor. He came over and set up the house for Dad. Lights, music, fire—you name it, all it takes is the proper wave of the hand." He shrugged ruefully. "Only problem is, sometimes I'm just walking through and the lights go on and off, the fire pops up and the house turns into a boom box with Frank Sinatra—my dad's favorite—blaring loud enough to wake the neighborhood."

"Oh," Sam murmured. "Well, I guess there's good and bad to everything." She took a seat on a little ottoman before the fire and extended her hands, grateful for the warmth.

"I'll take August upstairs and get the two of us into dry clothing. Why don't you give your cousin a call? See if she can escape for a minute with some clothes for you? Or I can whirl down the street and pick something up," he said, smiling. "If I take anything, I'll pay for it, don't worry."

"It's all right. I'll give June a call," she said.

August and Daniel started up the stairs. Sam gave her fingers another minute to thaw, then went looking for a phone, since her cell had drowned even if August hadn't. She found a landline and quickly dialed June's cell.

Her cousin answered after the first ring. The minute Sam identified herself, June said worriedly, "Sam, where are you? The party's already started."

"I'll be there soon, but I need your help," Sam told her.

"My help?" There was a touch of panic in June's voice. "I was hoping you'd show up soon because I could use *your* help. The Episcopalian priest, Father Alistair, brought his three-year-old, Tobey, because his wife isn't feeling well and can't watch him, but he's so busy having a heavy philosophical discussion with Rabbi Jenowitz that he's forgotten about Tobey, who so far has tortured the cat and nearly knocked over the Christmas tree," June said with dismay. "I did manage to save the Nativity scene."

"I'm so glad. Listen, is Katie Sue or Rebekah there yet?"

"Um, Katie Sue just came in."

"Good. Turn the party over to her and bring me something to wear really quickly."

"Okay, bring it where?"

"I'm at Daniel's house."

Sam supposed she shouldn't have been startled by the silence that followed. Even June—who had been away so much—knew that she and Daniel had been in love, and that he had broken her heart. She could hardly be blamed for wondering what Sam was doing at his house and drawing the obvious conclusion.

"It's not what you're thinking," Sam said hurriedly. "We found the biter, but he wasn't vicious, just heartbroken. Anyway, I can explain all that later. Right now I just need some clothes."

"But why?" June lowered her voice. "Daniel didn't… didn't…?"

"No! I told you, it's nothing like that. I'm soaked, that's all. We had to save the biter from trying to drown himself. Please, June, just hurry up and bring me something to wear."

"Okay." June sounded relieved. "Katie Sue can chase Tobey around the Christmas tree and save the cat. She's a complete emotional wreck, if you ask me. She wants to be on the beach by seven."

"Dead Horse Beach?" Sam asked dryly.

"Yes. So I'd better hurry or she'll have my head."

"Thanks," Sam told her, then hung up. She wasn't sure whether to be grateful, relieved or irritated. Who the hell fell in love with a selkie? Especially a selkie Keeper. Too bad no one had objected to Katie Sue's romance the way they had to Daniel and hers. *Seven years!* Way too long to miss a lover.

She could barely imagine it. She hadn't seen Daniel in nearly two years, and…

And seeing him again now only made her want him again. A world of time had gone by and everything had changed, and at the same time nothing had changed.

Because Daniel was still…Daniel.

She heard the knocking at the front door while Daniel and August were still upstairs. Sam hurried over and threw it open, and there was June. She was carrying a big, cheerfully decorated Christmas gift bag.

"It's your party clothes," June said. "It seemed like the best way to get it out of the house."

"Thank you, thank you!" Sam told her. Grateful that the men were still upstairs, she took the bag and hurried back over to the fire, where she stripped down to her underwear.

"You're going to leave those on? You'll catch a cold," June warned her. "I brought dry."

Sam glanced at her cousin. She wanted to run over and hug her. June was the sweetest soul in the universe. She cared, really cared, about people—and not only those she knew and loved, but everyone. And yet she still seemed nervous to be back here, dealing with her Keeper duties.

Sam didn't get a chance to answer as she quickly slipped into dry underwear. She realized she'd made a dumb move, changing by the fire instead of behind closed doors. She could hear Daniel and August coming down the stairs.

She swore softly.

What was she doing? Here it was Christmas, and she was swearing. What on earth was wrong with her?

She heard a sharp whistle. August was just ahead of Daniel as they came down the stairs. He was grinning ear to ear as he looked at her.

She looked up and met Daniel's eyes—and saw the fire that had always burned so fiercely in them when he looked at her.

His mouth curved into a little smile of amusement.

Sam left her wet clothing by the fire, clutched the bag to her and ran for the kitchen. As she struggled into the soft red sweater June had brought her, she could hear her cousin speaking with Daniel and August.

"So…Daniel. You're back in town."

"Yes. For the time being, at least."

"Ah."

"I'm afraid my work means traveling," Daniel said.

"Of course it does," June said sweetly. Hearing her, Sam smiled. Her cousins were always there for her. As sweet as it sounded, June's voice had the slightest edge.

"I'm August Avery," August said.

"How do you do?" June asked.

"Um, we've actually met, though I haven't seen you in a while. You look...very lovely tonight."

"Thank you," June told him.

"Like your cousin," August added. "I guess we Others are pretty lucky here in Salem."

Thank you, August. You were a jerk and made a wreck out of Christmas Eve, but you seem to have redeemed yourself.

Sam quickly slid into the silky black pants June had brought and hurried back out to the family room. Daniel was wearing a red sweater, too. And black pants. It almost looked as if they had dressed as a couple for the party.

She looked quickly away from Daniel and met August's gaze. "August, you look dry, warm and ready for a great party."

His smile wavered for a minute. "I guess."

"So we're ready to head back?" June asked anxiously.

"I just need two minutes," Sam said. She was carrying the socks June had brought, and she checked and found that luckily her boots had almost dried. In seconds she had them on. Not bad. She didn't even squish when she stood.

"Okay," she said cheerfully. "Let's go."

As Daniel locked the door behind them, he arched a brow at Sam. She shrugged, and he walked ahead with August.

"What's going on?" June whispered to Sam as they followed. "What's he doing here?"

"He's been sent back by the council. They're worried about the darkness."

June looked at her hopefully. "You think a vampire is causing it?"

Sam hesitated. June looked so hopeful that she hated to disillusion her.

No, I don't. I believe it's some kind of dark magic, she thought. *As in witchcraft.*

But she couldn't say that.

"I don't know, June. Vampires don't really have that kind of power. The whole council sent Daniel because he's a troubleshooter and we need a little help, not just because he's a vampire."

"And he came to see you because you're responsible for all of us?" June asked.

Sam set an arm around her shoulder. "We all have to be here for one another, right? And isn't that kind of the Christmas message? I mean, it doesn't matter where people come from or what they believe, the message of Christmas is all about peace and forgiveness and loving one another. So there you have it. We all need to be here for each other. Maybe that's how we'll disperse this darkness." June tried to smile, but Sam knew her cousin was worried. "I mean it. We'll all be here for one another."

She realized suddenly that they had reached her house, that Daniel and August had stopped and had heard her last words.

"Here for one another," Daniel repeated, his eyes on hers. They seemed to glow with that unique gold particular to his kind—a gold that couldn't be read.

"Well, we're here and I need to get inside," Sam said. "August, you *will* have fun, you *will* celebrate the spirit of the season—and you *will* find joy."

"Okay, okay, joy of the season," he said, though he didn't sound entirely convinced.

She linked her arm with his and started toward the house.

As she headed up the walk, the plastic Santa began singing again. This time the song was "Baby, It's Cold Outside."

"We'd all better stay inside, then, huh?" Daniel said lightly.

Sam refused to turn around.

What the hell was she thinking when she bought that stupid Santa?

As she walked inside, three-year-old Tobey went flying past her, carrying one of the garlands that had been on the tree. Katie Sue was racing right behind him, but she skidded to a stop when she saw the newcomers. Her hair was in slight disarray and she was panting.

"Thank God you're back!" she told Sam.

Meanwhile Tobey was heading into a part of the house where he had no business. Sam immediately went after him, sweeping him up into her arms. He let out a shriek and fought against her. "Oh, no, young man," she told him. "You are not going to single-handedly mess up a holiday tradition."

"Down!" Tobey shouted.

"No," she said firmly.

With the wriggling child in her arms, she returned to the entryway. Katie Sue was getting into her coat and scarf. "Thanks," Sam told her.

"I just… I'm sorry, I have to go. Seven years is a long time," Katie Sue said softly.

Something about her cousin's face touched Sam deeply. In fact, her insides seemed to be knotting up.

That was love. Nothing interrupted the feeling for

Katie Sue. Not time, distance, the cold—or the darkness of winter.

It was love.

It was faith.

"Go, go. Happy, happy Christmas Eve," Sam told her cousin. "Love you."

Katie Sue kissed June and then stopped dead. "Daniel! Daniel Riverton. You're—you're back in Salem."

"In the flesh, Katie Sue," he said. "We'll catch up later—right now you better hurry," he said. He was smiling, as well.

He knew about Katie Sue's situation, of course, Sam thought. He hadn't been gone that long. Not as long as Katie Sue had been waiting.

Katie Sue turned to look at him with a broad smile. "Of course, we'll catch up. It's wonderful that you're back."

"He isn't back," Sam snapped.

"Of course he is," Katie Sue said. "Anyway, I'm outta here. Catch you all later. Merry Christmas, August," she added, and then she was gone.

At that moment Tobey connected a smart punch right against Sam's jaw.

"Down!" he bellowed.

She controlled her temper—barely. She supposed she should have been paying more attention to him.

"No, Tobey, you're not getting down right now. And if you hit me or anyone else again, I'll put you in a really, really long time-out. Do you understand?"

Just then Father Mulroney came over and greeted her with relief. "Oh, thank the Lord. There you are, Sam. I'm afraid that the Wiccans and the Baptists are about to get into it. We have such a wonderfully diverse crowd here, but when they're discussing the darkness… Well, I begin to fear that one group might accuse the other group of bringing it on and—"

"I'm coming," Sam said.

She hiked Tobey onto her shoulder and marched into the parlor, then paused. The tree looked beautiful, and for a moment she did nothing but revel in the spirit of the holiday.

"Hey!" she said loudly, drawing everyone's attention, from those sitting comfortably to those milling around the dining table, visible through the archway, and those who were standing around as they sipped their eggnog and enjoyed the food. "Merry Christmas Eve, everyone, and welcome to my home. What's going on here? I'm not hearing any Christmas music. Father Mulroney, will you be so kind as to grace my piano with your presence?"

"I'd love to," he said.

He quickly sat down and began to play. Looking at Tobey in Sam's arms, he began with "Jingle Bells."

Sam was pleased when June walked right in and started singing with her beautiful voice. She was quickly joined by others in the room. In a minute Mrs. McClellan, an ardent Baptist, was standing arm in arm with Sally Canfield, priestess for one of the Wiccan covens. After "Jingle Bells," Father Mulroney looked at Rabbi Solomon and began to play "Dreidel, Dreidel, Dreidel."

Lars Anderson, an Elven who had recently arrived from Norway, walked over to the piano and suggested "O Little Town of Bethlehem."

Tobey's father came and retrieved him from her arms at last. She stepped back, letting out a soft sigh of relief.

A minute later, June was back by her side. "Shall we bring out more refreshments?"

"Yes, let's carve the turkey, shall we?" Sam said.

Together, they headed to the kitchen, where she found

Daniel already carving the huge turkey that had been roasting all day, layering the tender meat on the waiting serving platters. He was being watched by August and a young Wiccan named Sally Smith, who worked for Mica.

"Thanks for the help," Sam told Daniel.

"No problem," he said, continuing to carve.

"I'll get out this first platter," June said.

"We've got them," August said, turning to smile at Sally.

"We do— Oh, Mica is running a little late, Sam," Sally said. "But she'll be here—she wouldn't miss it for the world."

They left, and June stood there for a moment looking from Daniel to Samantha.

"I, uh, feel a song coming on," she said, and fled.

Sam stared at Daniel across the kitchen table. The smells of baked goods, cinnamon, pine and all things Christmas wafted between them.

Suddenly the kitchen seemed far too small and Daniel far too close, despite the table that sat squarely between them.

"What do you want?" she asked him, and her voice sounded more needy than she would have liked.

But before he could answer, Tobey came barreling into the kitchen and headed straight for a bottle of champagne sitting on a tray surrounded by delicate crystal glasses.

"No!" Sam gasped, diving for Tobey.

"I've got him," Daniel promised.

But Tobey ducked, and they both missed him as he sped by, sliding under the table and banging into the counter.

The champagne and the glasses clinked and rattled as the tray began to fall.

Chapter 5

Samantha gasped.

Daniel amazed himself by moving fast enough to catch the champagne tray before it could fall.

Samantha dived under the table and emerged victorious, grasping the unrepentant toddler in her arms.

"Out, mister!" she told Tobey. "And you better behave yourself. Do you remember that time-out I was telling you about?"

August came running into the kitchen, colliding with Samantha's back.

"I'm sorry—I'm sorry!" he said. "Sandy and I were watching him, but we didn't move fast enough."

"It's okay. This kid moves faster than a speeding bullet," Samantha told him. "I say let his dad watch him for a while." She walked out of the kitchen. Daniel followed quickly behind her. She walked straight to Father Alistair and politely but firmly interrupted his conversation with Elsie Beamish, an elderly shapeshifter.

"Father Alistair, I believe this young man has been looking for you," she said.

Father Alistair looked momentarily startled, as if he'd

forgotten bringing his son. Then his eyes cleared, and he smiled. "Tobey, did you see the beautiful Christmas lights?" he asked, reaching for his son.

Tobey went straight into his father's arms, his radiant smile making him look as sweet and docile as a cherub.

"Excuse me, Elsie," Father Alistair said. "I'm going to hang on to my little one for a minute here and show him the magic in this house." He smiled at Samantha gratefully, as if she had shown him something wonderful. Perhaps she had.

Sam smiled back and said, "Time to toast the tolerance and peace of the season, Father. I'll be back with the champagne—and some juice for your son."

Daniel followed her back into the kitchen, hoping to get a chance to answer her question. Did she really wonder why he was here? It seemed so obvious…but Sam felt the mantle of responsibility heavily on her shoulder, and though she wore it very well, he could see that she was letting it come between herself and her emotions.

No chance to say anything. June was right behind him, and Mica had arrived and seemed determined to help to make up for being late. And there was August, of course, who had been intent on destroying himself just a few hours before, yet now seemed to have a new crush on Sam for saving him.

"Grab the glasses, please," Sam said. "And the champagne. Thank you, everyone."

Daniel picked up the tray he had saved earlier. As they stepped back out to the parlor, there was another arrival.

It was the old werewolf Victor Alden, who had dressed up as Santa for as long as Daniel could remember and came to Mycroft House to hand out gifts.

"Ho, ho, ho!" Victor said, bearing a big red bag. "Why,

'tis Samantha Mycroft. My dear, you have been very, very good this year. I have a lovely gift for you."

"Oh, Santa, that's wonderful—but you have to come toast with us first."

"Don't mind if I do."

Victor set down his bag. "Everything going well here?" he asked.

"Yes, thank you," Sam said.

He nodded. "I was hoping...I was hoping the darkness wouldn't ruin the night."

"No," she said firmly. "I will not let the darkness ruin the night."

She smiled and headed out with Daniel. Victor followed them into the parlor, where both Others and humans of all faiths filled their champagne glasses and stood together to toast the holiday.

"To love, tolerance and understanding," Father Mulroney said.

"To you, dear guests, who understand that goodness is in the love a person spreads, and not in the words he chooses to describe himself," Samantha added.

"To Mycroft House," Daniel said, looking at Samantha as he lifted his glass. "A place where Sam has carried on the tradition of the true meaning of the Christmas season. All of us, no matter who—or what—we are learn here that love for our fellow man is the greatest gift we can bestow."

"Hear, hear!" Father Mulroney said, and began to play "Amazing Grace," his beautiful tenor voice so powerful that even Tobey went silent and listened.

Everyone applauded when he finished, and Rabbi Solomon said enthusiastically, "Please, someone keep it going."

This was his chance, Daniel thought. Maybe.

He walked over to the piano. "I know one—Samantha and I used to do it together all the time when we were younger. If she'll join me…?"

She looked as if she had given up on Christmas cheer and just wanted to kill him.

But everyone in the room began to applaud and urge her on, so she forced a smile and walked over.

"'Baby, It's Cold Outside,'" he announced.

Her smile was brittle. But Father Mulroney began to play, and she began to sing.

They were immediately in sync, taking their parts, and the song was fun and a little bit sexy.

It was as if they had never been apart, as if they had sung together every day, as if they hadn't missed a beat in their lives….

But of course, they had. And when the song was over, people laughed and patted him on the back as they complimented him.

And he lost sight of Samantha.

Determined, he looked through the house. He found August and Sally in the kitchen, chatting as they set the desserts on trays.

"Looking for Sam?" August asked him. "I think she went outside."

Daniel hurried to the front door, then paused. He looked back into the parlor. Father Mulroney was still playing, but now with Tobey on his lap and Father Alistair sitting next to him. Everyone had a suggestion for a carol. The room seemed to be ablaze with lights, a beautiful beacon against the darkness that had settled over Salem.

He slipped outside. Sam was there, staring up at the pale sliver of a moon that had somehow made its way through what seemed to be an eternal darkness.

"Sam," he said softly.

She turned to him. Her eyes looked huge and luminous. When he moved, the plastic Santa began to sing "All I Want for Christmas."

"Oh, for the love of God— Please pull the plug on that thing," she begged.

Laughing, he stepped through the snow and found the cord.

Santa went silent.

"Not a bad song," he said lightly, walking over to her.

She didn't move. They were alone at last. Now the only singing was coming from the house.

"You're doing a great job here," he told her.

"So great that they sent you to check up on me," she said.

"Sam," he said, and set his hands on her shoulders, seeking her eyes. "They sent me because every one of us needs someone sometimes. But…"

"But what?" she demanded.

"They needed to send someone," he said, then inhaled deeply. "They sent me because I asked to come here. I requested this assignment."

"Oh? So I'm an assignment now?"

He laughed softly, but he felt as if there were a vise around his throat. "Sam, I asked to come after I spoke to your father—and mine. I told them that they were wrong to have suggested that we couldn't be together and still perform all the duties that would fall our way. I told them that I was sorry, but I couldn't serve if we couldn't be treated with respect and understanding." He realized that she might laugh in his face for taking a stand that might no longer represent her feelings. But he didn't care. He was willing to risk everything.

He caught her hand and went down on one knee. "Samantha Mycroft, I am incredibly, incurably in love with you. Nothing in my existence matters without you. I realize that in this day and age I'm supposed to ask you first, but I happened to be with your father so I asked him for your hand. Well, not really. I *told* him—and my father—that if you would have me, I was going to marry you with or without their blessing. So…I realize that this is awkward, but I can't see a way of making it better if I don't just tell you the truth…if I don't try to make you understand that I was a fool, afraid that you were more responsible than I was, that you would reject me…that you would move on happily without me. But I know now that while you may still reject me, I can't go on with life without at least begging you to forgive me…without telling you that you are everything to me, that I love you with every fiber of my being. Sam, will you marry me?" He took a deep breath. "You don't have to answer right this instant. I'm sure you really want to shove snow in my face, but…you asked what I want…and…"

She was staring at him incredulously. He had no idea what she was thinking.

"All I want for Christmas is you," he whispered.

She flushed. A beautiful shade of red. It went well with her sweater. And her hair, and her eyes and…

"Sam?"

"Get up, please! Someone might walk out here and see," she said.

He got to his feet. "I'm sorry, Sam. I had to tell you."

She started to turn away. "It's this darkness," she said. "I know I'm not the right person to handle it, but I have to be here, to try."

"But I could be here with you," he told her. "I know I left you before—but you told me to leave, remember? Two years ago I came here…confused. My father, your father…both of them were so determined that we couldn't be together, that we had to be strong and do our jobs. Well, Sam, my strength came from knowing that I was going to come back here and be with you, if you'd have me. They wanted us to stand alone—but they were wrong. None of us stands alone. I told them that. I pointed out that the council only exists because no one really stands alone. We need one another. And we need love. Nothing shows us that as much as this time of year. Love is the greatest gift in the world. I love you, Sam. I have since I met you. I will into eternity—no matter what the future may bring."

"What?" she gasped.

"I love you. And I will love you forever."

She stood silent, staring at him. And then she began to laugh.

He frowned, watching her.

"Is that…a no?" he asked.

But it wasn't. She suddenly threw herself into his arms. And she kissed him.

She kissed *him*.

It was the kind of kiss he had dreamed of through long nights away. It was an easy kiss, a passionate kiss, a natural kiss, a wet, sloppy kiss that was the most erotic kiss he had ever known. It was filled with intimacy and promise.

She broke away at last and stared up at him.

"Um… Is that a yes?" he asked her huskily.

"I've never been all that anyone wanted for Christmas before," she told him.

He smiled. He looked up at the sky.

It was still dark, of course. No matter what, it would be dark now.

But somehow the world around him seemed to be filled with brilliant light in a rainbow of colors.

"It feels like the sun just broke through," he told her.

She leaned against him. He smelled the faint, soft scent of her perfume. He thought about the woman who had plunged into icy water to save a foolish boy, the woman who could bring together a room of people and Others, the woman who instinctively knew what a child needed. And he was more than ever in love.

He reached into his pocket. "I, um, happen to have this. In case you said yes," he told her.

"Let me see!" she begged.

He popped open the box. It wasn't a huge diamond, but it was a beautiful one. Radiant light seemed to stream from it.

"The light is inside us," she said.

"Pardon?"

"That's what Father Mulroney told me today. He said the light is inside our hearts. We can fight the darkness." She looked at him and smiled slowly. "Yes, Daniel Riverton, I will marry you. I will certainly have a few choice words to say about the way we parted, but then I suppose you might have a few, too."

"Well, you are pigheaded and proud, and you did tell me to get out."

"You were supposed to know I didn't mean a word of it. I was just giving you an out."

He smiled. Her temper was already flaring deliciously.

"May I?" he asked her.

She nodded.

He slipped the ring on her finger.

"Let your light so shine...." he quoted softly. "Matthew 5:16," he added with a smile and a grin.

"No, let *our* light so shine," she said.

From the house, they could hear Father Mulroney's voice raised in song: "Joy to the World."

"There are dark days ahead," she murmured.

"We'll be here to face them. Together."

She nodded solemnly. "However, I'm forecasting a brilliant night."

"Oh?"

"Let's go inside and join the guests. They'll go home. Eventually. And since I'm a Christmas present… Well, traditionally, you do get to unwrap one gift on Christmas Eve. And I plan on being the best gift you ever get."

They kissed again beneath the sliver of the moon, and radiance seemed to be all around them.

Light and love came from within.

And Daniel knew it was going to be a beautiful Christmas morning.

Because there would be love. And love, he believed, was light.

And as the saying went, love conquered all.

"Merry Christmas, Sam," he said huskily.

And she said the best words in return.

"Merry Christmas, my love."

* * * * *

THE FRIGHT BEFORE CHRISTMAS
CHRISTMAS
—
DEBORAH LEBLANC

Dear Reader,

We hope you enjoy this wonderful holiday anthology! I had such fun writing the short story for this collection and was very honored to work with the remarkable authors whose stories created the very pulse of this book. A huge, heartfelt thanks also goes to Heather Graham for allowing me to be part of her project. Not only is she a fabulous author—she's a remarkable person and has enriched my life tremendously simply by being in it.

So thank you, dear reader, for choosing to add this anthology to your book collection. May all of your holiday seasons be filled with joy, laughter and love!

Deborah LeBlanc

For Pookie—who keeps the joy of Christmas in my heart all year round.

Chapter 1

The cut burned, the wound bled and Rebekah Savay bit her tongue to keep a stream of curse words in check. She'd been in full power-walk mode, heading for the stone gazebo in Salem Common, when her boots had hit an obscure patch of ice on the sidewalk. Her feet had gone one way, her hands another as she grabbed for anything to keep herself upright. Unfortunately, that *anything* had been a metal No Parking sign with dinged edges tacked to the side of a light pole. She felt stupid for not having been more careful, but didn't wallow in it. After all, she'd come from Malta, where winter lows dipped down into the midsixties and lasted all of three weeks. She simply wasn't used to maneuvering on ice and snow, much less in the dark.

It was midafternoon, and the sky appeared blanketed with night—a moonless, starless night. Only Christmas lights twinkled in the gloom. It was the very sky that had greeted her when she'd arrived in Salem earlier that morning. The lack of sunlight during the day felt weird, but the gloom that seemed to have settled over the people here felt actively disturbing. Nearly everyone she'd encountered on the streets seemed to carry an energy of irritation. Being an empath, she'd felt it bubble and bleep on her emotional radar. Although shoppers and visitors chatted and smiled, she sensed that everyone wished they could scurry away, anxious to get out of the cold and gloom and into any warm and well-lit haven. Not that she blamed them. She wanted to do the same but couldn't.

The darkness had brought her here.

Her cousin Samantha Mycroft, Keeper of the Vampires here in Salem and unofficial chief among all the Keepers, had contacted her about the problem plaguing the town. Since Rebekah was the KOFE, Keeper of the Five Elementals, Sam wanted her to join her and their two other cousins, June, Keeper of the Witches, and Katie Sue, Keeper of the Selkies, to find the culprit responsible for the darkness. They suspected a rogue sorcerer was the cause of the problem, but Sam didn't want to make that suspicion an assumption. She'd asked Rebekah to do an extra sweep of the elemental elders and the charges that reported to them to see if there had been any unusual activity.

Rebekah had agreed without hesitation and immediately summoned the elemental elders to her base in Malta. She had questioned all five at great length, and after a long verbal battle of wits and wills and shameless finger-pointing—which happened more times than not when she brought the elders together—everything appeared to be in order. But she didn't dismiss the issue. Instead, she considered the resources available to her and contemplated enlisting the elders' help. They and their charges would provide thousands more eyes and ears with which to help find a rogue sorcerer—or anyone else, for that matter.

After checking with her cousins and getting their approval, Rebekah had called a second elders' meeting, this one to be held in Salem so they could witness the darkness firsthand. Sam had offered her home for a meeting place, but Rebekah had declined. The location would have been convenient, since she would be staying there, but Sam had a large Christmas Eve party planned for tonight and Rebekah didn't want to add an elemental invasion to the preparty mayhem. More important, it was one thing to gather the core elements of what basically constituted the makeup of the earth into one place, but restricting the space surrounding that collective unit was quite another.

The elders, like most people in positions of great power, were very territorial, so she typically met with each of them individually. On the rare occasion when she did gather them together, it wasn't uncommon for egos to swell and tempers to flare, making the group a challenge to rein in. To minimize the risk of an elemental apocalypse, she had devised a meeting mandate: take on human form, or else. The physical body acted like a check valve on the elders, reducing the force of their powers. Even at half throttle, however, a gaggle of angry elementals was not something you wanted trapped between four walls. So she'd chosen an outside location for the meeting. The venue might be public, but that was nothing an illusion veil couldn't fix.

After standing and finding solid purchase on the sidewalk again, Rebekah realized she had no tissue and wondered if sticking her wounded finger in the snow that bordered the sidewalk might staunch the bleeding. She dismissed the thought. Not only did the snow look dirty, she really didn't have the time to stop and pamper an injury that appeared no more severe than an oversize paper cut. She *had* to be at the gazebo by three, and it was already thirteen minutes till. Fortunately, she was only a couple minutes away.

Rebekah shook the dripping blood from her finger and took off, jogging. A crosswind brushed against her face, making her shiver. She hated the cold.

When Rebekah finally reached the steps of the gazebo, she took them in twos. She'd spotted only a couple of people in the park so far, and both appeared to be passing through on their way to somewhere else. With any luck the park could very well be empty by the time the elders arrived.

No sooner was she inside than she saw Faylin, her fire elemental elder, leaning against the south end of the railing. So much for luck.

"You're late," Faylin said, folding her arms across her chest.

"Uh…and you became my Keeper, when?" Rebekah glanced at her watch. Nine minutes to three. "That's a scratch on my being late. You're early."

Faylin tsked. "Well…whatever."

From a distance Rebekah heard a man whistle in the dark. The kind of whistle some men gave when they saw a beautiful woman. She had little doubt it was meant for Faylin. The lamps attached to the dome of the gazebo shed a soft white light across the pavilion, making it easy for anyone looking in this direction to see her.

Then again, in human form, Faylin was hard to miss in any lighting. The elder stood about five foot ten and looked to be in her late twenties. She had eyes the color of swirled cinnamon and a shock of thick auburn hair beneath a blue aviator's hat, complete with earflaps. She wore a blue, skin-tight ski suit over a body most women would have killed for.

"You think you could have worn something a little more…subtle?" Rebekah asked.

"What?" Faylin looked down at herself. "What's wrong with what I'm wearing?"

In that moment a man's face suddenly appeared behind the railing on the west side of the gazebo. It was Walter, her water elemental elder. Before Rebekah could advise him otherwise, he had climbed over the railing to get into the gazebo instead of taking the stairs. He stood a couple of inches shorter than Faylin, and had a slender build, shoulder-length hair the color of bleached sand and green eyes that looked too large for his narrow, pale face.

As soon as Walter landed inside the gazebo, he gasped like a little girl who'd happened upon a spider. The sound echoed throughout the Common.

"What happened to you?" he asked Rebekah, putting a hand to his chest. "Oh…oh…" He pointed to her feet. "You're… It's… Is that…?" He backed up against the railing.

Puzzled, Rebekah looked down to where he had pointed. She saw a few drops of blood on the floor near her right foot. Her finger had started to bleed again.

She heard a loud retching sound and glanced up in time to see Walter puking over the side of the railing.

"Oh, for the love of light!" Faylin said in disgust. "It's only a little blood."

Somewhere in the distance, far enough away so the darkness kept him hidden, Rebekah heard someone say, "Friggin gross!" The voice sounded male and young—early to mid-twenties.

"That really was a wussy move, Walter," Faylin said. "Totally embarrassing."

Walter pulled himself upright and patted his lips with the back of a hand. "Leave me alone. It's not like

I planned it. It just sort of happened." He looked over at Rebekah. "Are you okay? Do we need to find somebody to look at your finger? You know…in case you need stitches or something? I'm worried. It… I mean, that's real blood."

"I'm fine," Rebekah assured him. "Really. The cut's small and wasn't even bleeding a minute ago. I probably caught it on the railing while climbing the stairs."

"Take this, then," Walter said, and removed the beige cashmere scarf he had wrapped around his neck. He handed it to her. "Wrap it around the wound. It'll stop the bleeding for sure."

"There's no need. Look, the bleeding's stopped again." Rebekah had never seen the water elder react to the sight of blood that way. It puzzled her, but there were bigger things for her to worry about right now. "Really, it's no big deal. No blood, no worries. Okay?"

Walter gave her a reluctant nod.

"That's a relief," Faylin said. "I have to admit I was starting to get a little worried about you myself."

Rebekah gave Faylin, who was better known for surliness than empathy, a questioning look. "You, worried?"

"Of course. Blood's a tough stain to get out, you know. Had it dripped on that beautiful white coat of yours, it would've totally ruined it."

"You can't be serious," Walter said. "The woman nearly cuts off her finger and all you're concerned about are stains on her coat?"

Faylin glared at him. "And that's your business because…?"

He tsked. "You're so shallow."

"Better shallow than a wuss," Faylin shot back. "And quit blowing things out of proportion. The woman simply nicked her finger, Walter. Nicked, as in tiny cut. Nowhere near cutting it off."

"You think you know everything about everything."

"Okay, both of you, stop right now," Rebekah demanded. "You're acting like five-year-olds."

Faylin huffed, then glanced about as though seeing the inside of the gazebo for the first time. "Well...call me pretentious."

Walter did a double take in her direction.

"Not me, you waterlogged puke-ninny. The gazebo. It's architectural overkill for a town this size, if you ask me."

"No one did," Walter said, then scowled. "I don't think it's overkill at all. It's beautiful. Very grand and elegant."

"Yeah, yeah, whatever." Faylin let out an exasperated sigh and turned to Rebekah. "Let's get on with this gig already. I need to get out of this body. It itches, and putting clothes all over it makes the itching worse. I have important things to tend to, you know. Besides, I don't like being this close to so many humans. They smell funny. And why aren't the others here yet? Those three yahoos are late."

"Do you ever stop complaining?" Rebekah asked. "Like, ever?"

"No," Walter said. "She doesn't."

"Shut up, you old wart-nosed water lily," Faylin said. "What do you—" She suddenly cocked her head, then aimed her chin to the east. "Guess airhead Ariel finally decided to join us."

Rebekah squinted into the darkness and spotted movement.

"Where?" Walter asked. "It's so dark. How can you see anything out there?"

Faylin rolled her eyes, then did a quick flip of her right

wrist. A small ball of fire suddenly appeared in the palm of her hand. "Uh, hello, water brain, I'm fire. Fire means light…remember?"

When Ariel came into view, Rebekah was relieved to see that she had chosen a relatively "normal" human body for the meeting. The air elder stood at average height, had a slender build and long, platinum-blond hair. She wore a pastel yellow coat over a white dress and white flats. Relatively subtle in appearance—except for one thing. Instead of walking, Ariel literally floated toward them, three inches off the ground.

"Whoa… What the…?" From the sound of it, Rebekah figured the young man who'd verbalized his disgust with Walter's puking earlier had just spotted Ariel floating their way.

Shouting out to Ariel would only have drawn more attention to her, so Rebekah quickly sent her air elder a telepathic message. *Use your feet, Ariel, walk! The floating's drawing too much attention.*

Ariel immediately complied.

"And here comes boulder butt," Faylin said, pointing to the north.

In that moment Rebekah felt the gazebo floor vibrate ever so slightly beneath her feet. Definitely Eric. He soon came into view, all six foot five of him. He looked like a bodybuilder, with massive shoulders, shoulder-length brown hair, deep-set brown eyes and a serious expression, which he maintained every time he had to make an appearance in human form.

Eric climbed the steps of the gazebo only a second or two behind Ariel. At least they had the good sense to use the steps instead of jumping over the railing the way Walter had, or simply appearing like Faylin. Still, steps or not, it was difficult, if not impossible, for the lot of them not to draw attention.

"What are y'all doing here?" Eric asked Faylin and Walter when he arrived.

It always amused Rebekah to hear the voice Eric chose to go along with his human physique—baritone, with a Southern drawl.

"That's a stupid question," Faylin said. "Why do you think we're here, pebble brain? Same reason you are— because Rebekah wanted us here. Only *we* were on time."

"I'm not late!" Eric turned to Rebekah, his brow furrowing deeply. "Am I?"

His expression read of near panic. Eric had such an exacting, plodding personality that, for him, being late meant he'd committed an unconscionable and unforgivable act.

"Of course not. When are you ever?" Rebekah tapped the face of her watch to reassure him. "You're right on time."

Eric looked at Faylin. "Then you got here early."

"Yeah, so?"

"Why?"

Faylin cocked her head, a sly grin spreading over her face. "Because."

Knowing that a nonanswer like *because* would drive Eric crazy and that Faylin had probably used it for just that reason, Rebekah stepped between them, using herself as a pattern interrupt before things escalated out of control.

"Hey, I'm really sorry about floating earlier," Ariel said. Her voice had a breathy, high-pitched quality that Rebekah found annoying. "I forget about using feet. You know, humans have it tough. It's not easy getting around on those things."

"Look, can we cut the chitchat and get down to business?" Eric asked. "We're wasting time."

"Where's Quentin?" Ariel asked, scanning the gazebo. "We can't get to business without Quentin."

"He's not here yet," Walter said.

Unable to take it any longer, Rebekah asked, "Ariel, why on earth did you choose that voice? It's annoying. You sound like Marilyn Monroe on helium."

Ariel blinked rapidly, appearing stupefied. "Who's Marilyn Monroe?"

"An actress from a long time ago. Doesn't matter. Just change the voice, okay?"

"Sure, but if I change the voice, I have to change the body, and that's going to take a while. It's a lot of hard work, putting all these human parts together. You've gotta make sure—"

Rebekah held up a hand. "Never mind. Keep the voice. Just try not to use it too much, please."

Eric huffed. "We're wastin' time."

"Yeah, I'm ready to skate," Faylin said.

"We're supposed to be a team, and Quentin's part of it," Ariel said. "We have to wait for him."

Eric arched a brow. "Getting kinda prissy, ain't ya? Whether we wait for him or not is Rebekah's call."

"Well…well…of course!" Ariel said, looking utterly embarrassed. "I didn't mean to step out of bounds or anything. I was just saying…"

Rebekah heard two people talking in the distance, in the dark. She couldn't make out what they were saying, but would have bet her left arm that the five of them were the topic of conversation. They probably made quite the spectacle, illuminated in the middle of the gazebo by the Christmas lights the town had hung. She had to do something before they drew even more attention and half the town of Salem showed up at the gazebo to gawk at the "weirdos."

Rebekah turned to Faylin. "There're two guys talking to each other somewhere nearby. Can you see them?"

"Sure. Punky types. Kinda young. They've been watching since I got here."

"Let me know the second they both turn away from us, okay?"

"No problem," Faylin said. "You're going to do the curtain thing, aren't you?"

Walter shuffled around impatiently. "I'm bored. Do I have to keep standing? My feet hurt. Are there chairs around here? Can I—"

"Quiet for a moment, all of you." Rebekah held up her right hand, palm out. She was relieved to see the cut was no longer bleeding. At least Walter wouldn't be puking over the railing again—she hoped. She closed her eyes, certain that her stance looked strange to whoever watched in the dark. But she had no other choice. Once Faylin gave her the signal that the young men had turned away, she would have only a few seconds to produce the illusion veil.

"Okay… Now," Faylin said.

At her word, Rebekah quickly walked the perimeter of the gazebo floor, all the while creating the illusion veil using her mind's eye. The veil would allow anyone who happened by to see only what Rebekah allowed them to see. In this case, an empty gazebo. The only problem was that whoever had been watching them was in for a shock. Once the veil was in place, it would appear that the five of them had simply vanished.

No sooner did that thought cross Rebekah's mind than she heard, "What the hell?"

She opened her eyes and grinned. "I guess the veil worked."

"No doubt," Faylin said. "The guys out there are just a couple of punks anyway. Want me to cook 'em?"

"No!"

"But they're all up in our business."

"Not anymore," Rebekah said. "The veil's up, so their show's over." Only another elemental or a Keeper had the ability to see through the veil, so for now, at least, they were safe from prying eyes.

Rebekah glanced at her watch again. Six minutes after three. It wasn't like Quentin to be late. The quintessence elemental elder always made a point of being on time. His tardiness worried her.

"You know," Faylin said, leaning against the railing, "humans say that a criminal always returns to the scene of the crime. Maybe that's not true when it comes to elementals."

"What are you talking about?" Rebekah asked.

"Quentin," Faylin said. "Think about it. Who better to produce this kind of darkness than an elemental who can easily position himself between the sun and the earth?"

"Hmm, I never considered that," Walter said.

"You really think it could be Quentin?" Ariel asked.

"That's stupid," Eric said. His loud baritone made Rebekah glad that the illusion veil came with a sound barrier. "Quentin wouldn't do such a thing. Besides, if the sun was blocked from up there, it would affect the whole earth, not just Salem."

Faylin did an eye roll. "Okay, so maybe he just stuck a foot between the sun and Salem, then."

"Now, that's just ridiculous," Walter said. "First of all, Quentin doesn't even have feet."

"All of you, give it a rest!" Rebekah demanded. She

closed her eyes again and tried to tune in to Quentin telepathically.

Quentin, where are you? Everyone's at the gazebo waiting for you.

No response.

"Hey, y'all, we've got company," Eric said.

"Is it Quentin?" Ariel asked.

Rebekah peered into the darkness and saw two men headed for the gazebo. Intuitively she knew one of them was the guy they'd heard earlier. The one who'd seen Walter puke over the railing, Ariel floating instead of walking and heaven only knew what else. It only made sense that they'd come to investigate. After all, moments earlier five "people" had been in the gazebo. Now...no one.

"They sure are nosy," Faylin said, obviously seeing and identifying the same men. "Come on. Let me cook 'em—just a little."

"No," Rebekah said firmly.

"What's wrong with you, always wanting to cook people?" Walter asked Faylin. "Do you always have to be so dramatic? I mean, really, if—"

"Shut up, drippy dick. I'll do what—"

"Stop." Rebekah quickly held out her left hand, palm up, and drew an imaginary line across it with her right index finger. A repellent field. She didn't know why she hadn't put one around the perimeter when she'd set up the illusion veil. The repellent field acted more like an alarm system than a physical barrier. If a human even thought about coming toward the gazebo, the repellent field would trigger their internal alarm, making them think twice, insisting it would be better if they stayed away—far away.

Seconds later, she noticed two tall, lanky shapes scurrying away.

"Ooh," Faylin said, sounding more amused than surprised.

"What?" Rebekah asked.

"Um… Someone else is coming."

"Who? Quentin?" Rebekah squinted into the darkness and saw movement.

"*Is* that Quentin?" Walter asked.

"Uh…no…" Faylin's eyes had turned a bright sienna—a sure sign of mischief on the way.

"Then who?" Rebekah squinted harder. The person heading toward them was definitely male. The few times she'd seen Quentin in human form he'd always chosen something delicate, a small-boned physique that reminded her of a Michelangelo or a da Vinci painting. There didn't appear to be anything delicate about this man.

Suddenly recognition sent Rebekah's heart racing into her throat. "No… No way… It can't be."

The man drew closer, removing any doubts. The tall, muscular body, collar-length black hair, olive complexion; his walk confident, purposeful; jeans, a black pullover and a black leather jacket. The sight sent a chill through Rebekah that felt colder than any winter wind Salem had to offer.

Walter gasped. "Is…is that Vaughn Griffith?"

Rebekah didn't answer. She couldn't.

"Oh, my!" Ariel said, her voice breathier than ever.

As the man came into full view, Rebekah saw an easy smile spread across his face, which made the cold drilling into her bones immediately vanish. In its place rolled a wave of white-hot anger.

Vaughn Griffith in the flesh.

Maybe she would take Faylin up on her offer to *cook 'em* after all.

Chapter 2

As he neared the steps of the gazebo, Vaughn Griffith couldn't remember the last time he'd felt this breathless. Being so close to Rebekah after all this time—her waist-length, raven-black hair, those large, violet-colored eyes, her flawless complexion, her body so slender, so perfect—was hitting him harder than he'd expected. The sight of her would suck the breath out of any man. Even the anger he saw in her eyes didn't mar her beauty. If anything, it enhanced it.

"What are you doing here?" she demanded even before he reached the top step. She quickly brushed a stray hair away from her face and he noticed her hand trembling ever so slightly. It belied the sharp edge in her voice.

"I came to help," he said, then turned and nodded to the elders. "Good to see all of you again."

"Uh…yeah, s-same here," Walter said with a stutter.

"It's definitely been a while," Faylin said, then arched a brow and grinned. "Time's sure been good to you, buddy."

"That's true," Ariel said. "Oh, that's so true."

Eric simply nodded to acknowledge Vaughn's greeting. His expression remained, as always, stern.

"No one asked for your help." Rebekah's frown deepened. "Or did they? Did my cousins contact you, ask you to come here?"

"No, no," Vaughn said, holding up a hand. He took a cautious step onto the gazebo floor. He knew Rebekah well enough to know that if he pushed into her personal space before she was ready, she would either coldcock him or command Ariel to wrap him up in a tornado, spin him away then drop him in the middle of the Atlantic. "I heard about Salem, that you'd called for an elders' meeting. Thought you might need a hand, that's all."

Rebekah's eyes narrowed. "How long have you been in town?"

"Not long. Few hours, maybe."

"Where…? What…?"

He saw the frustration on her face and the questions in her eyes. He answered her unspoken questions as quickly and as best he could—save for the one he knew she really wanted to ask but wasn't ready to verbalize.

"I'm staying at the Salem Inn, not far from Sam's. I went to your cousin's first, looking for you. She told me I'd probably find you here. You know, Roe—"

"Don't call me that," Rebekah said.

"Aw, why not?" Ariel asked. "Pet names are so cute, don't you think?"

"Oh, for the love of light, Ariel," Faylin said. "You're gonna make me puke."

Eric cleared his throat, then asked Vaughn, "You seen Quentin?"

"No, why?" Vaughn quickly scanned the gazebo for the quintessence elder, then turned to Rebekah. "He hasn't arrived?"

"Isn't it obvious?"

Vaughn frowned. It wasn't like Quentin to simply not

show for a meeting. "No word from him at all? Any idea where he might be?"

"Probably hiding under a rock," Faylin said, not giving Rebekah a chance to finish.

"No, he ain't," Eric said. He tapped his broad chest with a finger. "Earth elder, remember? I'd know if he'd be under one of my rocks."

Rebekah glared at Vaughn. "Quentin's my problem, not yours. And how in the hell did you see us through the illusion veil? You're not a Keeper and definitely not an elemental, so how…?"

Vaughn smiled softly. The fact that he'd been allowed to compete for the KOFE seat nearly three years ago meant he possessed more abilities than the average human, and Rebekah knew it.

"Oh, never mind." Rebekah's eyes blazed with fury. "Why now, Vaughn? Huh? Why? I've called the elders together before for natural disasters far worse than this. What makes you think I need, much less want, your help *now?*"

The more she talked, the angrier she became, and the more Vaughn ached to kiss her.

"What? Do you think I've suddenly lost my abilities as Keeper?"

"Of course not." Vaughn stepped toward her, reached for her shoulder.

She pulled away, avoiding his touch.

Her rejection felt like a taser to his heart. "I know you're angry, and you have every right to be. I—"

"You don't know squat. And you don't have a say over what I have a right to be," she said. "Especially over what I feel or think."

"Roe, listen—"

"I said don't call me that."

Vaughn took a step back to give her more personal space. Roe might have had a fiery temper, something he'd always found endearing, but in the many years he'd known her, he had only seen it in full bloom—like now—a handful of times. It happened when someone she loved was threatened, when the weak were taken advantage of, when she confronted blatant injustice or when she'd been deeply, deeply hurt. And judging from the look in her eyes now, Vaughn knew the last reason was to blame for this flare-up.

The last thing he'd ever meant to do was hurt her.

"Oh, this is getting good," Faylin said, grinning. She rubbed her hands together.

Vaughn shot her a look. The fire elder lowered her head, but her smile remained.

Eric chuffed. "Do you think the two of you can quit peeing in each other's boots until—"

Suddenly a loud *thunk* echoed from the dome of the gazebo, making everyone look up.

A groan of pain followed the thunk, then a pair of wing tips slid into view below the east end of the roof. Within seconds a pair of legs clad in tuxedo trousers followed the wing tips, and before anyone had a chance to say a word, a man dropped onto the gazebo floor.

He stood about five-eleven, and had a thatch of wild salt-and-pepper hair, a tangled beard and an unevenly trimmed mustache and cobalt-blue eyes that appeared wild with fear. The rest of his ensemble included a red sports coat and a brown button-down shirt.

"Quentin!" Ariel squealed, then clapped her hands like an overzealous fan girl.

Vaughn did a double take. It was undoubtedly the quintessence elder, but he'd never seen Quentin disheveled before. It had an oddly disturbing effect on him.

Like stepping outside and discovering the sky had turned green and the grass blue. Something was off here—way off.

"About damn time," Faylin said.

Eric flipped a hand toward his peers as if to silence them, then said to Quentin, "You're late. You were supposed to be here at three. Everybody at three."

Rebekah hurried over to Quentin, put a hand on his arm. "What's wrong?"

The wild-eyed elder's lower lip trembled. He glanced over at Vaughn, then around to the others before his eyes settled back on Rebekah. "Tee-zee's missing."

"Uh-oh," Walter said.

"Uh-oh what?" Vaughn asked. "Who's Tee-zee?"

Walter shrugged. "I don't know, but if he's missing that can't be good."

"He's one of Quentin's charges—and a black hole," Rebekah said. "He's also responsible for the positioning and sizes of the other black holes in this galaxy."

"I knew it," Faylin said. "Didn't I tell you it was him?"

"What're you talking about? You didn't say nothing about no Tee-zee," Eric said. "You said Quentin."

Quentin spun around, looking from Faylin to Eric. "What about me?"

Faylin waved a dismissive hand. "Nothing. We were doing a little speculating, that's all."

Walter huffed. "We? A little speculating? You all but said he was the one who'd brought the darkness to Salem."

"You…you thought I… How could you?" Quentin's eyes welled up as he gave Faylin a questioning look.

She tsked. "What? It's not like I did or said anything bad or wrong. I speculated, that's all. If you'd been here on time, there would have been nothing to speculate about. Rebekah told us to be here at three. You were late. Not my fault. I got here early."

"Leave him alone," Rebekah said, then turned to Quentin. "How long?"

"How long what?"

"Has Tee-zee been missing? When did you last call for him?"

"About an hour, maybe two hours ago in human time. I wanted to check in with everyone before coming here, but he didn't respond." Quentin's lower lip trembled even more. "I don't know where he is."

Faylin snorted. "Maybe he got sucked into one of his black holes."

"That's not funny," Vaughn snapped.

Rebekah shot him a hard look.

"Sorry. Didn't mean to step on your turf. But you do know what could happen if Tee-zee's really missing?" Vaughn wanted to kick himself for asking the question. Of course she knew what it meant. She was a KOFE.

"So what if the twerp's missing?" Faylin said. "What's the big deal? We just find him and slap his wrists, right?"

"It *is* a big deal," Rebekah said. "Everything in the universe has its proper place and serves a purpose in that proper place. If the black holes are not where they're supposed to be at the time the earth rotates to make way for high tide, there will be no high tide. There will be no tide at all. And without the ebb and flow of the tides, every body of water on the planet will eventually grow stagnant, lose its oxygen. Fish will die, plants, too. Then eventually, inevitably, animals and humans—even elementals."

Faylin tsked in disbelief. She looked at Vaughn.

"She's right," he said.

Rebekah glanced at her watch. "We have about two

and a half hours before the next tide. Not much time to find him."

"But isn't Tee-zee a black hole?" Walter asked. "How do you lose a black hole? It'd be like someone losing this darkness. How do you lose the dark?"

Quentin opened his mouth as if he meant to respond, then snapped it shut.

"That's a very good question," Ariel said. "'Cause you can't lose the dark, really, right?"

Vaughn saw the depth of worry on Rebekah's face. He wanted to hold her, assure her that he would be by her side no matter what they had to face. But this wasn't about what he wanted. It had to be about what Rebekah needed, right now more than ever. Lives depended on her—as did the future of the whole damn planet.

Rebekah looked at her watch again, only to see too many minutes going by too fast.

She'd tried to collect her thoughts, narrow her focus to the challenges ahead.

Originally, when Salem's darkness first came to her attention, she had in fact feared that one of her charges might be responsible for it. The darkness seemed too big an event for a sorcerer. She'd yet to know one with enough power to affect the well-being of the universe. Many sorcerers had the power to produce darkness by casting an elementary magic spell. But those spells only created illusions, like pulling a shade over a sunlit window. The darkness here had no break in continuity, a sure sign that it wasn't an illusion. It sat heavy over the town like the lid of a casket. Because of that, she had to consider the possibility that Tee-zee might be responsible. Had the elemental gone into hiding after he heard Quentin was headed for Salem to meet her and feared being found out? As much as she hated even considering the possibility, there was only one way to know for sure. They had to find Tee-zee.

But how?

She communicated regularly with the elders telepathically and knew they stayed in touch with their charges the same way. It was possible that Quentin was too upset to get a telepathic fix on Tee-zee's whereabouts. If their telepathic powers were combined, they might be able to tune in to the lower elemental and make contact.

Rebekah turned to Quentin and held out her hands. "Maybe we can find him together. Take hold of my hands."

"Good idea," Faylin said. "Power in numbers."

"What numbers?" Walter asked.

"Are you always this dense?" Faylin asked.

"Huh?"

"Just shut up and pay attention, leaky lips."

"Quentin?" Rebekah said, capturing the elder's attention. She motioned, and he took hold of her hands.

"Now, please, I need the rest of you to be quiet," Rebekah said.

"Can I help?" Vaughn asked, taking a step toward them.

She glanced up at him, and in that second, memories and images from the past came rushing into her mind, too many to dismiss or brush away...

She had always taken her role as KOFE seriously. Although her parents had been KOFEs and she carried a Keeper's birthmark—hers a pentacle, a word Rebekah preferred over pentagram, since most people associated the latter with evil—she had not automatically inherited her position the way her cousins, Samantha, June and Katie Sue, had inherited theirs. The Order of Antiquities demanded that KOFEs earn the title through hard work, study and absolute dedication. Rebekah had done just that after the untimely deaths of her parents. She had committed herself completely to the cause of becoming a KOFE—or dying in the attempt. She knew no better way to honor her family.

The race to occupy the open high seat had not been an easy one, especially with Vaughn Griffith nipping at her heels. She'd known him since childhood and had carried a secret crush on him throughout her teens. He was smart, ambitious and handsome in a rugged, outdoorsman sort of way. As she'd grown older and life had taken a more serious turn, her crush on Vaughn had turned into frustration. She'd seen him as a relentless tease and felt he needed to take life more seriously. She hadn't really been surprised when he'd stepped up to challenge her for the KOFE position. She'd figured he was doing it simply to get a rise out of her.

Throughout the competition, he had demonstrated multilevel supernatural powers with uncanny ease. He seemed to take those powers for granted, which angered her, because her own powers had developed only after relentless practice and sheer, dogged determination.

In the end, when the title of KOFE had officially become hers, she suspected that she'd won by the smallest of margins. But it was still a win—and no small feat, considering that had been nearly three years ago, when she'd been twenty-five, the youngest KOFE on record.

The competition had been exhilarating, but not because she'd been a woman who'd beaten a man. It had nothing to do with gender or physical strength. It was because she knew Vaughn hadn't given her an inch. She'd earned the title fair and square. She remembered the look of absolute sincerity on his face when he'd congratulated her on the win. How her breath had caught when he'd leaned over and kissed her unexpectedly. And how, almost immediately afterward, for no apparent reason at all, he'd seemingly disappeared from the face of the earth. She hadn't seen him since. Until now.

Now—out of nowhere—Vaughn Griffith had traipsed into Salem, Massachusetts, and offered to help. She wanted to tell him to take a flying leap off the nearest cliff.

But she didn't.

Her responsibilities as KOFE took precedence over pride. And whether she wanted to admit it or not, she couldn't deny Vaughn's amazing telepathic abilities. She'd witnessed them firsthand during the KOFE competition. Refusing his help now would be childish on her part—and irresponsible.

With a sigh, she freed her right hand from Quentin's grasp and offered it to Vaughn. He immediately took hold of it, then linked his other hand to Quentin's, completing the circle. The heat of his hand in hers made it difficult to concentrate.

"Quentin," Vaughn said, "you know your charges better than anyone. What are we looking at here? A breakdown in communication? Or do you think Tee-zee's hiding because he caused this darkness?"

A look of embarrassment crossed Quentin's face. "If you had asked me that this morning, I would've bet the universe that none of my charges could possibly be responsible for it. When I told them I was coming to Salem and why, many of them wanted to help, Tee-zee especially. Now that he's missing, though… I don't know. I just don't know." His eyes filled with pain. "I'm really sorry, Rebekah. I lost track of him and let you down. I'm so sorry."

She squeezed his hand. "I'm not faulting you for any-thing, so stop beating yourself up. You're a good elder, Quentin. Sometimes a person—even an elemental—gets an idea or plan stuck in his or her head and there's noth-ing we can do to change it. They'll do what they want to do regardless. We may be jumping the gun here, any-way, and we have precious little time for speculation—an hour and forty minutes until the tide is due to roll in. Let's just concentrate on finding Tee-zee, and we'll deal with the rest as it unfolds."

"Whoa!" Walter suddenly sprang to life as if he'd been jabbed with a hot poker. "An hour and forty minutes? That's not enough time! If the tide doesn't come in, my mermaids and all the undines will get sick. They might die!" He started to pace. "This is simply disastrous, be-yond crucial. We've got to find Tee-zee."

"Get a grip, water boy," Faylin said. "We talked about this earlier. Why are you freaking out about it now?"

Walter's pacing picked up speed. "Because... I don't know. I guess it just sank in."

"Well, take a breath, bubble belly. It's not the end of the world yet."

"Easy for you to say," Eric said. "You and yours are sittin' at the planet's core, so you've got a little time. Wal-ter don't. His charges are gonna be hit right away if the tides stop. Then mine are gonna follow, 'cause when the water elementals start dying, ain't gonna be nobody left to water the earth. Won't take long then before this big ol' blue ball starts crumbling away. And when that happens, you'll see. Only a matter of time before you get snuffed out like a candle at a kid's birthday party."

"He's right," Ariel said in her breathy, high-pitched voice. "Planets will tumble out of their orbits and crash

into each other. A lot of people are going to die. Well…
all of them will die, actually."

Faylin arched a brow. "The earth's going to crumble
for real?"

Vaughn nodded. "If the black holes aren't in place for
tide, the natural order of the universe gets disrupted. We
know what the repercussions of that are. We can only
guess at the time it will take for them to occur."

"If it's so important, then why don't you take his place,
Quentin, and go play black hole?" Faylin asked.

"It doesn't work that way," Rebekah said. "As a quintessence elder, Quentin's natural form is literally the con-
stituent matter of the heavenly bodies, meaning he and
the governors who are responsible for the other galaxies
basically keep everything in the universe orbiting in its
proper place. He can't do that and be a stationary black
hole at the same time."

"You're our Keeper. Can't you change that?" Faylin
asked.

"No way. Number one Keeper rule: don't change
what's already in place. My job is to make sure what's
in place stays there—meaning all of you—and functions
as a cohesive unit."

"Well…damn," Faylin said, frowning.

"Yeah, that really sucks," Arial agreed.

"Okay," Faylin said, "so nature gets disrupted, then
what?"

"We're gone," Eric said.

"Yep," Walter said, sweating profusely now. "Gone."

Faylin swiped a hand over her mouth nervously. "Then
what the hell are we waiting for? We've got to find this
twerp and set him straight!"

"That's my plan," Rebekah said. "But all of you need

to stop babbling so we can concentrate and try to reach him."

Wide-eyed, Faylin mimed zipping her mouth shut. She motioned to her peers, and Walter, Eric and Ariel mimed the same.

"Ready?" Rebekah asked Quentin.

He nodded.

"Yes," Vaughn said. The sound of his voice made her acutely aware once again of his hand, warm in her own. It sent a tingle through her body that she had to mentally block. Otherwise she would never be able to focus and connect with Tee-zee.

Rebekah closed her eyes, and in that moment she felt a surge of energy flow from Quentin's hand into her left arm and the same coming from Vaughn on her right. As her energy flowed into them in return, she felt like a new fuse in a circuit breaker—alive, connected. In the center of her mind's eye a ball of brilliant white light appeared— the Circle of Knowledge. Without it, telepathy, along with several other powers, would not, could not, exist.

Tee-zee, where are you? As your Keeper and your leader, as Quentin's Keeper, I command you to reveal your location.

The only thing Rebekah heard in response was a dull hum—telepathic white noise. She felt Quentin's grip tighten on her hand and she gave his a small squeeze for reassurance.

Tee-zee, she went on, *I command you to make your whereabouts known immediately. If you don't—*

Wait, Vaughn said suddenly, his mental voice booming in Rebekah's ear.

Startled, she struggled not to open her eyes so she could find his shin—and kick it.

Do you have to be so loud?

Sorry—but I hear him. I hear Tee-zee.

Rebekah strained an internal ear, stepped closer to the Circle of Knowledge. There—just beneath the hum of the white noise—she heard a muffled voice. Low, too low for her to make out the words, but she heard it. For the words to be clearer, she would have to move even closer to the light, which might prove dangerous. The Circle of Knowledge acted like a magnet, pulling all those who sought its knowledge toward its center. Too close and you could be sucked in and made part of it—your old self ceasing to exist completely.

I hear him, too! Quentin cried.

Frustrated with the poor reception, Rebekah chanced another step toward the light.

That single step made a difference. The mumbling beneath the white noise took on just enough clarity. A small voice, like that of a child—and an unmistakable cry for help.

Chapter 3

Quentin had obviously heard the cry for help as well, because he immediately shouted, *Where are you, Tee-zee? We can't help if we don't know where you are.*

Rebekah heard more mumbling and took another step toward the light.

You're getting too close, Vaughn warned.

No choice. I can't make out what he's saying. Have to find out his location.

He's my responsibility, Quentin said. *I'll do it.*

No, you will not, Rebekah said. *We need you, Quentin—me, all of the ethereal elementals.*

Yeah, but isn't that like six of one, half a dozen of another? If I don't get Tee-zee in place, there won't be anything or anyone left for me to lead.

Rebekah's mental alarm suddenly went off as she thought more closely about Vaughn. In the short time she'd been preoccupied with Quentin, Vaughn had managed to make his way dangerously close to the Circle of Knowledge. Her heart started beating triple time.

Vaughn, get back! She tried mentally pulling him away, but he didn't—wouldn't—budge. *Vaughn!*

He nodded, but not at her. *Where?* The question wasn't for her, either. He'd obviously found a much stronger, clearer communication line with Tee-zee. *Yes, I can hear you…How big?…We will…It'll be okay, I promise…We'll find you.*

And then Vaughn took a step back and the Circle of Knowledge abruptly vanished. In the physical realm he let go of their hands, breaking the connection.

Rebekah's eyes sprang open. "What the hell were you thinking, getting that close?" she asked Vaughn.

"We needed information, and that was the only way to get it."

"So something like that is only foolish and irresponsible if I'm the one doing it. Is that it?"

"No." His eyes briefly broke contact with hers.

"Yeah, right. You never could lie worth a damn."

"I—"

"Forget it," she said. "What about Tee-zee?"

Four impatient elemental elders suddenly appeared at her side, all of them talking at the same time.

"Did you—"

"—find him?"

"Where's—"

"For the love of light, everybody shut up so we can hear what they found out!"

In the following two seconds of silence, Quentin managed to ask, "Where is Tee-zee?"

"As best I could decipher, trapped under the ground," Vaughn said.

"Under…" Walter began.

"Where?" Quentin asked. "What ground?"

"How on earth did he get stuck underground?" Rebekah asked.

Vaughn shook his head. "From what I pieced together,

Quentin was right. Tee-zee really wanted to help here in Salem. He knew you mandated that the elders take on human form, so he tried changing into one."

Quentin gasped. "He's never done that before."

"Obviously," Vaughn said. "Seems like he got confused midtransformation. I'm not clear on why he went underground in the first place, but I do get that whatever small space he's in now wasn't so small when he first got there. He probably finished the transformation inside of whatever hole he found, and now he can't make his way out."

"But where beneath the ground?" Rebekah asked. "Did he fall in a hole? Is he under a reef in the water? Did—"

"Judging from Tee-zee's description, I think he's in a cave," Vaughn said.

"A cave *where,* though?" Quentin said.

"Yeah, there must be thousands on this continent alone," Faylin said. "But if he's trapped inside because of a stupid human body, why doesn't he just revert back to his elemental state?"

"I don't think he knows how to revert back," Vaughn said. "And I get it about the caves, but he's got to be relatively close. Otherwise I wouldn't have been able to connect with him so clearly." He turned to Eric. "Are there caves in Salem?"

"Not right in Salem, but close by," Eric said. "Maybe thirty to thirty-five miles west of town."

"Great, we've got caves," Faylin said. "Why are we just standing here, then? Let's go get him."

Ariel, who'd been unusually quiet up to now, asked, "But how do *we* get him out when he's mutated into something too big to get out on his own?" She looked flustered and began to wring her hands. "Huh? How?"

"Good point," Walter said. "But I'm sure with all of us together, we'll come up with something, don't you think?"

"For sure," Faylin said.

"We're not going to be together," Rebekah said.

"Huh?" Eric said.

"Why not?" Ariel asked.

"Because I need each of you in other places."

"I don't get it," Faylin said. "We finally know where Tee-zee is and you don't want us to help get him out?"

Now that the elemental had been located, Rebekah immediately leaned hard toward her cousins' initial suspicion that a rogue sorcerer was responsible for the darkness. Which was frightening even to consider, because it meant the sorcerer would have to be more powerful than any she'd run across before. And she knew some *very* powerful sorcerers.

"That's the point," Rebekah said. "We *know* where he is. Even though it's important that we get him back into position for the tides, that still leaves someone—maybe some uber sorcerer—playing 'who's got the light' with Salem. That's where I need you, looking for this guy. We need as many eyes and ears as we can get out there, so he can be found and stopped."

Faylin pouted. "I don't wanna look for some stupid sorcerer." She suddenly brightened. "Hey, I can light up the cave so you can see where you're going. Good idea, right?"

Rebekah shook her head. "Think about it, Faylin. If Tee-zee is in a place too small for a human body to escape, that means you wouldn't be able to get in, either. You'd have to revert back to your elemental form to get anywhere near him. The last thing we need is a fried Tee-zee. As for the sorcerer, if that's who's creating the

darkness, he's anything but stupid. We're probably looking at someone very powerful. I mean *really* powerful.
The sorcerers I know can only do silly hocus-pocus illusions. None of them have the ability to screw with the
sun, even in a controlled setting like Salem. No matter
who's doing it, or how, it's serious. No illusion. And if
he, she or it is not stopped soon, the darkness will keep
growing, moving beyond the borders of Salem into the
next town, then the next state. We're talking perpetual
darkness eventually covering the entire Earth. That has
the same potential for planetary devastation as a mis-
placed black hole."

"Wow, I didn't think of that," Ariel said.

"Yeah," Faylin said. "Pretty heavy-duty stuff."

"What about me helping with Tee-zee?" Walter asked.

"Same problem with your human body and your elemental form, only you'd wind up drowning him."

"When you're talking caves, though, you're talking my
turf," Eric said. "I should be there, because I can move
the earth out of the way to get to Tee-zee if we have to."

"Sorry, Eric, afraid not," Rebekah said. "It's not that
simple. A shift in the earth could cause a cave-in and bury
Tee-zee alive. It could even facilitate an earthquake. We
can't take that chance."

"Okay, so what, then?" Walter asked. "What do you
want us to do?"

"I need you to take your undines, nymphs, mermaids,
all of them, and head west of town. Have everyone keep
an eye out for suspicious activity, underwater or otherwise. Faylin, you collect your salamanders and go
south. Same thing applies—eyes and ears, as many as
you can put together. Eric, you and your charges look to
the north."

"I guess that leaves me looking east, huh?" Ariel said.

"Yes, get all of your sylphs together, especially the fairies, and monitor the east end of Salem."

"Okay, but…how are you going to get to the caves and still have time to get Tee-zee out? And *how* are you going to get him out?"

Ariel's helium-filled, Marilyn Monroe voice might have been irritating as hell to listen to, but the air elder was far from being a dumb blonde.

"I know the timing will be tight," Rebekah said, "but we'll manage. I'll figure it out."

"Well…I could get you there really quick. You know, like in a tornado or something. You'd be at the caves in no time."

"Thanks for the offer, but no tornadoes."

"But—"

"No buts. Just head east like I said. With everyone covering so much ground, I'm sure we'll come up with some solid clues pretty quick. I'll take care of Tee-zee." Even as she said it, Rebekah wondered how she would manage it. Heaven only knew what kind of human form Tee-zee had chosen. The bigger the body, the more difficult it would be to revert him back to his elemental state, especially in a small space.

"*We* will take care of Tee-zee," Vaughn said. "I'm going with you."

"That's not necessary. I can—"

"Rebekah…*we'll* get Tee-zee," Vaughn repeated softly.

She sighed and gave him a slight nod. The sigh had been one of relief, but she would never let him know. For the first time since she'd spotted him headed for the gazebo, she was glad he was here. If ever there was a time she needed backup, it was now.

"I'm definitely going, though," Quentin said. "Tee-zee's my charge. I can help him change back to his natural state."

"I wish it was that easy, Quentin," Rebekah said, "but you can't be the one to do it. In order to revert him to an elemental state, you'd have to be in your natural form. Two quintessence elementals in that small space, especially with one being an elder, would act like a detonator to a mountain of explosives. It would cause an underground explosion far worse than anything that might happen if Eric started moving the earth around. Just hang tight, okay? Keep tabs on the rest of your charges and make sure everyone has their attention focused overhead. I promise you'll be the first to know when we get Tee-zee out."

Rebekah looked over at her elders. "Once you and your charges have covered your assigned territories, I want you to switch. If you had the north end of town, take the south. I want fresh sets of eyes and ears looking and listening at all times, until all four corners of Salem have been covered by all of you. Meanwhile, as soon as we find Tee-zee and get him repositioned, we'll come and help you. And I'll bring more troops if I can—my cousins are Keepers, too, and their charges can help." She hated the thought of having to bow out of Sam's party, which was scheduled to start at seven-thirty, only an hour and a half after the tide. Realistically, though, she didn't see any way they would make it back in time.

"That's all fine and wonderful," Walter said, "but I still don't see how you're going to get Tee-zee out of the cave. If my human body won't fit, yours and Vaughn's won't, either."

"I'll dig him out if I have to," Vaughn said.

"What's the difference between you digging him out and me moving the earth?" Eric asked, frowning.

"Big difference," Ariel said. "Like a summer breeze and a hurricane. No disrespect meant, Eric, but Vaughn can dig slowly and move little bits of dirt at a time. Your way would be quicker for sure, but it might kill Tee-zee, too, like Rebekah said." She glanced over at Rebekah. "Right?"

"Yes."

Eric harrumphed.

"Okay, we're wasting time rehashing this," Rebekah said. "Everyone get into your directional positions and—wait. Eric, I need the coordinates to the caves."

He squinted, as if trying to read a faraway sign. "Forty-two degrees, sixteen feet, forty-four point one inches north. Seventy-one degrees, twenty-four feet, fifty-nine point eight inches west."

Rebekah nodded, committed the coordinates to memory, then dismissed the elders. "Go. I'll see all of you soon."

In the time it took her to blink, the elders vanished, leaving her alone with Vaughn. All that remained as evidence that the elders had even been there were a red sports coat, a pair of tuxedo trousers and a blue aviator's hat, complete with earflaps.

With Rebekah's back momentarily to him, Vaughn chanced a smile. She hadn't put up a fight when he'd insisted on accompanying her to the caves. That had to mean something, hopefully that her heart was softening toward him.

One of the things he'd always admired about Rebekah was her willingness to put the needs of others before her own. He knew sometimes that meant her pride had to take a backseat as well, as it had earlier. He'd seen the internal struggle on her face when he mentioned the caves.

Her fierce independence had wanted to tell him to take a hike, but instead she'd chosen to follow her head as a responsible Keeper and hadn't pushed back when he'd insisted on helping. She might not always have been great about asking for help, but when a situation became serious, hitting the point of no return, she graciously accepted help when offered.

She'd matured into a remarkable Keeper. Her tenacity, determination and sheer dedication—all of which he'd witnessed during the KOFE competition, as well as secretly over the past two years—had only grown.

He knew the responsibilities that came with the KOFE title, understood the seriousness of the position. It was why he'd competed for the KOFE seat in the first place. Not because he didn't think a woman could handle it, but because he wanted to protect Rebekah. It had always been about protecting her.

After the competition, the Order of Antiquities had held a party in Rebekah's honor, and he had sought her out to offer his support and to congratulate her. There'd been so many in attendance, though, that he'd found it virtually impossible to get her alone. Later that evening he'd found her standing in the garden, staring off into space. When she'd spotted him, she'd given him a soft smile. It had been the smile of someone who'd been contemplating something bittersweet. He'd returned the smile and held out a hand, intending to bring her close for a simple hug. But something had happened the moment their bodies connected. His lips, as if acting without his control, had immediately sought hers.

The kiss had been electrifying, all consuming. It had erased time and space. All that existed or mattered was Rebekah, the feel of her, the taste of her. Their kisses became hungry and urgent. To this day, he couldn't recall if he'd offered her words of congratulations. If they hadn't heard someone calling out for Rebekah, insisting she was needed for yet another speech, he was certain things between them would have gone much further than a kiss.

It was then that Vaughn first contemplated leaving Malta. Being a KOFE would require Rebekah's full attention. He didn't need to be panting after her like a thirsty puppy at a time when she needed to be highly focused.

He had never been able to bring himself to leave the island, however. Instead, he'd simply moved out of sight. For two and a half years he'd watched her from afar, always waiting to step in if she got in over her head or was in serious danger. It had been one of the most difficult things he'd ever had to do—staying away from her. She'd been so near, yet so far away.

He'd done a lot of soul-searching before following her to Salem. He'd anticipated her asking "Why now?"— which she had—and he wanted to offer a viable answer. He'd considered using the elders as an excuse because the lot of them could be a handful when gathered in one place. But he'd witnessed, albeit secretly, her handling them collectively before, and she'd managed perfectly. But combining their unruliness with the darkness and the potential threat it posed had provided a viable platform from which to step back into her life. Or so he'd hoped. The missing black hole and the ticking tidal bomb it created certainly didn't hurt his cause.

No matter the plausibility of his excuse, appearing in Rebekah's life again was a gamble. She could easily have ordered him away. This was a woman who knew what she wanted. Strong, capable and very aware of who she was. She didn't need to be attached to a guy to find or hold on to her identity. What Rebekah needed was a man confident enough in himself not to be intimidated by her strength. Vaughn knew he was that man. He just needed a chance to prove it to her.

"Ready?" she asked, shaking him from his reverie.

"Always."

She turned in a slow circle, scanning the Common.

"What are you looking for?"

"People. I have to lift the illusion veil before we teleport and I don't want our sudden disappearance to give someone's grandma a heart attack. You do remember how to teleport, right?"

"Absolutely."

She studied him for a moment, searching his eyes. "You sure? It's been a long time since the competition. Have you practiced since then?"

"Sure. A few times, actually." In truth, it had been way more than a few times. He'd teleported almost every day. It had been the only way he'd been able to keep track of Rebekah and stay out of sight at the same time.

"Okay…good," she said a bit hesitantly.

Not wanting to step on her territorial toes again, he said, "I'm ready whenever you are. Lead the way."

She brushed a few strands of hair away from her face, then turned away from him, raised her right hand, palm out, and began to walk the inside perimeter of the gazebo. When she returned to his side, she dropped her arm, balled her hands into fists and, with no more fanfare than that, vanished.

Impressive.

Vaughn chuckled. She'd always been better at teleporting than he had. No matter how many times he did it, he couldn't make it *pop* the way she did. She had the instant disappearance thing down pat. His "takeoff" looked more like the flicker from a dying lightbulb.

Vaughn repeated her ritual and mentally prepared to

teleport. Instead of concentrating on the coordinates Eric had given them, he focused on Rebekah. He didn't need the numbers to get to the cave. She was already there. All he needed was her.

All he'd *ever* needed was her.

Within a matter of seconds Vaughn's mind's eye saw nothing but Rebekah's face. Her beautiful, violet-colored eyes, high cheekbones and small nose. Her sweet, full lips. Those lips... He would follow them anywhere and for the rest of his life. He felt the tingle that always came with teleporting race up his arms and spread across his chest.

Vaughn couldn't help but think of the pain he'd caused her and how much he regretted it. She had no clue that his intentions back then were honorable and for her benefit. All she knew was that he had disappeared. Unfortunately, hindsight didn't give him any clues as to how he might have handled things differently. The problem back then had been him—his inability to give Rebekah the space she needed to grow and mature as a Keeper. He always longed to touch her, to hear her laughter, even to watch her sleep. He was still the problem. The biggest difference between now and then was Rebekah's growth as a Keeper. It was clear that no one—himself included—had the power to distract her when duty called. He hoped—prayed—that the damage he'd done wasn't irreparable. At least her acceptance of his offer to help was a start. He had to find a way to get through the wall she'd built around her heart so she would know how he truly felt.

His world had always revolved around Rebekah. It still did. In fact, had it not been for her, he might very well be spinning mindlessly through some other dimension right now. Earlier, when he'd moved closer to the Circle of Knowledge to hear Tee-zee's words more clearly, he had felt the light's incredible, unmistakable pull. It had mesmerized him, taunted him to come closer. It had been so tempting to let go, to simply fall into its warmth and be lost forever. The only thing that had kept him from doing that was Rebekah, the knowledge that if he succumbed to the light's temptation he would be leaving her again, only this time for real, no hiding in the shadows. For real and forever.

He remembered the feel of her skin when he'd held her hand earlier as they linked to Tee-zee telepathically. It had taken a Herculean effort not to lean over right then and kiss her. He remembered so well how her lips had tasted that night in the garden. Thinking about it now sent a different sensation vibrating below his belt, which he, regretfully, had to staunch. In order for him to reach Rebekah at the caves, his entire being and mind had to be centered on her. He didn't want to botch the teleportation by allowing his other head to share the focus— because it never shared. It always took over.

The teleportation tingle traveled down his back, his stomach, his legs. He no longer felt the cold wind of Salem's dark winter afternoon. In real time, teleporting took only a few seconds. Right now, though, it felt like a lifetime. He couldn't wait to be standing beside her again.

As the tingling sensation reached his feet, Vaughn heard a man in the distance shouting, "Holy crap, look! Did you see that?"

Damn. Obviously someone had seen him flicker away. As far as he was concerned, though, that voice could have come from another universe. It was faint, but in this state he wasn't able to tell if the voice came from ten feet away or a thousand. Regardless of the distance, he was too far along in the process to stop it now. Even if he could, it would be a stupid thing to do. The person had already seen him disappearing. The shock of seeing him solidify again might send the guy to the loony bin.

But right now he didn't have time to ruminate on the guy's mental state. He had to maintain his own. He had to get to Rebekah. Always Rebekah...

Had he seen a softening in her eyes when she'd looked at him just before she disappeared? Had it been a look of forgiveness? Or had his mind played a trick on him, creating its own illusion veil, showing him only what his head and heart wanted to see?

Either way, he was about to find out.

Chapter 4

The cry for help still sounded muffled, but it was definitely closer, which told Rebekah she'd landed in the right place even before she opened her eyes. When she did open them, she found herself standing in the middle of nowhere. Open fields covered with snow were to her left and large, equally snow-covered waist-high mounds of tightly packed dirt stood on her right. The mounds were littered with branches, but through the clutter she spotted a small opening in one of them. It appeared barely big enough for a small child to wiggle through.

"*These* are the caves?" she asked aloud, surprised.

She didn't know what she'd been expecting. When Eric had said there were caves thirty-five miles from Salem, her mind had automatically pictured deep, dark wells made of rock, each filled with stalactites and stalagmites and little streams of water.

Even more surprising to her was the sight of the setting sun. It made her realize just how devoid of light Salem had been. Seeing the horizon painted in different hues of orange, red and purple filled her with a simple joy and appreciation. To never have the opportunity to see a sunset like this again would be a travesty.

"Beautiful, isn't it?"

Startled, she whirled around and found herself nearly nose to nose with Vaughn. The sight of his handsome face suddenly filled her with more joy than she wanted to admit.

She made a show of checking her watch. "What took you so long?"

He grinned. "You mean the three or four seconds longer than you? I—"

Somebody get me out of here, please! I can't see, and I can barely breathe. I'm gonna die. I don't know what I'm supposed to do.

The cry for help snapped Rebekah back into Keeper mode. She wanted to kick herself for allowing her attention to be diverted in any way while Tee-zee sat frightened in the dark. It was one thing to have your mind wander through the colors of a sunset, quite another to have it captured by a man who'd deserted you two and a half years ago.

She hurried over to the opening she'd spotted and started pulling branches away from it. Even cleared of debris, the opening was still too small for her to make it through.

"Tee-zee, this is Rebekah. I'm here and I've brought help, and we *will* get you out," she shouted into the mouth of the cave.

"Bless you," Tee-zee called. His voice sounded childlike, presumably a reflection of the body he'd chosen. "I'm so glad you're here. I'm sorry I've caused all this trouble. I didn't mean to. I just wanted to help."

"I know. It's okay. Now look around you, Tee-zee. Is there any way for you to crawl out?"

She heard a whimper, then, "No. I can't see anything. It feels like I'm sitting on the ground, but these…legs… these legs I have are dangling off the edge of something. I can't feel anything under the feet that I can stand up on."

Rebekah crouched down and peered into the hole, but saw only blackness. "Can you see any light from where you are? Any light at all?"

"I can't see anything but dark in here. I'm scared."

"What human form did you take, Tee-zee?"

"I…I don't know."

"Is it big? Small?"

"I can't tell. I've never had a body before. I saw Quentin change a couple times, so I just tried to do what he did."

Rebekah knew that for an elemental to take on a human form they had to have a specific gender and physique in mind. Without a specific vision, they could wind up with a hodgepodge of body parts—a head four times the width of the shoulders. Hips the size of ankles. Part female, part male. Half adult, half child.

Vaughn suddenly appeared on his hands and knees beside her.

"Tee-zee," he called into the cave. "If you saw how Quentin changed into a human, didn't you see how he changed back?"

"N-no, that's the problem. Please—please help me!"

"We're going to have to dig our way in and get him," Vaughn said to Rebekah.

"Depending on how far in he is, there may not be time. The only sure way is to have him revert back to his elemental state."

Vaughn let out a frustrated breath. "What about rope? If I can find some rope, maybe we can feed it down to him and drag him out."

Rebekah straightened, brushed her hair away from her face and shook her head. "That won't work, either. Tee-zee isn't used to having a human body. He wouldn't know what to do with the rope, and I doubt he's strong enough to hold on to it. Plus, we don't know how big the cave is, how deep, how labyrinthine. All I know is that we have to get him out somehow. If Tee-zee's human body dies, he dies. And if *he* dies, the black holes go haywire and we all die."

"But if he managed to get in as a human, shouldn't he be able to get out with that same body?"

"I don't think he *did* get in, not the way you're talking about. I think he miscalculated his destination and accidentally ended up in there when he changed."

Rebekah got on her hands and knees and stuck her head as far as it would go into the cave. It barely fit. Even this close, she couldn't make out its depth or width.

She heard whimpering and a sob from deep inside the cave, and it made her heart hurt. The elementals were like her children, and what she wanted more than anything was to take Tee-zee into her arms and comfort him. She pulled her head out, saw that Vaughn had gotten to his feet and followed suit.

"I'll teleport back to town and find a shovel. We can make the opening a little wider, at least. Maybe then we can see what we're dealing with."

"We don't have time for that," she said matter-of-factly. She glanced at her watch, no show about it this time. Forty-five minutes until high tide. "I'm going to have to transmutate. It's the only way I'll be able to locate Tee-zee, help him transmutate himself and get him out in time."

"No!" Vaughn said, his eyes widening. He took hold

of her shoulders, forcing her to face him. "No. It's too dangerous."

She'd only transmutated once before, and that had been at the competition for the KOFE seat. It involved molecular restructuring, and the person transmutating had to have a concentration level that was absolute. Otherwise it could be deadly. And it was the one thing Rebekah knew Vaughn was unable to do. Ultimately, it was the reason she'd won the KOFE competition.

The problem was, she didn't know if she would be able to reach that deep level of concentration with Vaughn nearby. Feeling his hands on her shoulders created such conflict inside her. She wanted to pull away, refuse his touch. And at the same time she wanted to draw closer to him and lay her head on his chest. She forced herself to stand still and do neither.

"We don't have a choice or the time to do anything different," she said softly.

"But—"

"There are no buts," she said. "We can't leave Tee-zee down there, and it's the only way to get him out. Besides, it's my job as his Keeper. I appreciate your concern, but I'll be fine."

This time she did pull out of Vaughn's grasp. She knelt again at the mouth of the cave, closing her eyes for a second. The part about needing to get Tee-zee out had been the truth. The part about being fine, not so much. She had no idea how this would turn out. It had been far too long since she'd transmutated, and she simply didn't know if she'd be able to do it successfully.

She glanced up and saw worry on Vaughn's face. "If something happens to me—"

"Roe, please, don't."

Oddly enough, the nickname didn't bother her this

time. "I'm not saying anything will. It's a just in case thing, you know? If something does, keep tabs on the elementals, will you? You're a little too arrogant for my taste, but you'd make a hell of a Keeper." She smiled.

He didn't return it.

"*You* are their Keeper, Rebekah Savay. Not me or anyone else. They need *you*. *I* need you. I know you're going to do this whether I like it or not, but you have to be okay. You have to make it work and be okay."

Vaughn's *I* was not lost on her, but she didn't allow herself the luxury of pondering the extent of what he'd meant by it. Time was running out, and she had a serious task ahead of her.

"Tee-zee," Rebekah called into the cave, "can you hear me?"

"Y-yes, I can hear you!" the quintessence elemental cried.

"I'm coming in to get you, but for me to find you, I need you to talk in a human voice, like you have been, and keep talking. Say anything, it doesn't matter what. I just need to hear your voice so I can get a specific fix on your location. Telepathy is too cerebral. It won't work in this situation. Do you understand?"

"I understand," Tee-zee said in a voice that sounded as if it belonged to a five-year-old boy. "What do you want me to say? Can I sing? Is that okay?"

"Singing's fine. I just need to hear the sound of your voice. It's so dark in there I won't be able to find my way to you otherwise. Once I'm down there, you're going to have to use your elemental voice to talk to me, got it? Just like you talk to Quentin every day with your mind."

"Okay…okay, got it. But I'm gonna sing now. Just don't laugh at my singing, okay?"

"I promise I won't."

With that, Rebekah heard a child's voice begin to sing off-key.

Rebekah sat back on her haunches, tuned in to the small voice and blocked everything else out of her mind. She allowed the sound of his voice to pull her to her center, which it did in a matter of seconds.

In her mind's eye, the brilliant ball of light from the Circle of Knowledge appeared front and center. It seemed bigger than ever before. From this point on, everything became internal. Whatever was happening around her was irrelevant.

Mentally, Rebekah lifted a hand and reached for the ball of light. The rays streaming from it seemed to stretch, elongate, vibrate toward her.

Now all she had to do was stay tuned in to the light and Tee-zee's voice and allow everything else to happen on its own.

The light from the Circle of Knowledge wrapped around her hand, encircling it with what looked like gold-and-white-striped cords. Even though everything was happening on a mental and metaphysical level, she felt a physical sensation of simultaneous hot and cold.

Tee-zee's singing was a constant in the background as the hot-cold cords traveled up Rebekah's arm.

They moved to her chest, her stomach...

The next thing Rebekah knew she found herself traveling horizontally through the cave in a narrow tunnel filled with silver glitter. The glitter acted like tiny spotlights, allowing her to see parts of it she'd been unable to see before. She was surprised by its depth as the silvery tunnel drew her down...down.

The tunnel itself seemed to follow the sound of Tee-zee's voice, or maybe it was her own mind directing the movement—she didn't know for sure. Either way, she traveled smoothly, effortlessly through the cave, and must have been heading in the right direction, because Tee-zee's voice grew louder. She felt neither hot nor cold, wet nor dry. The only sensation she felt at all was that of…being.

Suddenly, the tunnel jogged gently to the left, then down, before bringing her to a complete stop and standing her upright. She had no conscious thought of arms or legs. The tunnel did all the work, acting like a cocoon, moving her in whatever direction or position she needed. Until finally, in the glow of the tiny spotlights, Rebekah saw him.

Tee-zee sat naked on a ledge a mere ten feet away. He had the chubby face of a five- or six-year-old, and his arms were crossed over his chest. The feet dangling off the ledge were a size more fitting to a forty-year-old man. He swung them back and forth as he sang.

Tee-zee, it's me. Rebekah. I'm here.

When Tee-zee heard her, he unfolded his arms and she saw that his fingers were disproportionate to the rest of his body. Long and slender, better suited for a grown woman.

You found me! And I can see you. You look like light. Tiny dots of silver light danced over Tee-zee's face and chest, and in that light she noticed that below his large feet was a dark emptiness, indicating a depth she couldn't measure. And the only opening she saw was much too small for him to fit through, even as small as his chosen body was.

Tee-zee had been right. In human form, he wouldn't have been able to get out on his own. One misstep and the pit below him would have swallowed him for sure, and he could never make it through the tunnel in the rock. Without question, he had to be reverted back to his elemental state.

Which presented yet another problem.

In order for her to help him regain his elemental form, she would have to transmutate back to human form. She couldn't assist him in this molecular hodgepodge.

Without warning, the tunnel suddenly drew her slowly downward about five feet, then stopped.

Wait! Don't leave me! Tee-zee cried. *Where are you going?*

Rebekah tried to comfort him. *Don't worry. I'm not going anywhere.*

Evidently the silvery tunnel was part of her consciousness because it seemed to understand that she needed a place to put her feet once she transformed back into her human body.

To transmutate this time, Rebekah focused on each part of her body in order to establish the proper order for the molecular restructuring. She thought about how it felt when she brushed her hair, the tug of the brush on her scalp, the feel of tissue on her nose when she blew it, the feel of water on her face, breasts, stomach and legs when she showered. The feel of her feet in sneakers when she went for her morning jogs in Malta.

As she concentrated on each part of her body, the tunnel and all its tiny spotlights began to diminish. When she finally felt the ground beneath her feet—her human feet—she took a moment to steady herself. Without the specks of light from the tunnel, the darkness in the cave was absolute. She brought her hand up to her face, close to her nose—which she touched to make sure it had landed in the right place—and still couldn't see her fingers.

Fairly confident that all her physical parts had been

put back together in the right order, she sighed with relief. *Tee-zee, can you see me?*

Uh-uh. It's too dark.

She couldn't see him, of course, but she'd hoped that
as an elemental he would have an acuity of vision she
lacked. No matter. She remembered that the tunnel had
placed her just below and about five feet away from the
ledge he sat upon.

*Tee-zee, I'm going to stretch out my arms and reach
for you. I want you to do the same. Don't lean forward,
though, understand?*

Uh-huh.

*In order for me to help you switch back to your ele-
mental form, I've got to touch you. So when you feel my
fingers, grab hold to them, okay? And the minute you feel
yourself back in your elemental form, I want you to go
straight back to your position. Everything in the universe
is waiting for you. High tide needs to happen, so you have
to get there as quickly as possible. Do you understand?*

*I understand, and I will. I promise. And I'll never do
this again. I'll never try this again. I'm so sorry, and—*

*Just get back into place as quickly as you can. We
don't have much time.*

Okay. Stretch my arms, then the fingers...

Rebekah held out her arms. *Talk to me, Tee-zee, so I'll
know what direction to reach.*

What do you want me to say?

Anything. Say, 'Here, here.'

Tee-zee did as he was told, and in a matter of seconds
Rebekah's fingers connected with his. She grabbed hold
of them and held tight.

*Okay. Now, I know it's dark in here, but I need you to
close your eyes and think about Quentin. Think about*

what you do for him every day. What it feels like to be a black hole.

That's easy because it feels really great. I feel wide open and free. I can breathe easily, not like in this human body. It's all stuffy in here, and I can't move around the way I want. The other way I can go anywhere and do anything, and I can see all the stars and the planets....

As he spoke, Rebekah sent a flood of energy from her body to his. It vibrated from her core all the way up to her arms and through her fingers. She saw what Tee-zee described, him in his natural form—a black hole. A vital part of the universal structure. She felt the freedom he talked about. To keep herself from being pulled into the conversion, she quickly closed a mental gate that kept her within her earthly realm and Tee-zee within his own, grateful for the gates given to a KOFE that allowed her to do whatever was necessary to help the elemental while protecting herself.

It's happening! It's working!

Hearing his excitement, Rebekah thrust every ounce of energy she had left through the gate and into Tee-zee.

Before she knew it, and without warning, she felt a heavy gust of wind hit her full in the face, startling her. It was then she realized she was no longer holding Tee-zee's hand.

Her eyes flew open. *Tee-zee?* No matter the direction she looked in, all she saw was total darkness. Her heart thudded painfully in her chest. *Tee-zee, are you still here?*

From what sounded like a great distance, she heard the echo of Vaughn's voice. "Roe, are you okay?"

"Yes," she called back as loudly as she could—which, to her ear, sounded barely above a whisper.

"You did it, Roe. You got Tee-zee out. I saw him—a

stream of black smoke came right out of the cave and headed skyward."

She let out a sigh of relief. "Good," she said softly.

"Roe, can you get out? Can you climb out?"

She shook her head in the darkness. She barely had the energy to lift her voice loud enough for Vaughn to hear her. She had no idea where she was. What she did know, though, was that she would have to transmutate again to get out of this dank dungeon. She hated to even think about it. The two transmutations she'd already managed had pounded her down to a point of exhaustion she'd never known before. But she had no choice. There was no other way for her to get out.

"Can you?" Vaughn called out again.

"No. No climbing out."

"What? I can't make out what you're saying."

"I can't," she said more loudly. They should have been using telepathy, less of a drain. Then again, if Vaughn felt anything like she did at the moment, it was simply wonderful to hear, in every sense of the word, the sound of his voice.

Maybe if she lay down for a little while and rested she might be able to muster the strength to get out.

"Roe, please answer me."

Drawing on what little strength she had left, she shouted, "I can't climb out. Going to have to transmutate again."

"No! Don't take that chance again. I'll come and get you. We don't have to worry about time now. Tee-zee is out. I can dig you out if I have to."

"But I don't know where *out* is," Rebekah said. "It could take you a week to reach me."

Too exhausted to explain any further, she squatted in place. She had no clue as to how far down in the cave she was or how far from the opening. She wouldn't even be able to tell Vaughn what direction to start digging in. The only reliable way was for her to transmutate, let the tunnel guide her out.

She lifted her head and spoke as loudly as she could. "Digging won't work. Going to transmutate. Need you to talk to me. Need your voice for direction."

She heard her voice weakening and doubted Vaughn had heard much of what she'd said.

So tired...

She felt around, trying to find a place wide enough for her to lie down. She needed to rest. Needed to close her eyes...just for a moment.

"Then you listen to my voice!" Vaughn shouted. "I won't stop talking till you're safe." Evidently he *had* heard her.

Rebekah just wanted to sleep. Close her eyes and take a short nap. The only thing that kept her from doing it was the fear that if she did fall asleep she might roll off a precipice and into oblivion.

"Listen to my voice and come back to me," Vaughn said. "Follow my voice, Roe."

She closed her eyes and listened. She focused on his voice, his face....

"Hear me, Rebekah Savay. I love you. I always have. I never left you back in Malta, do you hear? I didn't leave you."

Her eyes sprang open.

"I only let you think I did because I didn't want to get in your way. I knew you needed to concentrate on your responsibilities as a Keeper. I didn't want to be a distraction. But I was always there, always watching out for you, making sure you were safe. I'm so sorry if that hurt you. I can't be without you again, Rebekah. I can't. I need you to come back to me."

The sound of Vaughn's voice, his words, moved into the center of Rebekah's heart and took root there, filling it to capacity. She couldn't believe what she was hearing. It consumed her completely.

"I need you, and I can't live without you."

And with that the silvery tunnel once again became Rebekah's cocoon. It swept her up gently, then moved her slowly up and forward.

"I need you in my life. I'll never let you go again."

The tunnel drew her closer to the sound of Vaughn's voice. She might have been structured differently on a molecular level now, but the heart beating inside her hadn't changed. It heard him and filled with overwhelming joy.

The next thing she knew, her forehead was resting against Vaughn's leather jacket and his arms were wrapped tightly around her.

She couldn't move. Her exhaustion was beyond the point of comprehension. It seemed to take too much energy to even think.

"I've got you," Vaughn whispered. "I've got you, Roe." He cupped the back of her head. "Are you okay? Talk to me, please. I need to hear that you're okay."

Rebekah managed the slightest nod. She really didn't know if she was okay, though. She'd never felt this tired before.

"We need to get you back to Samantha's," Vaughn said. "She can take a look at you, make sure you're okay. You can rest there. Teleporting back to Salem is out of the question, though. Not in your state. Can you walk at all?"

Before Rebekah could even think of forming the words

to answer, Vaughn said, "Of course not. Look at you. You can barely lift your head. I wish I could teleport us both."

She breathed in deeply, her nostrils filling with the scent of leather and musk from the sweat on his skin. She wanted him to stop talking and hold her tighter. To never let her go. She wanted to take the panic from his voice.

"I can carry you there if it comes down to it, but thirty-five miles—that would take hours."

His words barely had time to settle in her mind when she heard him call for Ariel. She knew he had the ability to communicate with the elementals telepathically. The fact that he didn't have the right to was moot. She didn't have the energy to argue.

Ariel, we need you. Rebekah needs you.

Rebekah heard Ariel's reply. *Why are you calling me, Vaughn? Is she okay?*

I think so, Vaughn said. *She found Tee-zee and sent him back. But she's exhausted.*

Oh, I think I saw him, Ariel said. *He zipped right past me—this giant column of black smoke, right through the stratosphere. It was awesome.*

I need you to take us back to Samantha's, Vaughn said. *Rebekah is too weak to walk, and I can't teleport both of us. I can carry her, but it would take forever to get there. Make the wind move her, Ariel. Take us to Samantha's.*

"Is it okay with you, Rebekah?" Ariel asked, and Rebekah realized the elder had joined them. "Is it okay for me to do that? I don't mean any disrespect, Vaughn, but she's my Keeper. I can only take orders from Rebekah." A look of desperation crossed her face. "Is it okay for me to do what he asks, Rebekah? To bring both of you back to Samantha's?"

"Yes," Rebekah whispered. "It's okay to do what he says." She felt Vaughn's arms tighten around her.

In a matter of seconds Rebekah felt the prickle of air against her cheeks and arms, a rush of wind against her back. She closed her eyes and held on to Vaughn as the wind pushed her harder against him, her cheek against his jacket, his chest. The smell of him was the scent of safety, the feel of his arms around her a lifeline against what felt like gale-force winds.

A storm?

Even at that thought, she felt no panic. The safety she felt in his arms was absolute.

Let the winds blow....

Let them blow....

The last thing she remembered was the sensation of flying, her feet lifting from the ground....

And her mind drifting off into what felt like the most peaceful sleep she had ever known.

Chapter 5

Sandwiched between thick, dark, swirling clouds, Vaughn held tightly to Rebekah. Ariel had chosen to move them as he'd asked by way of a cyclone—not the wisest of choices, now that he thought about it. But there hadn't been many alternatives. Ariel couldn't exactly transport both of them over thirty miles on a breeze.

He might not have been a Keeper, but he knew enough to know that having an elemental mess with Mother Nature's weather cycles was extremely dangerous. It was the main reason elementals answered to only two forces— their Keeper and Mother Nature herself.

If Mother Nature decided to do a cleansing by sending a hurricane or tsunami, an elemental's responsibility was not to change it or keep it from happening. Their sole purpose was to make certain it happened properly—no matter the human lives at stake. And for the most part, all the elementals held to that task.

Of course, that didn't mean an elemental didn't pull a mischievous stunt from time to time. A sudden deluge that seemingly came out of nowhere as you walked the streets of town on a cloudless day. A gust of wind sent at the very moment a Boy Scout ignited his first, hard-earned campfire, blowing it out. Little things that kept humans on their toes.

But the big events like earthquakes and hurricanes were Mother Nature's call alone, and a Keeper's job was to make certain that all the elementals performed as needed to fulfill Mother's wishes. To stop these catastrophic events from happening—or to make them happen—might alter the future of the planet and its inhabitants in ways that were never meant to be.

All things and all people served a purpose on earth, of that Vaughn was certain. And right now his purpose was to protect the beautiful woman resting in his arms. Ariel understood that when she'd been asked to carry them to Samantha's, it had been an exception to every rule ever set for an air elemental. He trusted that the elder would take great care and make certain that no damage came to humans or their property in the process.

As they stood in the heart of the storm, Vaughn lowered his face to the top of Rebekah's head as she stood snuggled against him and breathed in deeply, inhaling the scent of her. Without a second thought he kissed the top of her head once, twice, a third time.

There was still so much to do. He knew that the moment Rebekah had rested, and her mental and physical strength returned, she would be back in action, hunting with her cousins to find the culprit responsible for the darkness in Salem. And that was fine by him, because he planned to be right by her side the entire time.

He couldn't believe his good fortune. Here she was, the love of his life, safely tucked away in his arms. It might have been utter exhaustion that allowed her defenses to fall away long enough for him to take command and get them back to her cousin's, much less to allow him to take her into his arms and hold her this way. Once this was all over, he hoped it wouldn't take another bout of exhaustion to bring her back into his arms. If not, and by some miracle she came willingly, he knew it would take a hell of a man to keep her there.

Which was exactly what he planned to be and do for the rest of their lives—if she would have him.

As the whirlwind settled into a gentle breeze, Rebekah opened her eyes and saw that they were standing mere feet from her cousin Samantha's home.

She blinked against the colored lights that twinkled brightly about the house and lawn, where a plastic Santa was singing "Winter Wonderland."

Christmas Eve.

In all the commotion, she had almost forgotten about the holiday.

Tomorrow, a day meant to celebrate the birth of hope and love for all mankind, seemed doomed to be shrouded by darkness. The gravity of the situation weighed heavily on her. They still had to find and stop whoever was responsible for this perpetual night before the damage that had already been done became irreparable. Or, worse, spread.

Oddly enough, despite the seriousness of the situation, she felt some hope. She knew the strength and special abilities her cousins possessed would be a powerful weapon against the forces of darkness, and Vaughn's talents were a given. Collectively, they were powerful enough to drop any enemy to his knees. Then the darkness would finally end, and light, along with all its virtues, would once again fill the sky and the hearts of the good people of Salem.

Hope reborn.

She didn't think any better gift existed.

Well…maybe one.

Still resting in Vaughn's arms, she glanced up and gave him a small, trembling smile.

"Merry Christmas," she whispered.

A smile tipped the corners of his mouth. "Merry Christmas, Roe," he said softly, his eyes bright, loving, searching her own.

Then his expression grew serious, and he cupped the side of her face with a large hand, stroking her cheek with his thumb. "I swear, you have to believe me—not a day went by that I didn't think about you and wish we were together."

Rebekah looked away. She wasn't ready for him to see the truth in her eyes: that she had wished for the very same thing, if not more, over the past two and a half years. So much so that she'd unwittingly allowed him to become the standard by which she'd measured every man she dated.

And all of them had fallen short. She had been left feeling empty, lonely and hopeless, destined to either settle for a man who was second best or be alone for the rest of her life.

Vaughn gently lifted her chin, forcing her eyes to meet his again. "I don't want to know the pain of missing you anymore. We're together again, finally, and I don't want to spend another moment without you ever again. I love you, Rebekah Savay. I've always loved you. Even when we were kids, you breathed life into me. You still do."

Rebekah stood speechless, heart hammering in her chest. The rest of her body felt paralyzed. She feared any movement might cause her to wake up from an unforgettable dream. How many nights had she tossed and turned in bed, unable to get Vaughn off her mind, wishing he lay beside her, longing to hear the very words he'd just spoken?

"Say you'll have me, Roe," he said, his voice softer now, huskier. "Now and forever." He leaned closer, his breath warming her face. "Say it and make me the happiest man on earth. Say it and I promise to live the rest of my life making sure you never regret the decision."

As if on cue, the plastic Santa started singing "All I Want for Christmas Is You." Once, the irony would have warranted a chuckle.

But not now.

Not while in the midst of a kiss, a deep, sensual kiss that seemed to melt the snow beneath her feet and spark light into the depths of her soul. It illuminated a basic universal truth she'd somehow lost sight of through the years.

Love expanded hope.

Hope empowered dreams.

And dreams blazed trails to a brighter, happier future.

Love truly was the greatest gift of all.

She pressed her body closer to Vaughn's and deepened her kiss. His arms tightened around her, drawing her closer still. In that moment the pain she'd carried over the past two and a half years fell away. And possibly for the first time in her life, Rebekah suddenly understood the meaning of forever.

She saw it in his eyes, felt it in his touch, heard it in the beating of his heart and tasted it on his lips.

And she felt her heart open fully to it, taking in every measure of the gift he offered.

Merry Christmas, Rebekah Savay.

Merry Christmas, indeed....

* * * * *

UNHOLY NIGHT

—

KATHLEEN PICKERING

Dear Reader,

Season's greetings during this most wonderful winter festival of love and light!

Creating *Unholy Night* was such an adventure. Leave it to Heather Graham to combine a traditional human Christmas with multiple paranormal species, honoring each other's differences while overcoming world darkness. Isn't that what the Christmas season is all about? Creating light in the world?

Unholy Night explores the gift of giving—setting aside our own desires to bring joy to others. Courage, faith and love fuel the actions of Selkie Keeper Katie Sue and her Selkie lover, Jett, in overcoming the conflicts that arise this Unholy Night in Salem. Through the spirit of Christmas, these mismatched soulmates learn that love requires balance, truth and, so many times, compromise. In today's world of challenges and self-regard, what better time than now to consider ourselves in the bigger picture—the Christmas world tapestry of which we are all a part?

Merry Christmas. God bless us one and all.

Much love,

Kathleen Pickering

To everyone who sacrificed for love...and won.

Chapter 1

Katie Sue Montgomery stood below the high-tide line in the dark, listening as the gently breaking surf offered the only sign that she was near the shore. Bathed in the unholy night that had become relentless for the past two weeks, she blessed her cousin Rebekah, aka Roe, Keeper of the Five Elementals, who had arrived earlier in the day and been miffed enough with the cold weather to coax the air elemental elder into calming the biting winds.

The quiet winter air would make the evening hours more hospitable when Jett, her selkie lover, returned from the sea this Christmas Eve. She was sure he would arrive at this appointed hour as he had promised to do seven years ago and seven years before that. Each time she spent another brief holiday season with him when he came ashore and transformed from a seal into a man, only to lose him again to the sea. As an ocean dweller in his seal form, Jett was truly himself. Yet only as a man could he be hers. His love for her had been powerful enough to bind her to him despite his absence during these irretrievably lost years, but she had been younger then. Today she struggled with different feelings.

Had she thought these days of darkness would clear just for her and Jett because she loved him so much? The dark had done nothing but exaggerate her loneliness without him. Now she entertained the awful possibility that Jett wouldn't show. Why would he, when he loved his selkie life so much more than his time on land with her?

Even though she knew that wasn't true, it was in line with the thoughts that had been torturing her since the darkness hit, and even more so while helping set up for the Christmas Eve party at her cousin Samantha's earlier this evening. Meanwhile, everyone who was aware of her situation had been doing everything they could to get her out the door to greet Jett in time.

She tucked the end of her sand-colored scarf deeper into the collar of her coat. Only yesterday she had crocheted the scarf, choosing a silk corded yarn to match her blond hair, which she had cropped short in a fit of doldrums two days ago. She hoped Jett liked it, though at this point it hardly seemed to matter. The bad feelings inside her remained. The dull misery afflicting everyone in town had to be an offshoot of this unholy curse—because the prolonged unexplained darkness could be nothing else but a curse—that had invaded Salem.

And so far, no Jett in sight.

This stygian pall not only had the town mystics, Wiccans and paranormal beings scrambling for an answer, but the absence of sunlight had eclipsed the townspeople's well-being. The normally friendly and tolerant villagers of Salem were starting to become frazzled and impatient with each other. They'd strung holiday lights around town and decorated their homes for the Yuletide season, but the holiday songs piping from shops and restaurants could only go so far toward cheering people up.

The longer Katie Sue waited for Jett's arrival, the

more she grew irritated by the unusual despondent mood haunting her thoughts. She, Samantha and the other Keepers knew the unusual darkness was fueling these moods. Katie clung to the thought of the upcoming precious moments with Jett as her lover to buoy her through this difficult holiday season. Tonight she'd taken the daring step of bringing a sleeping bag with her. The darkness and the cold could be damned. Maybe if she and Jett made love as soon as possible, she could forget—if only for this Christmas Eve—her angst over the crucial decision before her.

The decision. There lay the crux of her problem. Today was Jett's birthday. He returned to this place of his birth at this same time and date every seven years since reaching manhood. Before then, she'd had the luxury of spending every day with him while he lived at her family's seaside mansion as a boy. They'd grown up together. Frolicked in the sea for hours on end because of her surprising ability to swim underwater for a long time. But once his fourteenth birthday hit, he'd been driven by instinct to return to the sea to fulfill his birthright as a selkie or lose his ability to transform. Would she welcome him with birthday greetings when he arrived tonight, or would she be telling him goodbye?

At twenty-eight, she had spent only six weeks with Jett in fourteen years. Those six weeks had been the most precious days of her life, because they had finally become lovers, but she and Jett were no longer children. She could not live with a mere three weeks basking in Jett's love only to let him go and endure another seven years without him. She wanted a husband, home and hearth. Children of her own to share with the man she loved. Her heart could no longer bear Jett's prolonged absences—not when the world carried on after he was gone and everyone forgot him except her.

Damn the selkie rule of shed your skin forever and stay human or return to the sea for seven years' time. Then again, when she'd learned from her mother that she'd inherited the role of Keeper of the Selkies, she'd known that falling in love with one of her charges was breaking the rules. The birthmark of a cresting wave inside her left arm matched the one her mother carried on her hip, identifying the women of their descent as selkie Keepers. Her mother had been grooming her since she turned fourteen—the year Jett left for the first time— because Christina Montgomery was preparing to retire. She'd been invited to join the International Council with the other elders and felt she would be of most assistance there. Katie learned that as a Keeper, the women of her line carried the latent selkie gene, giving rise to the possibility of having a selkie child. There was even a legend that a selkie Keeper might have the ability to transform into a selkie. The gift hadn't shown up for hundreds of years, so no one knew if it was really true. Yet for over a hundred years, her family had used their state-certified home for troubled boys as cover for their true role as Keepers of the selkies, who also sometimes sheltered there when they were young and not yet fully bound to the sea, as well as other paranormal water creatures.

She and Jett seemed damned on all counts. If only a sliver of sun would pierce the sky, perhaps her heart wouldn't feel as frigid as the sand beneath her boots.

The tumbling waves would have disguised his arrival to less-trained ears. But as a Keeper, she had heightened senses and heard the splash of direct motion. She felt his presence in the dark before he said a word.

"Jett!" His name tumbled from her lips. She turned

YOUR PARTICIPATION IS REQUESTED!

Dear Reader,

Since you are a lover of paranormal romance fiction – we would like to get to know you!

Inside you will find a short Reader's Survey. Sharing your answers with us will help our editorial staff understand who you are and what activities you enjoy.

To thank you for your participation, we would like to send you 2 books and 2 gifts – **ABSOLUTELY FREE!**

Enjoy your gifts with our appreciation,

Pam Powers

SEE INSIDE FOR READER'S SURVEY

YOUR READER'S SURVEY
"THANK YOU" FREE GIFTS INCLUDE:
- ▶ 2 Paranormal Romance books
- ▶ 2 lovely surprise gifts

PLEASE FILL IN THE CIRCLES COMPLETELY TO RESPOND

1) What type of fiction books do you enjoy reading? (Check all that apply)
- ○ Suspense/Thrillers ○ Action/Adventure ○ Modern-day Romances
- ○ Historical Romance ○ Humour ○ Paranormal Romance

2) What attracted you most to the last fiction book you purchased on impulse?
- ○ The Title ○ The Cover ○ The Author ○ The Story

3) What is usually the greatest influencer when you <u>plan</u> to buy a book?
- ○ Advertising ○ Referral ○ Book Review

4) How often do you access the internet?
- ○ Daily ○ Weekly ○ Monthly ○ Rarely or never.

5) How many NEW paperback fiction novels have you purchased in the past 3 months?
- ○ 0 - 2 ○ 3 - 6 ○ 7 or more

YES! I have completed the Reader's Survey. Please send me the 2 FREE books and 2 FREE gifts (gifts are worth about $10) for which I qualify. I understand that I am under no obligation to purchase any books, as explained on the back of this card.

237/337 HDL F5D5

FIRST NAME	LAST NAME

ADDRESS

APT.#	CITY

STATE/PROV.   ZIP/POSTAL CODE

on her electric lantern but it cast a paltry ring of light in front of her. "I can't see you."

"I'm here, Katie."

His words vibrated straight through her, plucking her heartstrings with the smooth, velvet timbre of his voice. Immediately her frozen heart began to melt. She watched in the thin artificial light as Jett shed his selkie skin and stood naked in the freezing wind.

She held out a bag of clothes and the down sleeping bag for him to drape around himself for extra warmth. As he stepped closer, her breath caught in her throat.

Jett was exquisite.

When you grew up with someone, their changes day by day didn't have as profound an effect as they did after prolonged absence. At twenty-one, Jett had been merci-lessly handsome with his lithe body, chiseled face and crooked smile. His bright, coal-black eyes always seemed to be laughing. That long, inky-black hair that fell in a cowlick across his forehead always begged, as it did now, for her fingers to brush it away and perhaps rest beneath those curls at the nape of his neck.

Jett was pure male. Naked, with the winter wind scrubbing his muscled skin, he was breathtaking from his broad shoulders to the flat plane of his belly high-lighted in the dim circle of light. His smile did things to the pit of her being that no one in her lifetime could match. His beautiful seal coat of silver-gray lay draped over his shoulders like a nobleman's cape.

"Jett…"

He took the sleeping bag from her and grinned when he realized it was large enough for two. "Is this my birth-day gift?"

"No, I am. Merry Christmas, Jett."

Ignoring the offered clothes, he pulled her within the

circle of his arms, wrapping them together in the cocoon of warm down, and captured her lips in a profound and urgent kiss.

She wrapped her arms around his neck, and the dampness of the seal fur and the heat of his kiss sent a frisson of heat and cold shimmering through her.

He broke the kiss long enough to whisper, "Katie, my love."

Uncaring of the cold, they tumbled to the sand.

She had missed the strength of his arms, the salty taste of his kiss and the way his mouth plundered hers as if he were starved for her. How had she survived without the musky smell of his skin, the magic he created with his lips and the heat of his body?

She could never let Jett go.

Oh, God, she couldn't think of that. Not now. His heat compounded the intention of his hands on her body. Every nerve ending responded to his touch.

"Katie Sue… I… So long without you…"

He could hardly speak between kissing her, rolling her in a tangle of limbs and laughter within the sleeping bag that they'd managed to zip themselves into. She'd wriggled out of her coat, and they used it now as a pillow for their heads.

Suddenly, when they'd finally settled into a welcome, passionate embrace where they could fully explore and fulfill their needs, Jett stopped and turned off the lantern.

"I want you naked, Katie Sue. I want your skin burning against mine."

This was her Jett. Playful. Serious. Urgent.

This was where she had to draw the line.

"Jett. Wait."

He stilled his roaming hands. "What is it?"

The profound darkness made it easy to speak. She

didn't want to see the look in his eyes if she was going to hurt him. Not knowing exactly how to begin, she whispered, "I've missed you so much."

He chuckled. "That's good, because here I am. Now kiss me."

She inhaled the salty scent of him as he pressed his lips to hers, questioning whether she should be so insane as to continue.

She pushed him away. "No, Jett. We have to talk. I don't think we'll get a chance once we join the others."

He nuzzled her ear, his breath whisper warm on her neck. "Can't we talk later? You smell so good."

Her body began yielding to his in automatic response. She forced her mind to wait. "Jett, please. As much as I brought the sleeping bag for this exact reason, I've been wrestling with my feelings. I don't know if making love is such a good idea for us."

He grew rigid. "What are you saying?"

Her words tumbled out in a rush. "Jett, I love you, you know that, but the years when you're gone… Your voice fades in my mind, your face, your touch, fade from my reality. I'm strong for a while, but then I see lovers holding hands, mothers with their children. All the things I can't have. Your absence becomes so painful that I can hardly breathe. I can't bear the loneliness. If you leave me this time, I may have to give you up, if only to keep my sanity."

He pressed his forehead to hers. "I knew this moment would come, and I don't know how to change it."

Hope sank. She'd wished he would say he was willing to do anything to keep her love. Her heart felt ready to shatter any second. "I know it's unfair of me to ask you to remain human, but I want you to stay with me so badly."

Jett pulled her closer, if that were possible. "If I could

make my life different, I would, Katie. Every minute, day and year away from you drives me back to you with an ache that won't quit until I hold you again. I live to return to you."

"What can we do?"

The irritation that had begun haunting her since the darkness fell simmered too close to the surface. With every ounce of strength, she wanted to do what was right for them both, but damn it all, if he truly loved her then why couldn't he change for her?

He buried his face in her hair. "If I asked you to become a selkie, would you forsake your human side?"

She'd struggled with the same question over and over these past few years. If she were to discover she could transform, would she leave land for Jett's love, only see her family for Christmas once every seven years? There were moments when she believed she could, and others...

In response to her silence, desperation filled his voice. "Can't you just love me as I am, Katie? I'll take my chances on losing you, just please don't leave me now. *You* are my birthday gift. How could I possibly celebrate Christmas without you?"

Tears spilled down her face. "I don't have the choice. You do. Your mother stayed human for love, Jett. Aren't I worth it?"

He grew silent.

Something dark began uncoiling in her chest, unleashing the suspicion that perhaps he didn't truly love her but was only using her. She swallowed hard to tamp down the rising ugly feeling. "I'm sorry. I can't explain what's happening to me."

He cupped her face. He could see her. He had the eyes for night. "It's okay. We've been apart so long. And we both know my mother's choice to stay human killed her in the end. She begged me to protect my heritage. You know I can't deny her wish—or my own destiny."

The message in his answer was unavoidable, but the tenderness in his voice tugged at her emotions. His hands sliding down her body, gently exploring while a sigh of need escaped his lips, set her blood on fire, even though that angry sensation still pulsed in her chest.

"Please, Katie Sue. Love me. Now."

She squeezed her eyes closed, wanting to wipe away the heartache that she knew would follow, and wrestled with the anger that she understood was magnified by the cursed darkness. Responding to her sigh, Jett slid his hands to her hips, drawing her against him. The feel of him undid her wavering determination.

She'd loved him from the day they had first met on Christmas Eve twenty-one years ago, when her father had brought him to their home. That wasn't unusual, as their oceanside Victorian mansion had served as a shelter for troubled boys for over a century. What was unusual, however, was the way she and Jett had bonded immediately. Both of them had been only seven years old. Jett, with his glittering black eyes, eager smile and a focus that would have made another girl her age uncomfortable, had imprinted himself on her—and she on him. She hadn't known it at the time, but understood now that he had claimed her for his own way back then. They'd spent every waking moment together as children. Could she resist him now, even when she knew her desire for stability, home and, someday, a family with the man she loved might never come to be?

She shivered, unsure whether it was from the weather or her dread of never attaining her dream with Jett. "I'm cold."

He pulled the seal skin from his shoulders and draped

the pelt over the sleeping bag. With the selkie coat as a cover over their heads, the sleeping bag grew toasty warm. "Now, before I die from longing, kiss me."

Unable to resist the man who'd stolen her heart all those years ago, Katie Sue wrapped her arms around his neck, pressing her body against him.

"Happy birthday and Merry Christmas, Jett," she whispered, choking back tears.

"Ah, Katie Sue…"

He began kissing her once more, only he'd switched gears from ravenous hunger to a slow, devouring determination, shifting her scarf out of the way, then planting kisses along her jawline, down her neck to the soft skin exposed above the top of her cardigan. He exhaled. The heat of his breath against her skin ignited a fire deep within her soul.

Jett took one tiny pearl button on the sweater in his teeth.

"Do you remember how to unfasten buttons?" Katie Sue whispered, teasing, while inside she ached for this magical man who she would not deny—at least not tonight.

His low laugh rumbled from his chest. "If I remember correctly, buttons work this way.…"

He slid his hand underneath the sweater hem, molding his hot, strong, slightly webbed fingers to her skin as they explored from her stomach upward over her breasts to reach the top button from underneath.

He hummed in satisfaction. "You're not wearing a bra."

She'd felt deliciously decadent. She'd also touched Jett's favorite perfume behind her ears. Succumbing to his allure, she grinned, sure that he could see her. "I'm afraid my desire for you outweighs my good sense."

"Ah, sweet. What you do for me…"

Although she couldn't see him in the darkness, she knew he was keenly watching her face. His knowing fingers caressed her belly, lightly teased her breasts, all the while pressing the length of his need against her.

Jett's talent at arousing her was one of the memories that had carried her through all those lonely nights. Feeling him for real once more sent a thrill through her. "Jett…"

One by one, he released her buttons. With the palms of his hands he peeled her cardigan open. "Shush. Kiss me now. I'm aching for my gift."

Jett could not believe Katie Sue was wrapped in his arms again. Finally. Her scent strong in his awareness, he'd swum toward this beach—toward her—nonstop for two days. From the moment his feet had left the shore seven years before, he had longed for this hour to arrive. Now here she was, her body against him in this tight cocoon of down, her lips parted, eyes half-closed with need. He didn't miss the tremor of desire that ran through her now. For the past seven years he'd lived on the memories of how her body reacted to his. How could he continue to miss her for what seemed a lifetime and would only feel worse as the years wore on? While he felt devoted to his heritage, his selkie tribe and their life at sea, since leaving Katie Sue he'd lived simply to return to her embrace once more. Now he was on fire for her and she was talking about leaving him.

Not on his watch.

Not ever.

She was his. He'd claimed her when they were kids. She'd loved him since laying eyes on him. He knew it.

He *knew* it.

All he had to do was remind her of what he meant to her one more time and she would forget the silly notion of leaving him. When she breathed his name, his control slipped another notch. His eyes devoured her beautiful, creamy skin beneath the open cardigan, the tightened pink buds of her nipples crowning those perfect breasts. Resisting the urge to taste the sweetness of her skin, he plundered her mouth. He would kiss those words of doubt right out of her mind.

A sigh of abandon rose in her throat. He kissed her more deeply, his hands roaming over her familiar beloved body, driving him to want to possess her completely.

He broke the kiss. "Katie Sue, leaving me is never an option."

"Jett...don't. Just love me. I don't want to think."

When a tear slipped down her cheek, Jett's chest tightened. Perhaps she thought he couldn't see her crying, but she knew better. Didn't she understand? Love was supposed to be wonderful, not cause pain. He would show her the difference. Sliding his hand behind her head, he buried his fingers in her hair. "I love your hair. I love your face, your eyes, your lips." He kissed her forehead, each eyelid, her cheeks, her chin and softly teased her lips with his own.

Her scent urged him on. She'd cropped her beautiful hair, but he didn't mind. The lingering aroma of cinnamon and sugar caught in those honey strands cemented the fact that the season of love was upon them. All the more reason to give each other the gift of themselves as they'd promised to do every time they met. He wanted her naked, like him, as fast as possible. He couldn't wait a moment longer. He covered her body with his, methodically finishing undressing her in the awkward confines of the sleeping bag, transferring warmth from his skin to hers while the frigid night pressed in on them outside their down cocoon. His kisses trailed down the soft column of her neck. He lingered against her velvet skin long enough to inhale her perfume, only to have the scent drive his mouth back to hers while his body demanded more. Ah, Poseidon, she fit him perfectly.

While they kissed, the steam of their passion rose, heating their faces and igniting their need even further. She shifted her body closer, wrapping her legs around him, pressing herself fully against him. The heat of her essence, the feel of her thighs, the flat plain of her smooth belly, her breasts and hardened nipples grazing his skin, were more than he could bear. They had been apart for too long. When she caressed his face in the dark and brought his mouth to hers once more, he kissed her with all the passion that was in him.

She loved him so much that seven long years later, not even the freezing winter evening had kept her from waiting for him, bringing him warmth so they could make love in the cold before greeting any of the others.

Katie Sue sighed. "Jett, I love you more than I can say."

Capturing her hips with both hands as he gently urged her to mate with him, he breathed against her lips, "Then show me how much, Katie Sue. Show me now...."

Chapter 2

A gust of wind startled Katie Sue awake. She blinked against the pitch black to get her bearings. She felt so drugged from their lovemaking that it took a moment for her to remember that she and Jett were ensconced within the sleeping bag on the beach. She couldn't guess the time.

Jett rose on one elbow. "Why are you shivering? My coat is impervious to the cold, so it should block…"

He stopped speaking and reached outside the sleeping bag. Alarm filled his voice. "Katie. My coat. Can you feel it?"

She hurriedly unzipped the sleeping bag and they both scrambled from the down cocoon. Naked, on hands and knees in the cold, they felt around for the precious skin that under any other circumstances Jett would have guarded with his life.

His selkie coat was gone. Stolen.

How on earth had someone managed to come so close unnoticed?

He'd been careless with his precious coat because of her. She'd driven him to distraction with her pleas. Her need. Without his pelt he could never return to the sea. The guilt weighed like lead on her chest. "Oh, God, Jett. It's not here."

He didn't answer, just quickly dressed in the jeans and fisherman-knit sweater she'd brought, his movements agitated.

She shimmied into her clothes in the freezing air, aching for the passion they'd shared only moments ago. When she and Jett had met again as teenagers, she'd begged him to stay with her forever. He'd told her how his mother, Miranda, had given her selkie coat to his father as a pledge of her love. Katie's hopes had risen, only to be cruelly dashed as he shared the rest of his mother's story. Years later, his father had died unexpectedly without telling Miranda where he'd hidden her skin. She died of a broken heart from losing her lover and her only way back to the sea, forcing Jett to promise he would never make the same mistake. What a fool she'd been now to hope he might break that promise.

"Can you light the lantern?"

He spoke calmly, but she knew he was racked with turmoil. Within seconds the small area around them was illuminated.

No selkie skin anywhere.

"What the Devil?" He raised his face into the air. "Do you smell that?"

Katie Sue took a breath, noticing sand, seaweed and salt water. "All I smell is ocean."

"No. Wood smoke. Pepper. Flint." He sniffed some more. "Leather."

Their gazes locked in the lamplight. As a Keeper, she had an awful feeling in the pit of her stomach, because she knew what Other possessed that scent, but she didn't dare say the word out loud.

Jett did. "A shapeshifter."

Shapeshifters were one of the few paranormal species that posed a danger to selkies. Selkie pelts could be used to create powerful potions to enhance shifter abilities. While universal law stated that shifters would not prey on selkies, the occasional renegade broke the law, damning a selkie to an abbreviated life. In almost all cases, unless a selkie had a binding emotional tie to a human, a selkie stranded on land against his or her will perished from heartbreak. That made stealing a selkie skin tantamount to murder.

Katie Sue slipped into her coat, but that didn't stop Jett from wrapping them both in the sleeping bag. "I can smell his trail. Let's find the bastard before it's too late."

"Jett, he's a shapeshifter."

"He can hide himself, but not my skin. The wind is picking up. Hurry, or I'll lose the scent."

She matched his pace across the beach. Without so much as a star to light the night sky, and lacking his dark-adapted vision, she moved blindly within the small circle of light from the lantern.

She whispered, "A shapeshifter hasn't violated a selkie here in decades."

Ignoring her, he said, "What is with this blasted blackness?"

The curse was beginning to affect him now, too. She wanted to help him understand how the darkness could turn one's thoughts to turmoil. "The darkness may have spurred the shapeshifter to steal your coat."

"Whether it did or didn't, I'm not going to let my coat become ashes so some shifter can create a potion." He led the way toward a path into the woods on a low cliff above the beach. "This way." Then he stopped abruptly, facing the breeze. "He's gone. I lost the scent."

He turned to her and for the first time absolute horror filled his eyes. "If he burns my coat..."

He would be stranded. Human forever. Hers.

And nothing but torment reflected on his face.

Her heart sank in more than just sympathy for the only man she would ever love. His look said it all. He would never abandon the sea. She had to let him go. He would never be completely hers. The call of the sea was too great.

She laid a hand on his chest, determined to aid her lover despite her own pain. As a Keeper, she was obligated to do what was right for Jett. She could cry a woman's tears later. "Let's get back to the house. We'll call my cousin June. She'll know if a new shifter has settled in Salem."

Once at her home, she sat Jett before the roaring fire in the hearth, but his shivers increased. She wrapped her arms tight around his waist and tried to swallow the knot in her throat. His warm, strong arm draped over her shoulder with such familiar comfort that tears threatened once more. She swallowed hard. With his words earlier and his reaction now, Jett had given her the answer she sought. She would never be his first choice. It had been foolhardy to indulge hope for a life with Jett, since she'd always known his lineage would take precedence. They could part as friends, and he would never be the wiser as to how completely her heart was breaking.

Part of her believed she should be glad that Jett might be stranded. With no skin, he couldn't leave. But that knowledge left her empty. If he stayed with her, she would know for the rest of her life that he was only there because he had lost his way back to the ocean. That knowledge would slowly decay the precious love binding them. She pushed the thought from her mind. This horrible situation needed to be resolved. Her own dreams didn't matter at this moment. Jett's happiness did. After her husband had died, his mother had perished quickly without access to her selkie skin. With all her love for Jett, Katie could never want the same for him.

Oblivious to Jett and Katie's crisis, the boys who lived in Montgomery Home were busy preparing for the Christmas Eve celebration at Sam's. Katie Sue's cousin Samantha Mycroft, who was the unofficial Keeper of the Keepers in Salem, held a traditional Christmas Eve party at her family's colonial home every year. Bridgette, the housekeeper and cook for Montgomery Home, scurried behind the boys, barking orders with an Irish brogue that made even her sternest command sound pleasant.

Katie Sue's brother, Kenny, in a fisherman sweater and buff-colored suede jeans and boots, his long brown hair tied back, joined them at the fire. His frown reflected his concern. Their father had passed away several years ago and Kenny took his role as patriarch seriously. That included Jett. The two men had grown up together and felt a strong brotherly affection.

Katie Sue told her brother what happened, skimming over why they'd fallen asleep on the beach, wrapped in a sleeping bag. Katie and Jett's love for one another was no secret in Montgomery Home, even though their relationship wasn't exactly condoned.

"I'll ask Vaughn Griffith to come here instead of us all going to Sam's. If anyone can track a shapeshifter, Vaughn can. By bringing him here, we won't have to disturb her guests…yet." Kenny rubbed his chin, thinking. "We still have time, but not much. You know a shapeshifter has to do a prolonged ritual before actually igniting the coat to create a potion."

Jett shook his head, his jaw tight. "If he tattoos the skin with his markings before…"

Katie hugged him close, sharing her strength. "He won't. We'll get it back first."

Kenny shot her a concerned look when he saw her pull Jett close. Jett might be his friend, but Katie knew he shared the family's concern over her attachment to Jett—not only as Keeper of the Selkies but because of the way it had stunted her personal life for so many years.

Kenny had gone so far as to remind her at breakfast this morning to rethink her commitment to Jett. He, Christina, Sam and June had already discussed whether or not Katie should relinquish her position. No Keeper could show favoritism toward one charge over another. Her love for Jett could sway her decisions in the long run.

Her family wanted her to be happy, but they weren't convinced that Jett could give her what she truly needed in a life partner, especially if she forfeited her position as Keeper in order to protect the romance. Katie rebutted their concerns and said that she had no intention of stepping down. She argued that rules could be amended. That her love for Jett would not deter her from attending to the rest of the selkie population, and that with Jett beside her, she would actually have greater insight into the needs of her charges.

Hearing them give voice to her own fears had simply reinforced her knowledge that she had to make a decision—soon. Now, though, it didn't matter. Jett would no longer be hers. Once he reclaimed his coat, entered the sea and became a selkie again, he would stay that way forever. She could keep her precious Keeper status with no fear of recrimination. That would have to be enough.

Chapter 3

The front door opened. "Bah, humbug! I'd like to get my hands on the idiot who cast this darkness spell."

Bridgette's voice rose from the hallway. "Well, Merry Christmas, Juniper Twist. Why are you frowning while wearing the prettiest green velvet coat I have ever seen?"

"Oh, stuff it, Bridgette. Where is Katie Sue? And what trouble has she caused now?"

Bridgette's voice trailed off as she ascended the stairs. "Well, happy solstice to you, too, Miss Witch."

Katie Sue and her brother exchanged glances. Juniper—or June, as everyone called their cousin—had left Salem eight years ago to train as Keeper of the Witches, a role she'd openly expressed she didn't feel ready to inherit. She'd only been back for two weeks, forced to return after the death of her uncle, who'd been Keeper before her. Though they had all grown up together, Katie suspected that, given the choice, June never would have come back to Salem. She'd been burned in love and had shaken the dust of her hometown from her boots when she left. She'd returned only reluctantly to assume her uncle's role as Keeper, and to take over the family bookstore in town, Twists & Tales.

"We're in the parlor, June," Katie called.

June blew into the room looking like a petite fashion model. "Jett. Happy birthday. It's been a long time. My, you've grown."

Jett grinned in response to June's teasing. "I think we were fourteen and I ate all your Christmas pudding."

She waved a hand. "Hate the stuff anyway." She tossed her coat on a chair before sitting down. June's green dress, inset with fine lace around the neck and bodice, matched her coat, while her black boots looked like something a rock star would wear. Katie admired not only June's spirit but her style.

Pushing an errant lock of black hair off her face, June leaned in to speak quietly. "Vaughn told me what's going on, and I've checked with the four shapeshifters registered in Salem. I trust each of them implicitly. None of them would have done you harm, Jett. And none of them know of any other shifter who's come to town for any reason. What else could it be?"

"It was a shapeshifter, June. No mistaking his scent. Given the darkness and the fact that we were...asleep, I don't think he even bothered to transform. But the scent was strong. Masculine."

June frowned, her fingers smoothing the lace at her neck. "Well, that's a start, I suppose." She looked from Katie Sue to Jett and smiled. "Of course, if you hadn't seduced this poor guy within seconds after he came ashore, he wouldn't be in this mess. Not that I can really blame you."

Katie felt her throat constrict with guilt.

"The truth is, I seduced Katie before she could say

hello," Jett said. "I'm the one who neglected to protect my coat."

Kenny held up his hands. "It doesn't matter who seduced whom. The fact of the matter is that someone knew Jett was arriving tonight and waited to do him harm. And we have to figure out who that is."

Another gust of cold air followed the ringing doorbell. "Merry Christmas, one and all!" Vaughn's voice carried from the foyer, and in seconds he was in the room. Taller than both Jett and Kenny and looking every bit the modern wizard with his long black hair, casual aplomb and black leather jacket, he slapped Jett on the back. "Happy birthday, buddy. Got a bit taller since last time."

Jett laughed. "Always wanted to be able to look you in the eye. Mission accomplished."

Under other circumstances this would be a joyful reunion leading to a long, celebratory evening filled with eating, stories, gifts and more eating. Now their attendance at the Christmas Eve festivities at Sam's would be delayed while they scoured the village in search of the shapeshifter who'd stolen Jett's sealskin. Katie didn't know if the despair pressing like a weight on her chest was from Jett's loss, her breaking heart or the cursed darkness so thick against the windows that it felt like cloying ether that would soon render everyone unconscious.

She stood, shaking off her despairing mood. "Did you find out anything, Vaughn?"

His face grew grim. "Rebekah and I consulted with the elementals. Eric, the earth elder, believes that the shapeshifter may have left a psychic pattern imprinted on the ground that we can trace to where the thief is hiding. It will be best if we start from the original point where the pelt was taken to determine the imprint. We should head to the beach and start our search there."

Kenny said, "I'll get our coats." He glanced at Jett. "You won't mind wearing one of mine?"

"I'd welcome the warmth. Thank you."

June slid into her own coat. "I think I'll leave the tracking to the men and go nose around town for a while. I have a few hunches of my own. Maybe I'll manage to make my way over to Sam's later to cheer you all up."

They all waved goodbye, and then Katie Sue sighed. "Can't you guys feel the pressure? I know it's the darkness, but it makes me feel so anxious. Like there's no hope. It's Christmas, when faith should be at its highest point, and I feel awful." She turned to Jett and leaned against him, soaking in his strength.

The empathy filling his eyes did nothing to console her. "I can feel the agitation but I'm ignoring it. Instead, I'm concentrating on being here with you."

Vaughn slipped on black leather gloves. "Luckily you haven't been exposed to the darkness long enough, Jett. Hopefully we'll solve this crisis before it has a chance to affect you."

Kenny walked in with the coats. "Which crisis? We have two at the moment. And what's with June? Is she dodging her responsibility to help us?"

"Let's try to be understanding," Katie Sue said. "The blackness is affecting her pretty hard, especially given the loss of her uncle."

Vaughn smiled indulgently. "Always the peacemaker, Katie Sue."

She shrugged. "And if I am? So what? It's what a Keeper does."

As the men prepared to leave, she said, "I can't join

you until I finish rounding up the boys for Samantha. Will you be coming back here?"

Kenny shook his head. "We'll let you know where we are as soon as we get a lead. Meanwhile, let's try to act as normal as possible for the kids' sake, if nothing else. Christmas Eve should still be happy for them."

He and Vaughn left, but Jett stayed behind a moment longer. He cupped her face in his hands. "I'm worried about you, Katie. You look so unhappy. Don't you know how much I wanted you while I was away? You're all I dreamed about." He stared into her eyes, his own troubled and searching.

She pulled back. How could she tell him her heart was breaking when so much more was at stake? She tried to smile but couldn't—not when she felt seconds away from tears. "I dreamed of you, too."

He kissed her with such tenderness that tears slipped unbidden down her cheeks. "It's Christmas Eve, sweet Katie Sue. It's my birthday. And I'm here with you. We can still find joy in the night. As for my skin? Perhaps my mother is watching and will lead me to it."

Katie Sue hugged her arms around her waist as she watched Jett depart and whispered, "And with it your freedom."

Chapter 4

The shapeshifter passed a hand chapped red from winter wind over the silver-gray pelt lying across his lap. He brought the selkie head cover to his nose and inhaled deeply, then exhaled a slow sigh of satisfaction while gazing at the velvety fur surrounding the empty eyeholes and dark snout with the whiskers still in place.

Leo couldn't believe his luck. He'd smelled the selkie's fur on the air minutes after the Other had come to shore. The scent would have reached him even sooner if the winds hadn't died down today. No matter. The Other had been so engrossed with the Montgomery woman that he could have sat down beside them to watch; they were both oblivious to his presence while they made love.

That had been entertaining in its way, but it had also enraged him. He'd admired the sultry blonde with the almond-shaped eyes for the entire two years since he had been brought to Salem by his master. Yet other than a smile and a polite nod, Katie Sue Montgomery had never given him a second look.

After hearing the symphony of sounds from their lovemaking and having his body react in a way that shamed him, Leo was afraid he would never be able to look her in the eye again without her sighs and cries at the hands of the selkie ringing in his ears.

Damn that black-haired sea snake.

Leo had been too weak to shift tonight. Spending the day shielding his master as he moved through town, relishing the disaster he had wreaked on Salem, had drained him of his power to shift. Right around four o'clock, after returning with his master to his lair, the master had looked at his expensive watch and instructed him to go home by the beach road.

And, lo and behold, even in the dark he could smell why the master had sent him on that route. How the master had known the selkie would arrive at this time was another of his surprising talents. He seemed to know everybody's business in this tight-knit village.

The master knew that the scent of selkie skin to a shapeshifter with waning powers was like heroin for an addict. And the master knew him well enough to know he would succumb to his basest desire and commit the atrocity, despite the unspoken law that governed the shapeshifter community. Holding yet another damaging secret over his head would allow the master to bind Leo to him for another decade. The master always mocked the craving for the power that surged through Leo's system from the potion made exclusively from selkie skin, but the master was also more than willing to use it for his own ends.

Aah. Just visualizing the moment when he would inject the potion into his veins set his hands trembling.

In earlier centuries, the usually peaceful shapeshifters struck fear in their fellow Others because their ability to change form made them dangerous as adversaries. Only when laws on shifting were drawn up, with severe consequences for breaking them, did the rest of the Otherworld accept shapeshifters as brethren. Cannibalizing other paranormal beings for power potions was forbidden.

Leo thought differently. Humans used steroids to enhance their bodies. Rogue shifters like himself believed that refusing to use all the resources at their disposal, no matter what the source, was actually denying their true abilities. He was willing to risk the severe punishment for such a violation. Once he administered the virility potion, the Keepers would have to subdue him first, and that would be all but impossible once he was enhanced. He would be able to elude the most powerful Keeper or shapeshifter sent to strip him of his power, which would be easy for them to accomplish if he were in his natural form. His addiction to the intensely powerful potion had almost caused his demise in his last community. He'd survived only because the master had intervened and bound him as a veritable slave.

This time he would cast a spell to augment the potion's power, making him the strongest he'd ever been in his life. Powerful enough to turn the tables on the master and expose him to the Keepers of Salem, finally breaking the magical bond holding him captive to the master's every whim.

After finally eliminating the master, the last of his wicked bloodline, he would retire. He would occupy one of the mansions whose front doors he'd never gotten past. Shapeshift his way into a home he especially desired, then stay for as long as he wanted.

How convenient that he'd come upon the selkie whose lover was his very own intended target. The mansion he wanted was Montgomery Home. The inhabitant whose home—and heart—he wanted to possess? None other than the newest selkie Keeper, Katie Sue Montgomery.

He'd heard her cousins talking when he was working around town. Katie Sue was hooked on the foolish Other who preferred to be a seal instead of the man she needed.

He would be that man for Katie Sue Montgomery. He would use his powers to destroy Jett and shapeshift into the selkie's human form, then give her the happy ending she wished for: Jett as a man, forever. Then he would take her as he longed to, with the sultry Keeper of selkies none the wiser. And with Katie Sue Montgomery bound to him, his supply of selkie skins would never end. He could dominate the woman, and ultimately Salem, even more effectively than his master intended to annihilate them all with his spell.

Why the master hated the people of Salem was not his to question. What mattered was breaking the master's control over him. He ran a hand across the fine pelt in his lap. The master's obsession with his own plans to destroy Salem's inhabitants must have blinded the cruel overlord to the fact that his thrall knew how to turn his addiction into the master's own demise. This selkie skin could make that happen. The silvered markings along the neck proved that this particular selkie came from noble lineage. The effect would be sublime.

The excitement burning inside him was almost unbearable. He had the tools, the ancient spell written on its original parchment, which he had stolen from Twists & Tales, and the perfect flame to create the finest ash required for the spell.

The hunger gnawing at his insides subsided for the moment. Between his duties today for the master, his regular job and stealing the selkie pelt, the fatigue plaguing him now could cause an error in judgment. He had only one chance to create this potion, and if he made a mistake, everything would be ruined.

He would rest for an hour before he began.

Chapter 5

Katie Sue made a cup of calming tea as Bridgette herded the boys together. The woman was a miracle worker, Katie thought as she headed for the kitchen, drawn by the cinnamon scent of snicker-doodle cookies mingling with the savory smells of the different meat and fruit pies Bridgette had prepared for the celebration.

Katie snatched a cookie and smiled as Bridgette entered the kitchen. "These look wonderful. I can't believe you found time to do so much baking."

"I won't swear everything's edible," Bridgette said. "I just don't feel like myself these days."

Katie Sue exhaled. "It isn't only you. It's me, it's everyone—we're all so tightly wound." She set her tea and cookie down and gathered the other woman in for a hug. "Don't let this wretched blackness affect you, not on Christmas Eve. I love you too much to see you unhappy."

Bridgette rested her head on Katie's shoulder. "Will it ever go away?"

Katie shivered. *It had damned well better!* "Soon. My cousins are investigating, and you know we Keepers don't like to fail."

"And Jett?" Bridgette stepped back, patting her pink cheeks. "Will they find his skin?"

"They're out looking now. An earth elemental gave Vaughn some ideas for tracking the thief."

Bridgette untied her apron. "Let me get the logs from outside for tomorrow's fire, and then we can go."

"I can do that. Why don't you finish getting ready for the party? It will do me good to do something useful."

Before Bridgette could argue, Katie Sue pushed her from the kitchen. "Go. I'll meet you back here in twenty minutes."

Katie Sue carried a few logs topped with kindling into what had once been the original kitchen of the old Victorian home. Her parents had remodeled with modern appliances to accommodate the growing number of occupants. This cozy area now served as an informal family dining room with a long farm table and ladder-back chairs. An old stone fireplace along the outside wall offered light and warmth to penetrate the all-pervading darkness. A cast-iron log rack next to the hearth was used to dry the wood before using it.

With the load in her arms, Katie caught her toe on the area rug. She lost her balance and the wood tumbled onto the hearth.

The old fireplace had been fashioned from locally mined granite blocks of different sizes. Rectangular slabs of stone raised the hearth about a foot above the wood-planked floor. The apron of the hearth was paved with black slate.

Katie cleared the logs off the hearth, placing them one by one into the rack, only to find the end slate on the right side of the hearth had shifted from the impact, exposing an opening beneath the hearth.

"What the heck?"

Prickles of apprehension raced up her spine. Her mouth dried. She slid the square slab farther to the right, then peered inside the perfectly square opening to see half of a large oak box.

A secret compartment? Wow. Old houses held secrets, but this was her first time uncovering one. She reached in for the box, but it was too big to fit through the opening. She pulled on the outside piece of granite and it slid away to reveal more of the box. With the granite removed, she easily slipped the wooden receptacle from its hiding place. Clearly the box had been fashioned specifically to fit into the space. It had two small hinges and a flat hook and latch.

She slipped the hook free and opened the lid. Releasing a breath she hadn't realized she was holding, she frowned, not understanding at first what she was looking at. Inside the box lay a selkie skin, a beautiful silver-and-white coat. Not Jett's.

Katie Sue's heart hammered in her chest. Of course. Miranda's pelt.

The coat that Jett's mother never found. The coat she had died without. After all these years, she had found it.

What was it doing here?

Awestruck, she stared at the lush pelt. Miranda had been a selkie princess. Her father had ruled the selkie realm for almost a century. Returning this coat to Jett would finally close the circle on the mystery of his mother's lost skin. Jett could finally bury the dead. Unbelievable. Jett's last words before he left had been that maybe his mother would lead him to his coat, and this was almost as good.

Katie replaced the fireplace stones, then took the back stairs up to her room, carrying the box as if it were a child

in her arms. Miranda's selkie coat! But how—and why—
had it been hidden in Montgomery Home?

And Jett. If his coat was lost forever, he could try
using this one, since selkie coats adjusted to the wearer
regardless of gender—but then a wicked thought twisted
through her head. If this coat were to be destroyed, too,
he would be stranded with her. For life. Maybe she'd been
wrong earlier and she *could* make him happy as a mere
human. Maybe he *would* continue to love her, even if he
couldn't escape to his own world, which tugged at him
daily whenever he was on dry land.

Could she be so cruel as to deny him the chance to live
out his destiny just to appease her own desires? She swallowed hard, pushing the poisonous idea from her mind.
Love based on deception could never survive. Jett needed
to find his coat and return to the sea to fulfill his destiny.

She closed the door to her room behind her and laid
the box on her bed. The soft fur felt like silk to the touch.
The glistening silver shimmered in the soft light. The
musky smell was pleasant—almost like a mossy perfume. She lifted the coat from its confines and spread
it out on the bed.

It was exquisite.

She pulled her sweater over her head to change into
her party clothes, but once she was undressed she found
herself reaching for the selkie coat instead of the dress
hanging on her closet door.

What was she doing?

The skin seemed to draw her to itself, as if needing
human touch. She ran her fingertips over the head cover,
where the whitest fur ran along the snout and surrounded
the eye openings. As if mesmerized, she lifted the coat
and draped it over her shoulders. Gently, she fitted the

face cover over her own face, and the unexpected happened.

As if taking on a life of its own, the skin molded itself to her face, flowed over her neck and shoulders and began to seal itself along an invisible seam down her torso. Within seconds her arms and legs were bound. Panic bubbled in her chest and her breath grew labored as the skin tightened around her. Not that she was suffocating, but the odd sensations were making her hyperventilate. Even knowing full well that she would be okay, sheer incredulity forced her to fight the transformation.

Without legs to stand on, she fell to the floor, feeling her insides adjust to the new skin as she began transforming. Then, as if she'd been shocked by an electric current, pain rose up her spine and shot into her head. The struggle to breathe was the last thing Katie Sue remembered before losing consciousness.

Chapter 6

"Katie Sue, darling, wake up."

Katie's eyes fluttered open, but they felt dry. Crusty. Something wasn't right. As her eyes focused and adjusted to the light, she realized her mother was kneeling beside her. Behind her stood Bridgette, her hand pressed to her mouth, her eyes wide in shock.

"Mother…" She tried to speak, but the words caught in her throat.

"Shh, sweetheart. Rest a moment. You have to get your bearings."

Christina Montgomery rested a hand on Katie's forehead. "Katie, look at me and concentrate."

Bridgette whispered, "What if the children see her?"

Christina shook her head, smiling at Katie. "Please, Bridgette. She'll be fine in a moment."

Katie Sue felt as if she were returning from some distant place, struggling through a dark tunnel toward the beacon of light that was her mother's smile.

Christina focused her full concentration on Katie. "Sweetheart, I don't know how or where, but you must have found Miranda's beautiful coat and gotten curious. Something amazing happened. You transformed."

Katie was still lying there. She still felt bound and breathing was still difficult, as if the weight of her own body was oppressing her as she lay face down on the floor. She attempted to lift a hand, but no. *Something* moved, but it felt flat and awkward.

She gasped.

Christina laid a hand on her head. "I am going to explain how you can remove the skin, Katie, but please understand. Only you can do it. If I try to open the seam, you'll be harmed."

How had she become a selkie? That was impossible. She was a human. Oh, no. The legend! She needed her body back. Now!

Christina must have seen the panic in her eyes. "Sweetheart, calm down. You'll be restored in seconds."

She felt the urge to find water and slip into its comforting embrace. This body was heavy. In the waves she would be light and breathing would be easy. Her mother's voice brought her back to the here and now.

"Katie Sue, the seam begins just below your jaw and travels to the tail. When it gets to the fins, your hands will reform, and you'll regain your legs when you reach the tail. Now, think. You have to use your thoughts. The seam begins here."

Christina touched a point beneath her mouth. Katie felt her mother's fingers run along a thin line of skin running through the fur.

"Katie, I want you to concentrate on my finger. I'll go slowly. Imagine the seam is a zipper and my finger the zipper pull, opening the zipper as I go."

Katie closed her eyes to concentrate. "Ready," she said, but the sound was nothing like the word. It startled her eyes open.

Christina chuckled. "This is the first time in your life

you've been speechless. Now concentrate. Christmas Eve is waiting. A time of magic, even amidst this darkness. Your transformation is proof. We need you."

Katie Sue wanted out of the fur. It wasn't that she felt trapped, exactly. The sensation simply felt bizarre, as if one moment she was herself and the next, fifty pounds heavier with no arms and legs. And her tongue didn't feel right in her strangely shaped mouth.

Christina put her face inches from Katie's and held her gaze as she rolled her onto her side. "Okay. Follow my finger. You can do this."

Katie Sue closed her eyes and imagined her mother's fingertip was the fastener on a zipper. She made a *zzzzzip* sound in her mind to visualize the action. As she did, cool air filled the gap that was opening in the fur. She gasped. Feeling the fur opening sent a surge of alarm through her, as if flesh were lifting from bone.

"No, Katie. Don't struggle." Christina's voice was firm. "Now inhale deeply. Close your eyes once more. And concentrate. You'll be fine. Just imagine you squeezed yourself into a dress two sizes too small and we have to work you out of it. You'll be okay, I promise you."

She trusted her mother implicitly, but the sensation was unnerving. Tingling. Stressful. This must be how a butterfly felt while struggling from a cocoon, compelled by the urgent but daunting drive to emerge.

Katie jammed her eyes shut, forcing her mind's eye to follow the gentle trail her mother made down the center of her torso. As the air slipped in, she inhaled deeply and imagined Jett emerging from his coat. She'd watched as he lifted his chin high and the seam would magically begin to release. He never seemed to struggle to transform. Of course, he'd had a lifetime to learn the process, but she drew on that memory now to allow her mind to open the seam.

"Good, Katie. We're almost there. Can you free your hands?"

As the seam passed the flippers, she felt as if leather gloves were sliding from her fingers, pulling a bit at her fingertips. Immediately her fingers flexed and she reached outside the fur. The head cover fell back, and she sucked in a huge breath of air.

Christina stopped "unzipping" and helped Katie Sue to sit up. "You look like a mermaid."

Katie Sue felt dazed. "What happened?"

Christina glanced at Bridgette. "Tell her."

Bridgette dropped to her knees, panic still clear in her eyes. "I came in to tell you the boys were ready and found you out cold in that skin. Good heavens, I thought you'd died. I sat the boys down in front of the TV and called your mother."

"How long?"

Christina said, "About half an hour. You must have needed a nap."

Katie Sue laughed. Mother was always quick to lighten a difficult situation. Feeling her body reshape itself to conform to the pelt against her will had been surreal and frightening. "I think I mentally checked out from terror."

Bridgette sat back on her heels. "I would never have believed this if I didn't see it with my own eyes."

"Did I just do what I think I did?"

"Let's get you out of this coat, then I'll explain. We have to join the others soon."

What, Katie wondered, would Jett say when she told him about this experience? A tremor of excitement ran up her spine as she carefully wriggled the last of the skin from her feet. The enormity of this power flooded her.

She had the capability to transform. Heaven help her! She could leave with Jett—if she were willing to reveal that she could become a selkie.

Had Jett's mother inadvertently left her a gift? Could this be her destiny? Was she meant to be the mate of a selkie, rather than Jett becoming the husband of a woman? Her mind reeled.

Impossible. She was the Keeper of the Selkies. Only a human could claim that right. And even if she *could* permanently transform, would she? Would she be willing to give up her natural form for Jett's love—the very thing she wanted in her heart for him to sacrifice for her?

"Katie. You're pale. Don't forget to breathe."

She glanced at her mother. The same mother who hadn't seemed one bit surprised by finding her daughter as a selkie. "I need you to explain this now."

"Can you stand?"

Lightheaded, but empowered by the return to her human form, Katie stood. She inhaled deeply and realized she was physically fine. The selkie coat lay at her feet, the skin open wide as if waiting for her to return. She lifted the beautiful silver pelt and laid it carefully on the bed. "Bridgette, could you get me a glass of water? I'm parched."

Their cook seemed all too willing to escape the room. "Of course. I'll be right back."

Katie faced her mother. "Please…tell me."

"Can you dress while we talk? We really need to move. Sam phoned a few minutes ago and she asked me to tell you she's called a Keepers meeting for later. They have a lead on the culprit who cast the darkness. We need to be there."

"Okay, but, Mom, I found Miranda's coat in a secret chamber in the old hearth. Why was it hidden there?"

Christina's hand flew to her mouth. "In the hearth? Oh, my. Miranda's husband was caretaker of Montgomery Home. He must have hidden the fur when he repaired the old fireplace. Since he was always on the property, he could always have access to it." She closed her eyes. "If we'd only known, Miranda might have lived."

"No one would have guessed the fireplace had a secret hiding place, Mom. How could you have known? Let the past rest."

Katie slid her dress over her head. She wanted answers about her transformation before Bridgette returned. She dropped her voice. "I knew there was a legend, but I have never heard of a human actually becoming a selkie."

The look of pride in her mother's eyes almost floored her. "It's been generations since a human transformed."

"You knew this was possible?"

A small smile curved Christina's mouth. "The legend of the Viking king who loved a selkie princess is no legend. It's fact. Their son became a selkie and the daughter remained fully human. You and I are direct descendants of that girl, who grew up to protect her brother and his family from hunters. She became the first Keeper and taught us, her daughters, to do the same."

"Wait. You're saying that I—that we—have the selkie gene?"

"Yes, sweetheart. As Keepers, we've always had enhanced abilities in the water and can hold our breath longer than any normal person, but the possibility of transformation comes from the unusual recessive selkie gene in our lineage tracing back to Viking times."

Dressing forgotten, Katie Sue dropped onto the bed next to the selkie skin. "So it's true that I can become a selkie just as Jett becomes human?"

"Since it's a rare occurrence to find an abandoned

selkie skin, there have been few opportunities over the generations for us to transform. And not all of our lineage can transform. I can't."

"You tried?"

"Miranda and I were friends. She let me try her coat. Nothing happened."

"What does this mean?"

"It means that even if you were to marry a human man, you could very well have a selkie child."

Katie Sue froze as she imagined herself and Jett with a child.

"And you told these facts to Dad?"

Christina nodded. "Your father was a man of great compassion. When we met at college and fell in love, I brought him here, explained the Montgomery purpose and then explained my birthmark. He was skeptical until I showed him the family diaries the Keepers have kept throughout the centuries. He had been born and raised in Salem, so he already lived with the mystique of Otherworld possibilities. To find out they really existed was exciting to him. He more than met the challenge of becoming my husband and perhaps having a selkie child, and he was willing to protect that possibility with his life." Her smile was tender. "He would be so very proud of you, Katie Sue."

Katie Sue shook her head. Transforming and now learning of her heritage... It was overwhelming.

"Speechless again?" Her mother took her hand. "Just keep in mind that whomever you choose as your life mate will have to be a very understanding man."

"Or a selkie."

Her mother held her gaze, sadness filling her eyes. "Yes. Now that I see you can transform, I could very well lose you to the selkie realm. Although, if I remember correctly, you're not bound to wait seven years before you can return because you're human first, not selkie."

Bridgette returned, interrupting the conversation between the two women. She handed a glass of water to Katie. "Here, darlin'. You look like you've seen a ghost."

"Just feeling a bit shaky. I'll be fine." *Would she ever really be fine again?*

Katie drained the glass while her mind reeled with her mother's words.

Bridgette ran a hand over the pelt on the bed. "What shall we do with this?"

Christina carefully folded Miranda's coat and slipped it into a shoulder bag she took from Katie's closet. "It's not safe to leave this around. We'll bring it with us to Sam's."

Chapter 7

Jett ignored the biting chill as the small party worked its way along the shore to the place where he and Katie Sue had made love a few short hours before. The three men walked in silence, each caught up in his own thoughts. Jett's mind was full of self-recrimination for unknowingly putting Katie into danger the way he had.

His mind had been even more consumed than usual with Katie Sue during the long journey back to her. He'd carried her in his heart every day of the past seven years, trying to figure out how he could stay with her forever. Seeing her standing on the beach, hearing the familiar cadence of her voice when she called his name, had ignited a fire that blinded him to everything but her.

The darkness lying over Salem hadn't seemed an oddity at his first arrival. Five miles out to sea the sun had finished its trek across the sky and begun to set. Katie's scent, the pull of the path to his birthplace, the long years since he'd last been to shore, all drew him through the water like a magnet. It just seemed natural to take advantage of what he had thought was an early winter night.

If only he'd been more aware once he was on shore.

But his focus had been entirely on Katie, and he'd needed to make her his one more time before their common sense took over.

His acute selkie vision didn't require light to know they'd arrived at the spot. "Here. This is where we were."

Kenny was carrying a small battery-operated lantern because they wanted to draw as little attention to themselves as possible, and that meant avoiding the need for Vaughn to cast a fireball spell. Vaughn stepped in front of Jett, using the light to examine the sand. "Try not to disturb the surrounding area. Let's see what we have here."

Kenny stepped next to Jett and watched Vaughn pass his hands above the area. "What should we do?"

"Nothing."

After a moment Vaughn shot a grin at Jett. "The energy here is pretty potent, but I don't sense anything but you and Katie Sue."

Jett pointed up the beach from where they'd lain. "The thief came from this direction."

Vaughn nodded. "Again, if you can refrain from moving for just a moment."

Kenny said, "Do you need the light?"

"Not yet."

Vaughn moved slowly. The seconds dragged on as he used his hands to feel for any remaining pulse from the intruder's presence.

After the third step, he stopped. "Here."

"What is it?" Jett asked.

Vaughn looked troubled in the dim light from Kenny's lantern. "Your intruder stopped here and waited for the right moment to make his move."

A jolt of revulsion shot through Jett. "How did I not notice?"

Vaughn shook his head. "Buried inside a sleeping bag

with your mate for the first time in seven years? I'm surprised you remembered to breathe."

Vaughn was trying to make light of the situation, but it didn't help. Jett was all too aware that he'd put the woman he cherished more than his own life in danger. He shook off the guilt in order to keep concentrating on the task at hand. "As I said earlier, I tracked his scent into the woods up there."

"I sense the energy from the pelt, as well. As long as our thief remained on foot, we have a chance."

The men retraced the path Jett and Katie had taken earlier, then started moving carefully through the blackened woods. Kenny followed closely behind Vaughn to provide light while trying not to interfere with the other man's efforts to follow the shifter's trail. The woods ended at a parking lot adjacent to a state park bordering the Montgomery property.

"Vaughn?"

"Don't worry, Jett. The echo is still strong. Given the vibrations, I'd say the thief broke into a run right here. This way."

Katie Sue sat in the passenger seat of her mother's car, holding the bag containing Miranda's pelt in her lap. She'd refused Christina's suggestion that they put the coat in the trunk. Transforming might have been initially traumatic, but now Katie felt differently. She didn't want the fur out of her grasp, let alone her sight. It took every ounce of willpower she possessed not to open the bag and rest a hand on the silken fur.

Christina broke the silence. "The Keeper council has to be advised of your transformation."

"I understand."

What Katie Sue *couldn't* understand were the visuals that were bombarding her mind, as if wearing Miranda's coat had awakened something deep within her, something genetic that had been lurking inside her all along. A sense of euphoria surged through her as she felt the thrill of diving effortlessly through the surf into the deeper, canyon-blue waters out at sea side by side with Jett, chasing schools of fish or swirling through the water like a lover entwined with her mate.

If making love with Jett on land was a mind-blowing experience, how erotic would his touch be if they were weightless beneath the sea? She closed her eyes, imagining such an intimate moment with the man she loved more than anything in her life.

The silence beneath the waves. The softness of his fur brushing against hers as they swam. She would flirt with him by swimming close, curling herself around his body then swimming away. Jett would move quickly to catch her, nip her, bring her back to him by pressing himself against her underside and propelling her toward the surface.

When they broke for air, she would lure him to the beach. The beauty of selkies was that they were uninhibited in their sensuality. As a selkie female, she would lead Jett to a sunny stretch of sand just above the waterline and use her telepathic connection to offer her body to him. In her mind's eye she could see him follow her to a secluded spot behind some low rocks, because she would want to seduce him as a man. Just as she had seen Jett do before, she would raise her head to begin releasing her selkie skin beneath her chin. She would expose her throat to him first, then her breasts, her stomach, her woman's juncture, arching slowly, stretching her body along the sand. She would rest for a moment, half in, half out of her coat, watching his charcoal gaze burn with desire as he peeled off his own coat like a man removing his clothes and fully prepared to take control of her seduction. He would lean over her, using his mouth on her first until his hands slipped free to caress her exposed human form.

She would sigh at his touch. Oh, the sweet surrender of slipping from one existence into the other. She would go slowly, waiting until Jett had heated her to abandon, until only his touch mattered and his words of love in her ear overrode the ocean waves breaking on the rocks around them.

She loved that about Jett. His seductions were complete. He would tease her, taste her, touch her with the tender urgency that rose between them until she could no longer stand not having her legs wrapped around his waist to take him deep inside her. Maybe they would create their first child. Maybe their son or daughter would be born on Christmas Eve, just as Jett had been. The thought sent a frisson of delight through her.

Jett's body never ceased to thrill her. Her excitement always started with his mischievous smile beneath those penetrating eyes that knew every inch of her body and the secrets deep in her heart. She loved running her hands through his hair, the curls at the nape of his neck sheer seduction for her fingers. His athletic swimmer's body fit her perfectly. The flush she felt from his smooth skin, the rock-hard muscles in his arms, chest, abdomen and the legs that he used to drive her exquisitely into ecstasy, made her ache to be with him every moment of her life.

Now not only the possibility of living with Jett as a selkie tugged at her. Living among the enchanting presence of other creatures, the entire selkie population in motion to the summer feeding grounds outside the stone grottoes along the craggy Maine coastline had her ach-

ing to live the fantasy. She felt these memories flooding
through her from Miranda's coat as if she'd lived them
herself. The freedom and the beauty of these thoughts
exhilarated her. She understood now, more than ever before, why it was so wrong of her to ask Jett to choose between her and his life as a selkie.

So now she had an even greater dilemma. It lay within
her power to return Jett to his birthright, should he not
recover his skin. Given her new insight, she could never
deny him his selkie heritage. She would remain as Keeper
of the Selkies and stay as his human lover through the
rest of her life, given that she couldn't imagine ever loving anyone else the way she loved him.

Or, should Jett find his pelt, she could forsake her
birthright as Keeper and leave with him to live in the selkie realm. Could she really forfeit her position as Keeper?
Who would take her place? She was Christina's only
daughter. Her time was now. Could she abandon her heritage for something as selfish as love?

Despite everything, her attraction to a selkie existence
was growing. She understood why Jett could never give
up the sea. She found herself longing for the experience
as a traveler longs for the trip of a lifetime. But fighting
against this new desire was her common sense. Her destiny. Her humanity.

As they pulled into the drive of Sam's house, the lights
in the windows and Christmas lights decorating the porch
mere pinpoints in the cloying darkness, Katie Sue found
herself dreading this Christmas Eve, normally her favorite night of the year. After tonight, no matter which direction the answer pointed, her life would never be the same.

The three men reached the foot of Salem village, where
some of the oldest historic homes nestled along the wa-

terfront. Kenny doused the lantern, making the darkness more pervasive beneath the muted streetlamps. Vaughn straightened and stopped on the sidewalk, stepped out into the street then retraced his steps. A look of confusion crossed his face. "The echo is gone."

"Impossible." Jett didn't like the worry in his own voice.

"It's as if someone placed a blocking spell across the street. I sense nothing." Vaughn traced a path with his hand. "The echoes are strong all the way up to this point. Then they vanish."

Jett raised his face to the endless night and smelled the freshening air. "I can smell my coat...and the scent of the thief. They can't be far."

Vaughn shrugged and stepped back. "Lead the way."

Jett stepped up to join Vaughn, and then he, too, stopped, his gut knotted. "The scent is gone, just...gone. It was there, and now it isn't." How could this be? He and his pelt were connected by flesh and soul.

Vaughn said, "It has to be a blocking spell. Either some Other living in this neighborhood doesn't want to be found or our thief is covering his tracks."

"What if they're one and the same?" Kenny asked.

Vaughn shook his head. "No shapeshifter can cast a spell this strong. Someone else is either protecting him or hiding themselves."

He walked up to the point where the trail had stopped, laid his palms flat as if on a wall and said, *"Ostendo tex-isuperficies."*

Static electricity filled the air in a web of pale blue light running from his hands over the darkness like vines climbing a wall until the entire shape of the blocking shield was exposed. The force field lay like a dome over the neighborhood.

"What did you do?" Jett asked, awed by Vaughn's power.

"Added some illumination. I was hoping only one house would be protected. We'll have to go door to door."

Jett stilled. "We don't have enough time."

Kenny spoke. "Before he can burn it, he has to mark the fur with his brand and his intentions, and that will buy us some time."

"I'll kill him if he inks my skin."

Kenny checked his watch. "We've been out for an hour. Sam's house is close. Without disrupting Christmas Eve any more than necessary, let's consult the Keepers and make better use of our resources to find Jett's skin before it's too late."

Chapter 8

The oppressive darkness seemed to have seeped into Sam's house. Katie Sue frowned at how quickly the mood of the celebration had changed since she'd left three hours before. She, Christina and Bridgette had bundled their gifts and desserts into the appropriate hands, while the younger boys quarreled over candy canes and who would play video games on the big-screen television in the family room. Bridgette and a few of the mothers began losing their patience and putting the children in time-outs until they calmed down.

"Jingle Bell Rock" playing happily in the background seemed to mock the foreboding permeating everyone's conversations, and among the Others, that foreboding had been compounded by the news of Jett's coat being stolen. The savory aromas of roasted meat and fresh-baked bread coming from the kitchen should have bolstered Katie Sue's mood, but she knew she wouldn't be able to touch a morsel with the way she felt at the moment.

Sam caught her up in a huge hug and whispered that everything would be okay. The understanding in her eyes reassured Katie that whatever the results of tonight's meeting, Sam would be there for her.

Roe, Keeper of the Five Elementals and Vaughn's partner, joined the two of them and squeezed Katie's arm reassuringly.

"Once June gets here, we can get down to celebrating Christmas Eve."

Sam gave Katie a commiserating glance. "And Jett?"

"There's been a new development."

"His coat? Has it been recovered?" Roe asked hopefully.

"Not exactly," Katie Sue said. She hugged the shoulder bag close. "I found Miranda's selkie skin hidden in the fireplace hearth."

"What?" Her cousins spoke in unison.

"Can we see it?" Roe said.

Katie opened the bag and the women sighed at the sight of the beautiful cream-silver pelt. A tingle ran through Katie as she imagined herself inside the skin, and the longing to feel it wrapping around her became almost overwhelming. She gasped involuntarily and had to close her eyes.

At her sharp intake of breath, Sam laid a hand on her arm.

"Katie, what's wrong?"

"Something happened to me tonight," Katie whispered. "I...transformed."

Roe gasped. "Does Jett know?"

Katie shook her head, a knot forming in her throat. Her attraction to the pelt was becoming a craving. "No. It just happened."

She refused to tell them of the almost irresistible pull the skin was exerting on her now. She didn't want to jeopardize her role as Keeper, and if she revealed her feelings they would be bound to question her ability to keep the level head every Keeper needed.

"I know this changes the discussion about Jett and me, but I think it also enhances my position as Keeper. My ability to wear a skin gives me firsthand understanding of what's best for the selkie realm."

Roe let out a low whistle. "I want to be in the room when Jett finds out your news."

Katie Sue smiled, but inside her heart already ached at the impossibility of a life with Jett as a selkie. She was a born Keeper. Her love was already lost.

"I'm going to give Jett his mother's skin. It will be my Christmas gift to him, so please don't say anything to him yet."

Sam sighed. "That's so brave of you, Katie."

Katie frowned. "No, Sam. I'm Jett's Keeper. His well-being supersedes my needs. You know that."

"Yes, my sweet selkie Keeper, I do." Sam smiled.

Tears welled in Katie's eyes. Sam had just declared her confidence in Katie Sue's ability to remain a Keeper despite the questions that needed to be answered. It seemed her fate was sealed. Jett could no longer be hers.

The grandfather clock in the foyer struck the half hour as the search party arrived, grim faced. No pelt. No villain. Katie Sue's heart broke at the look of battered purpose on Jett's face.

She tucked the shoulder bag beneath the Christmas tree, then approached Jett. He opened his arms wide and she stepped into his embrace. How many more times could she allow this? She hugged him fiercely, and he trembled.

"Still no luck?" She pulled back to search his expression.

Pain filled his eyes. "We traced the echoes to the village. We're closer, but losing time."

Sam and Roe had followed her over, and now Vaughn

took Roe's hands. "Can you recruit a group of elementals? We discovered a blocking shield. We either have to
remove it or use a tracer to home in on Jett's coat."

Sam frowned. "A shapeshifter would have to be incredibly powerful to create a shield. The possibility is
slim, so that pretty much narrows the field to witches
or warlocks."

As she spoke, June barreled through the door, her face
flushed and her hair askew, as if she'd run all the way
from town. She was carrying a leather folder. "I know
who stole Jett's skin!"

"Who?" Katie Sue demanded as the others all moved
closer.

"That weirdo who does grounds maintenance for the
village."

"Leo Gantry?" Katie Sue asked. "He graded our driveway this summer. He seemed like a decent guy."

"He's the one. He was in Twists & Tales yesterday. I
was lounging on the windowsill when he came in."

"That doesn't make him a thief," Roe said.

Jett turned to Katie Sue. "She was lounging on the
windowsill?"

She whispered, "June likes to shift into a cat. It's a
little trick she uses to keep an eye on her patrons."

June held up the large leather folder. "It makes him a
thief if he stole the parchment that was stored in here—
a parchment containing the recipes for several ancient
potions, including the one for a potion that uses a selkie skin."

"How do you know it was him?" Jett asked.

"I saw him nosing around the rare items. I got to thinking after I left you all earlier, so I went back to the bookstore." She tapped the folder. "He didn't return this to
the proper place, so I took a look and saw that the parch-

ment was missing. I don't think there's any question as to who's got it—or why."

"If Leo Gantry is the thief, then he must be a shape-shifter," Katie Sue said.

"If so, he's not registered," June said.

"Does anyone know where he lives?" Katie Sue asked.

"I can find out." Sam reached for her cell phone.

Jett gritted his teeth. "I'll bet he's in the lower village."

Vaughn frowned. "Which would explain the blocking shield we ran into."

Sam added, "A shapeshifter can't cast a blocking shield."

June frowned. "But a powerful Other can."

"Then Leo's not here on his own," Jett said. "He's with someone who doesn't want anyone to know he's here or the powers he has."

Katie Sue had had several encounters with Leo. She'd offered him something cold to drink when he'd worked on their driveway last summer. He had spoken very little, but she remembered how he'd grinned when their fingers had touched when she'd handed him his drink. The look had made her feel uncomfortable, as if he was looking right through her.

More recently she'd been in town just before the darkness hit and had caught Leo watching her from his truck as she crossed the street. She had shrugged off his almost hostile look, since men sometimes found her aloofness off-putting.

Sam snapped her phone shut. "He lives in a cottage on Benson Street. Number nineteen."

The men scrambled for the door. Jett called over his shoulder, "Call the council leaders. Tell them to meet us here as soon as possible."

"Wait for me!" Katie grabbed her coat.

"I'm coming, too." Roe was already tossing her cape over her shoulders.

June held up a hand. "Make sure they don't kill him until you get my parchment back!"

Chapter 9

Nineteen Benson Street was invisible in the oppressive dark. From the sidewalk, the small, neglected house looked vacant. No lights shone from within. The blocking shield had not been removed, so Jett still couldn't detect the scent of his coat.

This house was his last chance.

Jett opened the gate, but Kenny stopped him.

"Jett, if he hears us, he'll shift and disappear."

Jett struggled to keep his voice low. "I don't care. I want my coat."

"If he didn't shift on the beach earlier, maybe he's too weak to change," Katie whispered.

Jett focused on the house. "I see a chimney. No smoke. I'm going in."

As he spoke, something brushed past his ankles and darted through the open gate. His excellent vision let him identify the shadow. "What the—a black cat?"

"It's June!" If Jett hadn't said anything, Katie would never have seen her. As a cat, June could discover what was happening inside the cottage without detection. This was what family did for each other.

Vaughn put a hand on Jett's shoulder. "Let her scope out the situation. We'd see smoke if your coat was burning."

Roe moved close to Vaughn, who put a protective arm around her. Katie Sue stood between her brother and Jett, linking arms with both of them.

Vaughn whispered, "Be still, everyone. We don't want him detecting our energy."

After only minutes, though they seemed like an eternity, June returned. Still in cat form, she jumped into Vaughn's arms. As he held her, she transformed into a woman, smiling with satisfaction when he abruptly set her on her feet.

"We don't have time for your antics, woman," he said.

Ignoring him, June turned to Jett. "I saw through the back window. Looks like he just woke up. Your pelt is laid out on the floor in front of the fireplace." She grimaced. "He's shaving a pentagram in the fur."

Jett bolted for the back of the house, and in seconds everyone else was on his heels.

"I'll take the front door," Kenny said in a hoarse whisper.

Through a window in the back door Jett saw Leo's bent blond head leaning over his pelt as he concentrated on shaving the fur to the skin.

Using every ounce of control not to howl, Jett kicked the door open and lunged for Leo.

The shock and disbelief in Leo's blue eyes offered little satisfaction. Rage tore through Jett like an exploding gun. He hit the shifter as he rose to his feet, knocking him to the floor.

Katie Sue grabbed Jett's selkie skin as Vaughn and the other women surrounded her.

Leo had disappeared beneath the weight of Jett's body, the razor he'd been holding clattering onto the wood floor.

"What the...?" Jett scrambled to his feet.

Leo was gone, as if he'd disappeared into thin air.

Roe slammed the door shut and sat against it. "If he thinks he's getting out, he has to get past me." She yelled to Kenny, "Leo shifted, Kenny. Guard the front door."

Jett spoke into the air. "It's over, Leo. We know you're not strong enough to hold your form right now. We can wait you out."

June shifted into a sleek Siamese cat, her intense blue eyes concentrating on the floor where Jett had struggled with Leo. She sniffed, then began scratching the floor, her sharp claws digging into the spaces between the boards. Within seconds Leo emerged. He'd shifted into a cricket, but couldn't hold the form with the pain June caused. He lapsed back into human form, his cheek and lips bleeding from where she'd scratched his face.

Roe and Vaughn opened their palms. Streams of static streaked from their fingertips and surrounded Leo like tightly wound ropes. He immediately grew weak and collapsed against Jett, who held him upright.

"I could kill you for what you've done," Jett said.

Leo let out a harsh laugh. "Doesn't matter what you do to me. The curse will have you all killing each other anyway."

"How do you know?" Katie Sue moved closer. "Who cast this spell?"

Leo's smile was ugly. "I'm not telling you anything."

Kenny headed for the door. "I'll go back and get the car so we can get this bastard back to Sam's."

Katie handed Jett his fur with utmost tenderness. Relief flooded him to have his selkie lifeline back. The compassion rising in Katie Sue's eyes showed that she would do anything for him—not only as his Keeper, but as his lover. The truth of his love for her hammered in his chest with each beat of his heart. Having his pelt returned was like receiving a second chance at life. He was free to decide his fate now. The next seven years without his only love would be intolerable. His mother's blessing washed over him. She'd gifted him with his pelt. He was now free to choose his direction.

He leaned toward Katie Sue, inhaling her sweet perfume. Kissing her softly, he whispered, "Now we can celebrate Christmas. Let's go home."

On their way back to Sam's, Leo lost consciousness in the backseat of the car from the energy constraint of his bindings. His weakness boded well for keeping him from shifting anytime soon.

As soon as they reached the house, the men hustled Leo in the back way and up the stairs. The women circulated through the rooms, greeting neighbors while seeking out the Others in attendance and informing them that there would be an emergency council meeting as soon as the party wrapped up.

Katie Sue finally escaped to the kitchen to gather her thoughts. Now that he had his coat back, Jett would leave her again, and she had to make a crucial decision for her personal well-being. If she let Jett go, the void in her heart would remain forever. Could she live with that decision? Earlier, it had seemed cut and dried. She'd been convinced she had no choice, but now that Jett had his coat and Miranda's pelt was free for her to use, her choices no longer seemed as clear. How could she keep her lover and remain as Keeper of the Selkies?

Sam entered a few moments later, her concern clear on her face. "Everyone knows we'll be meeting to decide Leo's fate after the guests leave. I'm so glad Jett's pelt was recovered in time."

Katie Sue took a drink of water to buy herself time, but she could barely swallow it. She pushed the glass— and her painful thoughts—away, drawing on the strength she possessed as Keeper of the Selkies. Besides, this was Christmas, the season of giving. Jett's well-being was paramount, more important than her own desires. She loved him so much. Only his happiness mattered. The smile she offered her mentor was straight from her heart. "Recovering his skin was truly a gift. We're so lucky that we all have each other to rely on." She met Sam's eyes, her own serious. "But we have to question Leo. I'm sure he knows who's behind the curse."

"Let's save that concern for the meeting." She reached for Katie's hand. "Come on. It's Christmas Eve. We're exchanging gifts. Let's enjoy the moment."

The house finally grew quiet close to midnight. Katie Sue glanced at the shoulder bag holding Miranda's coat. As she'd watched the others exchange gifts, she'd decided to present Jett with his mother's fur in private. His emotions might be too raw for him to receive the long-lost gift in front of others. The Salem council members convened around the fireplace while Jett recounted what happened when they recovered his skin. As always, Katie Sue marveled at the way these unassuming and familiar residents of Salem balanced their normal lives as shopkeepers, medical and financial professionals, parents and caregivers with their existence as members of the Otherworld.

One of the shifters said, "If you had to breach a blocking shield, that means someone was hiding Leo's abilities from detection."

"Which makes Leo someone's minion," Jett said. "Most likely we're talking witch or warlock here."

June took a deep breath, as if to steel herself against what was coming next. "Then as Keeper of the Witches, the burden falls on me to find the conjurer of this evil." She sighed and met the gazes of the group. "If one of my charges is behind this, I will deliver him or her. I promise."

Kenny put an arm around her. "We're all here to help, June. You're not alone. We'll get through this together."

As if on cue, Bridgette entered carrying a tray holding Christmas cookies, coffee and eggnog into the room. "Let's bring Christmas morn in with a final blessing and a toast to us all," she said.

Jett stood. "Before this Christmas Eve ends, I'd like to give one more gift."

He walked over to the tree and retrieved his selkie skin from where he'd tucked it so it was hidden from view. Katie Sue watched, eyes wide, as he returned to her, smiling that heart-stopping smile she cherished. Her pulse pounded as he knelt before her, and she could feel the attention of everyone in the room focused on them.

Jett placed the skin in her lap with the nobility of the royal line from which he came. She couldn't help but rest her palm on the soft silk of his gray coat, fully aware it could only be filled by the one man she would love forever.

Jett's eyes were filled with a passion she felt right down to her soul as he said, "Katie Sue, as my Keeper and my lover, you unselfishly set aside your own dreams tonight to help me recover my heritage—no, my life. In return, I offer you my heart. Forever. My selkie skin is yours. Marry me. I am prepared to remain human and give us the life we both seek until death do us part."

A hush fell over the room. Katie knew that Jett's willingness to forfeit the sea and become human was monumental, and that everyone else recognized that, as well. The fire burning in his eyes proved how serious he was about claiming her for his own. Only the ticking grandfather clock marked the passing moments as she soaked in the enormity of his words.

Tears fell shamelessly down her cheeks. Unable to resist this man she'd loved for what was essentially her entire life, she caressed his face with her hands and drew his mouth to hers for a kiss that sent a thrill through her. "Jett, I've dreamed of hearing you say those words. Thank you. Nothing would make me happier than to be your wife, but before I accept, there's something I have to tell you."

Jett sat back on his heels, confusion clouding his eyes. "Is something wrong?"

A bubble of laughter escaped her as she pushed that errant lock of black hair from Jett's forehead. "Not exactly, my love."

She glanced at her mother and smiled, then retrieved the shoulder bag from beneath the Christmas tree and knelt in front of Jett. "Here. This is for you."

Jett's hand stopped in midair when he opened the bag and saw the contents. Awe filled his face as he removed the skin for all to see. "My mother's pelt? Where did you find it?"

Katie Sue's pulse quickened. Telling Jett of her discovery would change the field of possibilities between them. Did she have the courage to become a selkie wife instead of a human one? She had wanted Jett to forfeit his heritage for her and he had done exactly that. Could she return the offer? The gesture would mean relinquishing her role as Keeper, her family and her life on land. Unless...

She rested her hands on Miranda's pelt, where it lay on Jett's knees. "I found it hidden in the hearth. And a little while later I felt this…this inexplicable urge to put it on, and something amazing happened."

Understanding filled Jett's eyes. His voice dropped to a whisper. "Tell me you transformed, Katie."

Her heart in her throat, she nodded. "Yes. I became a selkie."

Jett pulled her to her feet, wrapping her in his arms. "Oh, by the goddess! So the legend is true?"

She nodded, tears brimming in her eyes. "Yes. I have the gene."

He spun her around, laughing. "My Katie Sue is part selkie!"

The joy in his face was infectious. Katie Sue laughed with him. She could feel the energy flow through her body and into his as he held her close. They were one. The way he was looking at her proved there was no denying that simple, beautiful fact.

When he held her at arm's length, her smile grew serious. "I can choose now, Jett. I can leave with you, if you would prefer the life of a selkie to a life on land. I'm prepared to become a selkie wife. All I want is to be with you for the rest of my life."

Sam stood. "Okay, you two lovebirds, while this is truly a Christmas blessing, Katie Sue has raised a serious issue that affects us all. While Jett's choice to become human is a personal one, Katie's decision will affect not only her future but the entire Keeper and selkie communities."

Knowing how this discussion would go, Katie decided to make the process easier by speaking her mind first. She held up a hand. "In the hours since I discovered Miranda's coat, I've had the chance to consider the options."

Samantha nodded. "Go on."

Katie reached for Jett's hand. "I cannot live without Jett in my life. I also cannot ask him to remain human forever. That was a choice he was willing to make for my happiness, not his own."

Jett interrupted. "I did it for *us,* Katie."

She gave him a brief but heartfelt kiss. "I believe you, Jett. However, I have a proposal for the council." Squeezing Jett's hand for support, she addressed the others. "During the short time I was a selkie, something shifted inside me. I felt a freedom I've never known before. An organic joy seemed to flow from Miranda's skin into my body—and I want to experience that feeling again. I will always be human, but now I truly understand what it means, how amazing it is, to be a selkie. I've been blessed with the opportunity to be both, and I want to take advantage of that chance."

Sam said, "So what do you propose, Katie?"

"What better way to remain a Keeper of the Selkies than to live among them? Our purpose is to protect the Others in our care. As a selkie, I can better understand and help, and as a human, I can better represent them in our world. And the really wonderful thing is that since I'm only part selkie, I'm pretty sure I won't be bound to spend seven years away at sea. If I'm needed at home, I can return and transform as needed."

"I think that's a brilliant idea," June said. "And I intend to make sure our world survives. I will find and defeat the source of the darkness that threatens us." The light in her eyes reflected her commitment to achieving her goal.

Katie Sue smiled at June. "In the meantime, I propose that Jett and I marry before his time on land ends."

An elder vampire held up a finger. "Let's slow down

for a moment. Would she remain eligible to be a Keeper? A Keeper must be human."

Katie Sue opened her arms. "But I *am* human."

In the ensuing silence, Sam spoke up. "Shall we vote?" When everyone nodded their assent, she continued. "All opposed to Katie Sue remaining as Keeper, say *nay.*"

Jett pulled Katie Sue close while they waited for a verdict, his heart hammering beneath her hand resting on his chest. She held her breath in anticipation. Her future as Keeper was at stake, and heaven bless Jett for being as worried as she was over the outcome.

When no one spoke in dissent, Samantha grinned. "All in favor?"

Every voice in the room responded "Aye!"

A thrill ran through Katie Sue. Jett hugged her hard before draping his mother's fur over her shoulders. She immediately felt the warmth of Miranda's essence soothe her. Though she had never known Jett's mother, the woman's love continued to linger. And Katie intended to build on that shared love to make the world in which she lived a better place for everyone, human and Other alike. It was all she could do as Keeper of the Selkies. It was all she could do for Jett.

The others crowded around them, laughing, hugging them, toasting them.

When Katie Sue finally found her way back to Jett's side, she smiled into his laughing dark eyes. "Are you prepared for a whirlwind wedding, my love?"

He searched her face as he asked, "Are you prepared for a life spent almost entirely beneath the sea? Away from your loved ones?"

Katie Sue inhaled a fortifying breath. She'd already spent most of her existence without the love of her life. Spending time—years, even—away from the only home she'd ever known would be a walk in the park, especially now that they would be exploring his world together. Besides, she was free to return whenever her Keeper duties required it. Their future looked brighter than ever. She and Jett were going home.

She met his gaze, hoping every ounce of love she felt for him was reflected in her eyes. "For the first time in my life, my destiny makes sense. Yes, I am prepared to leave with you. Miranda's legacy is the most precious of Christmas gifts. I have not only discovered new possibilities for myself, but I get to keep you in the bargain."

Kenny lifted his glass. "I propose the final toast of this blessed Christmas Eve. To Jett and Katie Sue. May Christmas tidings be with them always!"

Jett pulled her into his arms and kissed her soundly while everyone around them cheered them on. Katie Sue couldn't help but imagine that the love generated in this house tonight could light the entire world. She had never felt happier. Hugging Jett close, she inhaled his familiar scent, knowing this was the best Christmas ever. She murmured, "Merry Christmas, my love." With Jett's arm around her shoulder, she lifted her glass and met the eyes of their family and friends to acknowledge their love. "A very merry Christmas to us, one and all."

* * * * *

STALKING IN A WINTER WONDERLAND

—

BETH CIOTTA

Dear Reader,

Greetings, and thank you for joining us on this dark ride through the brightest of seasons. For me, there's nothing more rewarding than sharing the gifts of joy, love and adventure. I feel especially blessed to be included in this intriguing anthology alongside some of the nicest people I know: Heather Graham, Deborah LeBlanc and Kathleen Pickering. Joining together, we've created four tales celebrating the many wonders of the paranormal realm and the power of hope, faith and love. My contribution, *Stalking in a Winter Wonderland,* comes from my heart and explores the magic of the season, the importance of family and the blessing of true love. I wish for you everything I write about—not just during the holidays but the whole year through. Peace and joy, my friends...always!

Cheers,

Beth Ciotta

To my fellow authors, Heather Graham,
Deborah LeBlanc and Kathleen Pickering,
and to our editor, Leslie Wainger. Thank you
for the inspiration, collaboration and the joy of
creating something magical!

Chapter 1

Typically Juniper Twist would be sound asleep.

Typically most everyone in Salem would be asleep. Except for the parents who were wrapping last-minute presents. Or the children peeking out of their windows in hopes of spying Santa and his reindeer.

Instead, in these moonlit hours before the dawn—at least, as measured by the clock—of Christmas Day, the citizens of Salem, human and Other, were restless. Sleep patterns had been disrupted. A sinister darkness had crept into their lives, and over the past few weeks, as the daylight hours had shrunk to mere minutes, an anxious desperation had seeped into their spirits. Would there even *be* a dawn? Ever?

June pushed aside the magical tome she'd been studying for the past hour and stood to stretch her tense muscles. Snatching her fourth can of Red Bull, she breezed by shelves crammed with sacred texts and literature to get to the frosty pane of the Twists & Tales, the bookshop she'd recently inherited from her poor deceased uncle.

Sipping the energy-charged drink, she peered into the black night. It had been just as black at two o'clock in the afternoon on Christmas Eve. On what had been a festive, sunny day everywhere else in the country, Salem hadn't gotten even a half hour of blessed light.

Scientists and meteorologists had pondered the phenomenon. The media had speculated like crazy. But none of them had suspected the truth, because, due to the code of silence, very few human beings knew of the existence of the plethora of supernatural beings occupying this planet. Vampires, selkies, shapeshifters, werewolves and fae, to name only a few. The Others had been living among humans for centuries, overseen by the Keepers, who helped them to peacefully exist in a world that had no clue as to their existence.

June was a newly appointed Keeper. The Keeper of the Witches. Witches with supernatural zing.

"Whoop-de-twinkly-do."

Once upon a time, her father had been Keeper of the Witches, but then he'd died and his younger brother, her uncle, had taken up the post. She had been marked for the future and had spent most of her young life looking forward to holding this distinguished position. Then she'd fallen prey to a spell. A *love* spell. Learning she'd been duped by those she'd respected and admired had altered her perception of witches. Oh, she still admired their magical powers and their affinity with the earth, but she didn't trust them. She'd spent the past few years overseas, studying vigorously and learning as much as she could about witches—the magical kind, not the religious kind—although she'd boned up on Wiccans, too. She'd planned on being fully prepared, knowing all their tricks and how to better detect deception, by the time she became a Keeper. She would become impervious to bewitchment. Yes, she had centuries' worth of knowledge to absorb, but she honestly hadn't expected to fill a Keeper's shoes for another twenty years. At forty-one her uncle Artemis had been in his prime—as a man and as a Keeper. She still couldn't believe he'd died of a heart attack. A *heart attack!* Considering the potentially dangerous and powerful individuals he dealt with on a daily basis, it seemed such a mundane way to go.

Hence, June had been contacted by her family as well as the council. She'd abandoned her ancient studies near Stonehenge and flown across the Atlantic to take up her inherited duty. There'd been little time to mourn Artemis's death because she'd landed smack-dab in the middle of this blackout crisis. It had been coming on ever since before the Winter Solstice and had gotten worse by the day. According to pagan beliefs, Yule was when the darker half of the year relinquished precedence to the lighter half. The days should have been getting longer, not shorter. It was as if their midwinter celebration had backfired. She'd even heard rumors that practicing witches and Wiccans were having a hard time keeping their Yule logs lit.

At first she prayed heart and soul that this pall was a freak glitch in nature.

And then she'd hoped some terrifying government experiment had gone awry.

When it became apparent the darkness was Otherworldly, she'd willed it to be the mischievous doing of an elf or a sick prank by a rabid vampire. She wanted it to be any other Keeper's problem but hers. Several of her cousins were Keepers. Katie Sue was Keeper of the Selkies. Roe was Keeper of the Five Elementals. Samantha was Keeper of the Vampires. Any one of them had more practical experience in these matters than June. All had keener leadership skills. All held more sway with their charges. Especially Sam. Heck, Samantha Mycroft was not only respected by the vampire community, she was beloved by the entire town, not to mention she was the de facto leader of all the local Keepers. June herself... Well, she was an outsider. Or at least that was how she felt. She'd been away for so long that she felt dismally out of touch. With her family, yes, but especially with the witch community.

Now she was back, and it was up to her to save the day—literally.

Due to three separate and very recent Other crises, there was no mistaking that the darkness sucking the joy out of everyone this holiday season had been brought on by witchcraft. A harmful spell cast by a magical witch.

One of June's charges.

Who was capable of such treachery? She couldn't imagine. Because she'd been away from Salem for almost eight years, she didn't yet have a keen lock on the dynamics of the local magical coven or the latest gossip within the Other community. She'd been in town for two weeks now. She'd touched base with a few of her charges, made her presence known throughout town, but she'd yet to call a formal meeting. Out of respect, she'd spoken briefly with the acting high priestess, if only to assure Esmeralda she was on the job. The one thing June hadn't done, the thing she dreaded most, was speaking with Esmeralda's grandson, Basel Collins, a powerful wizard and the next in line as high priest of the local coven. The bad boy who'd seduced her soul and stolen her heart.

Except it hadn't been real.

June tossed her empty can in the trash bin, blaming her racing pulse on the energy drink, not the memory of Baz's passion. His soul kisses and heated touch. His declaration of love.

None of it real.

Her cheeks flamed. That had been eight years ago, and she still felt the fool.

Her cell phone jangled with the theme from the old television show *Bewitched*. Not an original choice, but a sporadic reminder of her youthful naïveté. Crazy, but the song always put starch in her spine. Glancing at the incoming call, June paced while connecting. "Hey, Sam."

"You doing okay, kid?"

June flushed at her cousin's caring tone. Even though she had been nervous and tentative ever since her return, Sam, along with everyone else, had been doing their best to make her feel welcome. "Hanging in there, O Keeper of Keepers."

"I can't help it if I feel responsible for the well-being of my sisters-in-arms. Not to mention my cousins," Sam added with a smile in her voice. "I'm worried about you. When you rushed out of the council meeting—"

"About that. I'm sorry I didn't thank you properly for including me in your Christmas Eve party."

"You're kidding, right? You're family, June."

"Estranged family." Her gut knotted with guilt. "All that time I was away, I didn't work very hard at keeping in touch."

"You were busy," Sam said reasonably. "We all get caught up in our own lives from time to time."

"And since I've been back…I've been sort of distanced. Worried."

"It's the darkness. Everyone's on edge. About that, June. Before you left you promised you'd get to the bottom of this curse. I—we—just want you to know that we're here for you. Me and Daniel, Roe and Vaughn, Katie Sue and Jett. Just give a shout if—"

"It's the middle of the night."

"Anytime. Any hour."

"I appreciate that, Sam. I know I'm not qualified to be a Keeper, and—"

"The only one who thinks that is you." Sam sighed. "Okay. Time for some tough love."

"You really don't—"

"Yes, I do. As the eldest cousin and as someone who cares deeply for you, I'm compelled to tell you to grow some balls."

June choked on shocked laughter. "What?"

"Bear with me. It seems to be my running theme lately. Listen, honey, you were born to be a Keeper. You've been studying the history and traditions of Wiccans and witches for years. But you can't do this alone. You need to call a formal convocation and confer with your charges."

"I know."

"Your interaction with them thus far has been minimal, and now they're taking matters into their own hands."

June stumbled. *"What?"*

"Humans aren't the only ones rattled by this darkness," Sam said. "All the Others are affected, as well, and now that we've determined that a witch is the likely culprit, the pressure is on the local coven to rein in their own before the whole of Salem is at each other's throats."

"But it's only been a couple of hours since—"

"News like this travels like wildfire, June. You should know that."

"I do know that." June mentally kicked herself for wasting the past hour poring over the *Book of Spells* when she should have been consulting with the people who knew those spells best. She dashed for the coat tree and nabbed her coat and scarf. "I'll head over to Esmeralda's right now. I know it's late but—"

"That's part of the reason I'm calling. I just got word Esmeralda's down with some horrible virus. That's why she wasn't at my party tonight…last night…whatever. That's why she wasn't at the last-minute council meeting, either. She's put Baz in temporary charge."

Coat half on, half off, June froze. "What?"

"He's on his way over to Twists & Tales."

"Crap." If she had to speak with Basel, she would prefer someplace public. She wasn't ready to be alone with him, and her bookshop had been closed for hours. If she left now, maybe she could avoid him, call him later and name her own meeting place.

"Word of advice from someone who was also burned by my past love, cousin. Everyone makes mistakes."

"Love had nothing to do with what went on between Basel and me," June snapped. "Nothing."

"Good luck, honey," Sam said with genuine affection. "And Merry Christmas."

It took all the self-control June could muster not to reply, *bah, humbug.*

Chapter 2

"Happy belated solstice, June Bug."

"First of all, what's happy about it? Second, why can't you call me June or Juniper like everyone else?"

"Because you'll always be June Bug to me." Baz smiled, hoping to break the ice. There was plenty of it. Even though the sidewalk had been shoveled and salted, several deadly looking icicles hung from the gables of Twists & Tales. Then there was the frosty look in June's emerald-green eyes. "Cold as a witch's... Well, you know. Mind inviting me inside?" Although he wasn't sure it would be any warmer inside the old bookstore than out here on the street. He'd assumed he would get a chilly reception, but this was ridiculous.

For the minute June kept him waiting, he drank his slow fill of her. She'd always been cute, but now she was stunning. Stunning in a way that made him randy and resentful at the same time. He'd missed eight years of watching Juniper Twist blossom. She was still on the petite side—five-one to his six feet. Pale skin, vivid green eyes, lush black lashes. He liked that she still wore her straight hair long, although the thick bangs were new. The blunt fringe drew attention to those amazing eyes. Eyes that shimmered with…resentment? Anxiety? And, oh, yeah. There it was. A little female appreciation. Baz was pretty sure his friendly smile just turned cocky.

A frigid wind blasted his back and fanned several strands of her ebony hair. Shivering, she stepped back, gesturing for him to hurry inside. Once he was over the threshold she shut and locked the door.

"Going somewhere?" he asked with a cocked brow. She had one arm in the sleeve of her coat and a long scarf hung crookedly around her neck.

"I was on my way out to see Esmeralda."

"Ez is sick."

"I heard. I mean, Sam just called. I hope it's not serious."

"Nice of you not to hold a grudge."

"I'm not sure I'll ever forgive your grandmother for casting that spell, but I don't wish her ill, either."

"I appreciate that," he said, irked that she still couldn't see beyond that damned incantation. Her coat still hung from her right arm and shoulder. She seemed distracted. He moved in to help. "On or off?"

"What?"

"Your coat. On or off?"

"Oh. Off, I guess. Since you're here. Sam said you're stepping in for Esmeralda."

"Just while she's sick." He hung her coat on the antique tree near the cashier counter. Meanwhile, she shifted back and forth, rocking her weight while relooping her scarf. She was dressed in black from head to toe, except for that purple scarf and her knee-high purple boots. She was wired. He noted several empty cans of Red Bull in the garbage bin and another two on a table alongside a stack of books.

"Want some coffee?" she asked. "Hot tea?"

Like she needed more caffeine, he thought. "Got any wassail?"

"Why would I have wassail?"

"'Tis the season?" Baz shrugged out of his rugged leather bomber and hung it alongside her stylish velvet coat. "Not that you'd know it by the look of this place." He swept his gaze over the dimly lit room. He'd always loved Twists & Tales. A centuries-old building full of centuries-old books, most of them having to do with spiritualism, mysticism and the occult. "Artemis used to deck the halls."

"I'm not Artemis."

"Obviously." He couldn't help admiring June's sexy curves. The magicals' former Keeper had definitely been lacking in that area. Annoyed by his fierce attraction to the woman who'd mangled his heart, Baz focused on the crisis. "Artemis would have spent the past week spreading Yuletide cheer among his charges and friends. He would have visited each and every witch—Wiccan or magical—trying to ease their concerns regarding this black curse. Working with us, not against us."

She stopped shifting and gawked. "I wasn't working against you!"

"You sure as hell weren't *with* us."

"I've only been in town for two weeks. I've been easing into the position, gathering information. Plus I've had a lot going on. Moving in here. Settling my uncle's affairs. Reacclimating to the area. And then today, I mean, yesterday, Sam needed my help at her house. You know, with her annual party. And then there were the Other incidents."

"Let's start there," Baz interrupted. She was practically bouncing off the ancient walls. He caught her hand and finessed her toward the upstairs apartment.

"What are you doing?"

"I need you to brief me on that altercation with the shapeshifter. I especially want your take on the blocking shield. But first, I need a drink." He had climbed this narrow stairwell many a time before, but usually with Artemis. He missed his friend. He mourned the Keeper. As for June… Holding her hand brought back every intimate moment they'd shared with vivid clarity. Did she feel it, too? The connection? The energy? The soul-deep love?

She slipped out of his grasp as if reading his thoughts. *Or feeling the same unnerving jolt.*

"Water or brandy?" he asked as they reached the small kitchen. Either drink would counteract her caffeine high.

"I don't have any brandy."

"Yes, you do."

"Water," she said in a dazed voice. "I need my wits about me."

"As do I." Hopefully a snifter of cognac would dull his sensual buzz.

High on Juniper Twist.

Great. Just great.

He snagged a bottle of spring water from the fridge and passed it to her. Then he nabbed both a snifter and Artemis's stashed Rémy Martin from the corner cabinet. She'd stayed away so long, Baz knew this apartment better than she did. He noted the circles beneath her eyes as she screwed off the cap of her water and swigged. "When's the last time you slept?"

"Yesterday. I think. For a couple of hours. Or maybe that was the day before." She palmed her forehead. "The days and nights are blurring."

He ached to pull her into his arms. Instead, he sipped

cognac. "I hear you." He nodded toward the living room. "Come on, Bug. Let's talk."

June hated that Baz called her Bug. She used to love it. It made her feel special. June Bug was cute. *Bug* was special. A term of affection that made her insides all squishy. Even now.

How the heck was that possible?

She was over him. *Long* over him. Not only had their love been a sham, but he had cheated on her not an hour after the spell had been lifted.

"I can hear those wheels turning," he said as she sat on her uncle's butter-soft sofa.

"I've got a lot on my mind."

He sank down beside her.

She shot up and moved to the matching leather club chair.

Baz just grinned. The same knowing grin he'd adopted on the threshold just minutes ago when he'd realized she was checking him out. How could she *not* check him out? Basel Christopher Collins had always been sinfully gorgeous. But now…now there was an air about him that she couldn't quite pinpoint. A grounded confidence. A driven calm. It was…intense.

And incredibly sexy.

Even when he'd scolded her downstairs, he hadn't raised his voice. He hadn't lost his cool. He had always been a wild child. A bad boy. He still looked the part in his faded jeans and rugged boots, the snug black tee and the black-and-red flannel shirt—unbuttoned and tails hanging out. His chocolate-brown hair was windblown, and he needed a shave. His eyes, nearly the same color as that cognac, sparkled with something dangerous. Controlled, but dangerous.

She squirmed under his intense regard and that sexy hint of a smile. "We should be out there looking for whomever's responsible for the darkness spell."

"I know who's responsible."

"What?" She shot out of her chair, shocked and incensed. "How can you sit there looking so calm? Why didn't you tell me straightaway? Why—" Her voice caught when Baz grasped her hand—again—and gently tugged her down beside him on the sofa. She felt a zap as soon as their palms connected. Her nerves jumped like live wires. Real? Or magic? The effect, combined with his nearness, stunned her into silence.

"Correction. I'm ninety-nine percent certain of the culprit's identity. A warlock by the name of Marin Bryce. I just put the pieces together in the past couple of hours. What I don't know," he said while sliding her a disquieting look, "is his location. Even if I did, I couldn't force him to break the spell."

June wasn't familiar with the wayward magical. "Bryce is that powerful?"

"I'm not that ruthless. Violence isn't our way, June Bug."

"I know." She knew the way of the magicals, which was in tune with the Wiccans' "An in it harm none." "But there was a time…" She thought back on when Baz had used his powers to punish a boy who'd been terrorizing young girls. Disturbing, even though his intentions had been good. "You didn't always play by the rules."

"Still don't." He drank more brandy, then set aside the glass. "But this is bigger than anything I've ever dealt with. Anything *we've* ever dealt with. By lashing out and striking hard, by acting out in anger or desperation, we'd be playing into his hands and strengthening the spell."

"You've given this a lot of thought."

"Ez had her suspicions. I narrowed them down. We've been questioning members of the coven, quietly poking around."

"Which I would've known if I'd called a formal meeting." Head spinning, June chugged more water, then worked a kink from her neck. "When I think of the time I wasted hoping this was anyone's problem but mine…"

Baz squeezed her arm.

Another zap.

Unsettled, June cursed her squishy insides and tried to relax in his presence. Tried to absorb his calm. "If Christmas Day comes and goes without a sliver of sunlight…"

"We won't let that happen."

She glanced at one of the most powerful wizards she'd ever known, her stomach twisting with skepticism. As if Baz really needed her help. "We?"

"Between my practical experience and your extensive studies," he said, "together we can beat this."

"How can you be so sure?"

"Faith. In the power of good over evil. In us."

She didn't like the look in his eye. Well, she did, but she shouldn't. She had been short on faith and trust for some time now. Ignoring the sensual sparks flaring throughout her body, she summoned every practical, logical particle of her being. "Let's start with what we know."

Chapter 3

June faded, then finally fell asleep, in the middle of her rendition of the showdown with the shapeshifter who'd stolen Jett's seal coat—the skin that allowed his selkie self to return to the sea. Jett had already relayed the story to Baz, just as vampire Daniel Riverton had briefed him on the troubled vamp who'd bitten a young woman in the middle of a Christmas concert.

Still, Baz had wanted June's input on both events before revealing the details of his own suspicions regarding Salem's curse. She'd personally been involved in tracking the rogue shapeshifter, Leo Gantry, who everyone surmised was somehow connected to the fiend responsible for this sinister darkness. The tip-off had been the blocking shield, an invisible force field that deflected detection. The work of a powerful spellcaster. Someone who didn't want Gantry found. That hadn't gone well for Gantry or Marin Bryce—the warlock Baz suspected was at the root of the all-enveloping darkness.

Baz had been on the verge of sharing Marin's background when he'd noticed June nodding off. Her speech had slowed and her eyelids had drifted shut. One minute she'd been telling him how she'd sniffed Gantry out utilizing her keen feline senses, the next there had been silence.

He had shifted position just as June's head had lolled. Now he held her in his arms. Unexpected, but nice.

Lack of Red Bull, and Artemis's comfortable sofa had done wonders to help her relax. Baz hoped his presence had helped to ease her anxiety, as well. He blamed the bulk of her exhaustion on lack of sleep, but he also knew from Vaughn and Jett that she had shifted into cat form twice within a short period in order to help snag Gantry. When someone wasn't in peak condition, shifting could take a heavy toll.

Every Keeper was born with a "borrowed power," an ability linked to their charges' abilities. June had the mark of the paw, which signified her ability to shift into a witch's familiar—a cat. Only instead of being the companion and source of inspiration for just one witch, she'd been marked as a Keeper, her role to aid all witches, specifically the magical element of Salem. Her father and her uncle, rest their souls, had been marked as well, and as they were first in line to serve, no one in the community had thought it likely June would adopt the role of Keeper anytime soon, if ever. Growing up, Juniper Twist had been one of the sweetest souls ever to grace Salem. No one could imagine her as a guardian. In times of peace, sure. But when things got rough?

Baz studied June's lovely features. So angelic. So petite. He'd been stunned when Jett had described her aggressive role in Gantry's capture. Then again, this wasn't the same woman he'd fallen in love with all those years ago. She'd grown cynical since then, guarded. She'd never fully recovered from her parents' tragic deaths, and then not two years after she'd felt deceived by Esmeralda's well-intentioned spell and his own unintentional betrayal.

She stirred and moaned, and he held her a little closer, a little tighter. His body hummed with yearning. He wanted to kiss her, slow and deep. He wanted to peel away her winter layers, to stroke her curves. To make her purr. He wanted to bury himself inside her and re-claim the magic they'd once shared. He'd sworn he was over Juniper Twist.

He'd been wrong.

His groin tightened when she turned into him, drap-ing one leg over his lap. He remembered her flexibility with aching clarity. He struggled to temper the erotic vi-sions dancing in his head. Struggled to smother the lust-ful inferno raging through his blood. For the love of...

June snuggled into his embrace. Apparently she didn't despise him as much in her dreams. She even smiled a little when he smoothed her hair from her face. He fix-ated on that mouth, the same mouth that had whispered her undying love, only to curse him to hell when she'd caught him in a lip-lock with Lolita Dorring. The biggest bonehead move of his youth. He admitted it. He'd apolo-gized for it. Lolita had caught him at a bad time, working her seductive wiles the same day June had spurned him, and he'd rolled with it. If he had been tempted and had taken the kiss further, then his "love" for June would have been false. A spell-induced illusion. That experimental kiss had fallen flat, just as he'd anticipated, but June had walked in before he'd had a chance to end it. His expla-nation regarding the need to prove the genuineness and depth of his love for June had fallen on deaf ears. *June's* deaf ears. In hindsight, he'd acted rashly. But he'd been angry and desperate. Back then his lack of control was downright famous.

He had spent years reining in his impetuous streak. Now he thought before acting—and he was thinking about taking advantage of this moment and brushing a kiss over June's tantalizing lips. Just a taste to appease his hunger. He dropped his face closer to hers and, as if sensing his intention, as if welcoming his affection, she wrapped her arm around his neck.

Heart pounding, Baz froze. She was asleep. A fatigued sleep. She could be snuggling with anyone in her dreams.

His thoughts took an ugly turn. She'd been away for eight years. She was vibrant and beautiful and smart. *Passionate.* He had been June's first. He didn't want to think about her in any other man's bed. But he couldn't stop himself.

She stirred then, as if sensing his tension. Her lashes fluttered, and she looked up at him, all soft and dreamy.

He knew the moment lucidity hit. He could read her thoughts as clearly as when she was in her cat form. Communicating telepathically. Just one of the boons between a witch and familiar.

She didn't trust him.

"I—"

"Let's take a walk." He didn't take her by the hand this time. He couldn't risk the connection. For the first time in ages, he wrestled to maintain calm. June peeked at the clock hanging over the cashier's counter as Baz helped her into her coat.

3:30 a.m.

Normally dawn would break in four hours, but she wasn't counting on it today. In the two weeks since she'd been back in Salem, sunrise and sunset had been erratic, the days shorter and shorter. There hadn't been even a glimpse of daylight yesterday. The most dismal Christmas Eve ever. A chilling fear had begun to worm its way under her skin. The fear that if they didn't break the spell pronto, if the sun didn't shine for even a minute on Christmas Day, Salem would be doomed to darkness forever.

"I can't believe I fell asleep in the midst of this crisis." June pulled her sweater cap over her head, angry with herself, angry with Baz. "Why didn't you wake me?"

"If we're going to go up against Marin, you need to be alert and aware," he said as he pulled on his bomber jacket and gloves. "Being hopped up on stimulants and sugar doesn't count."

"I'm aware of that," June groused. "And I know my job."

"I'm not questioning your abilities. Just pointing out it's hard to stay sharp when you're exhausted, which you were."

Baz opened the door, allowing June to move outside ahead of him. He was irritated. She could feel it, see it. She chalked it up to the oppressive darkness. Everyone was edgy and off. Even so, he retained his manners. Even in his bad-boy days, he'd always been a gentleman.

Sexy.

Her stomach fluttered along with her pulse, but it was nothing compared to what she'd felt when she'd realized Baz was about to kiss her. Worse, she'd wanted that kiss. She'd dreamed about that kiss. Her cheeks burned as she thought about the way she'd practically crawled onto his lap. He was here on business. They had a job to do.

Plus she didn't trust this electric attraction. She didn't trust Baz. She knew through the grapevine that his magical skills were more powerful than ever. Along with a few key witches from his coven, surely they could bring down this spellcaster. Why did he want to team up with *her,* especially given the bad blood between them? Just because she was his Keeper? She didn't buy that. Not only had she not proved herself in any way, her failure to bond properly with the coven upon her return had suggested a lack of confidence or, worse, incompetence. Shame washed over her, and she silently vowed to make amends.

Her mind raced as they walked toward the corner of Howard and Brown. Between the catnap and the frigid wind, she was feeling alert and aware. Four o'clock in the morning, yet almost every house and business sparkled with some sort of illumination. Candles, strings of multicolored holiday lights, icicle lighting, frosted globes, LED snowflakes, stars and Santas, twinkling garlands and wreaths.

So much for saving on the electricity bill.

It was as if everyone, human and Other, was desperate for the enlivening presence of light—even the artificial kind. June could sense the fear pervading the town. The fear of complete darkness and the evil associated with it.

"I need to know more about this Marin," she said, her breath coming out in billowy plumes. "So stop putting me off." She didn't care that her frustration was obvious in her voice. "Why would he do this? What's his motivation? His goal?"

Baz had steered her left toward Washington Square. "1692 to 93. More than two hundred people were accused of practicing witchcraft." He cast his gaze to the dark, starless sky. "The Devil's magic."

She shivered, unsure where he was going with this, but knowing the story well.

"One hundred and fifty imprisoned," he went on. "Nineteen condemned and hanged."

Nineteen innocents.

"The Salem witch trials," June joined in. "Spurred by the fits and ravings of three young girls."

"Who, after a doctor blamed the fits on bewitchment, accused three women of afflicting them."

"Which ultimately led to mass hysteria and a massive witch hunt."

"A dark time for Salem and its people."

June's stomach knotted as they stopped in front of the Salem Witch Museum—a former church that had been built in the mid-1800s and steeped in religious controversy. The historic brownstone had been a favorite haunt of June's when she was a kid. She glanced up at the statue of Salem's founder, Roger Conant, a stunning work of art that was often—and mistakenly—referred to as "the wizard's statue."

In her youth, when June had been enamored with witches, she hadn't thought Conant worthy of the appellation. There had been nothing magical about Roger Conant. That wasn't to say she didn't admire the man. He'd been a hard worker and a visionary. Conant and his followers were considered the founding fathers of Naumkeag, renamed Salem for "shalom" or "peace." How sad and ironic that his noble vision had been forever tainted by the heinous and infamous witch trials.

And now this. This unnatural darkness resulting in a similar hysteria. A curse inflicted by a contemporary warlock. If Baz had brought up the trials, he must have established a link.

"What are you thinking?" he asked.

"I'm pondering the connection between Marin and the witch trials."

"And?"

"By invoking darkness, and thereby the Devil, he's hoping to incite paranoia. Chaos."

"The logical assumption."

"But why?" June scrunched her brow. "To incite hatred and fear of witches? That makes no sense. All the human residents think it's just some weird meteorological phenomenon, and none of the Others seem to have taken against witches en masse. Besides, he's one of you."

"Marin was cast out of the coven last spring. He was dabbling in black magic, manipulating the universe for his own ends." Baz dragged a hand through his already rumpled hair, then leaned against the iron fence surrounding Conant's statue. He angled his head as though deep in thought. "Marin was fine when he operated as a local defense attorney, but last year he was recruited by a big-name law firm. You were away and would have missed all this, but he brought in several lucrative cases and was promoted to partner within months. That and the media coverage brought him to the attention of several key figures in Boston politics, and it became evident that Marin had developed his own rather lofty political aspirations. Marin's arrogance was famous within the coven, as was his ambitious nature. His flawless and speedy rise to glory raised suspicions.

"Artemis was the one to home in on the fact that Marin was using black magic to tamper with evidence and influence judiciary decisions—all in the service of attracting personal wealth and power," Baz continued. "Long story short, Marin was given the choice to change his wicked ways or hit the road *or*...we'd crush his dreams."

"Let me guess, he hit the road."

"No. He dug in. We conferred with Artemis, and the decision to use a spell to banish Marin from Salem was unanimous. Artemis also sent word to magical Keepers in other major cities to be on the lookout for a rogue warlock. We don't know where he went, but I'm quite certain he's back and behind this darkness."

"There's an argument that banishing spells are black magic." June raised a brow. "Wasn't that hypocritical? Not to mention dangerous?"

Baz grinned. "I was careful and quite deliberate with my choice of words."

"You cast the spell? Not Esmeralda? I would think as the high priestess—"

"Ez hasn't been faring well for the past year or so." Baz looked away, but not before betraying a somber expression. "She's not as strong as she used to be."

"So you've been helping out."

"That's what we do for one another around here, Bug."

Again, June felt a wave of shame. Whether she'd wanted the position or not, she had it now. She was the Keeper of the Witches. She had responsibilities. She should have addressed her new role head-on instead of pussyfooting around. "So what happened?" she asked, eager to focus on the crisis instead of her personal issues. "If *you* cast the banishing spell, it had to be powerful. How could Marin get back in?"

"I'm not sure. Some sort of counter spell. Maybe a loophole. Looks like he had help within city limits and the Other community."

"Gantry."

"For one. There could be more."

"If there was a counter spell to banishment," June said reasonably, "there must be a counter spell to this unholy darkness."

"A powerful talisman would help. Something connected to Marin or to the root of his—"

An explosion rent the air. June gasped and turned in

the direction of the ear-splitting boom. Her pulse tripped as the night sky glowed. "Sunrise!"

"Fire."

Baz grasped her hand, and together they raced toward the sound of sirens and chaos.

Chapter 4

The Episcopalian church that stood a mere block from Twists & Tales was ablaze. June looked on in horror as the sacred building burned.

Firemen were already on-site fighting the mounting inferno. Curious onlookers had gathered in spite of the late hour. Searing heat and uniformed cops kept them at bay. Baz had a firm grip on June's arm. Not that she felt compelled to rush into the burning building, but she *was* curious.

"Curiosity killed the cat," he said, as if reading her mind.

June grinned. "Lucky guess." Yes, they'd communicated telepathically in the past, but only when she'd been in the form of a cat.

Just then someone burst out of the inferno, laughing maniacally and waving what looked like a fuel can. "The Devil came to me and bid me serve him!"

June gawked. She knew that saying and she knew that man—but what the hell was he doing running free? "Gantry!"

Baz readied for action just as two cops rushed the

crazed shapeshifter, who hadn't even bothered to change form as a means of disguise.

Out of nowhere, lightning struck.

A crackling, blinding bolt that scored a direct hit to Leo Gantry.

The electrical charge knocked him off his feet and sent him flying. He landed flat, flesh smoking.

The onlookers reacted in various ways—some screaming, some gasping—then fell into stunned silence.

All but one, a dazed woman who mumbled, "Struck down by the hand of God."

June shook her head. "I sense malevolence," she whispered to Baz. "Magic."

"Marin." Baz scanned intently the faces in the growing crowd.

So many people, all of them bundled in layers of outerwear including sock caps, ski masks and scarves. Hard to tell one person from the next. Human from Other.

"I'll sniff him out," June said.

"Don't…"

But she'd already dropped her mitten and stooped to retrieve it, then disappeared into a sea of boots as she shifted into cat form. As a feline with a heightened sixth sense, she could better detect negative energy. Marin was both wicked and powerful. That kind of energy would be unmistakable.

Sleek and swift, June serpentined through the growing crowd, brushing ankles, reading vibes. Mostly human, some Other. A vampire, a werewolf, a witch. Plenty of negative energy. Too much for the holiday season, but everyone was anxious because of the oppressive darkness. And now this horrible fire. But there was something… Something powerful, evil, just over…*there!*

Shift back, Bug.

Baz's voice boomed in her head as loudly as if he'd spoken directly in her ear. Years apart hadn't diminished the strength of their telepathic bond.

I know you can hear me.

I feel him. June homed in on the energy with her psychic radar, her four paws sliding over ice as she zipped toward the source. *He's a she!*

What?

The source. It's...

No. It couldn't be!

June skidded to a stop two feet from the source of the evil energy, shocked and disbelieving.

It's what? Who? Dammit, Bug. Where are you?

Old Cemetery, she managed—just before her cousin Sam, Keeper of the Vampires, zapped her with a surge of electricity, knocking her back a dozen feet and straight into a gravestone.

June might have yowled. She couldn't remember. Dark became darker as her lids drifted shut, her last memories the sound of chaos and the smell of singed fur.

With a wink and a chant, Baz teleported to the Old Cemetery of St. Peters. He spied June immediately—a small black cat sprawled unmoving against a stark slate tombstone.

Her cousin Samantha Mycroft lay close by, crumpled and unresponsive.

Daniel Riverton, a powerful vampire newly engaged to Sam, swooped in on the heels of Baz. "What the—"

"I don't know."

"Let's get them back to Mycroft House," Daniel said.

Baz didn't argue. He felt dazed and sickened as he gently scooped June's limp body into his arms. He smoothed his hand over her sleek fur, speaking his thoughts aloud. "Wake up, baby. Shift back." She didn't respond, but thank the universe, she was breathing. By the time he turned, Daniel had already flown off with Sam. Baz rarely teleported, honoring certain magical skills by regulating them to dire or special circumstances.

For the second time in less than a minute, he didn't think twice.

If it had been any other Christmas, everyone would have been in their own homes at 4:15 a.m., fast asleep. But there was nothing normal about this Christmas. Mycroft House was buzzing with activity. Sam and June's Keeper cousins, Roe and Katie Sue, were present. As were their partners, Vaughn and Jett. Pooling their knowledge, they suspected magic had played a role in Gantry's escape, enabling the slippery shifter to instigate the church fire and additional chaos. They'd arrived at the scene just in time to see Gantry zapped for his efforts. After splitting off but finding themselves unable to pinpoint additional clues, they'd returned to Mycroft House to find Samantha, who'd been placed on the sofa and covered with a quilt, just coming around.

June was still out.

Baz stared down at the beautiful cat curled in his lap—his familiar, his Keeper, the great love of his life. He racked his mind for a spell or a blessing to expedite her return to consciousness and transformation back into a woman. Aside from a patch of singed fur, he didn't see any external injuries, but he couldn't be sure until she was in human form. Not only that, the longer she remained a cat, the more difficult the reverse transition.

Katie Sue squeezed his shoulder. "This is the third time June's shifted in less than twenty-four hours. She's exhausted. Let her rest."

"She'll rally," Roe added.

Sam roused with a groan and, with the help of Daniel, rose into a sitting position. "What happened?" she asked in a croaky voice.

"That's what I'd like to know," Baz snapped.

Daniel shot him a glance, warning him to chill. "Regardless of what June reported, Sam's not to blame." The vampire wrapped the quilt around her shoulders and pulled her close. "She wouldn't harm family. She wouldn't harm *anyone*."

Noting Samantha's dazed expression, Baz tempered his frustration. "I know. Trust me. My mind's not traveling that road. This is the work of a rogue warlock, who somehow managed to possess her or control her or—"

"As long as you're aware—"

"I'm aware."

"Well, I'm not." Samantha pressed a palm to her forehead and eyed everyone in the room, including her feline cousin. "I'd appreciate it if someone would clue me in."

Baz felt June stir, felt the increasing weight of her in his lap as she shifted before everyone's eyes. His heart hammered as her sweet body, her human body, appeared unscathed except for a charred patch on her coat. One mitten on, one off, she smoothed her hands up his chest, wrapping her arms around him and snuggling her face into his neck. Her contented purr was all female.

The looks on the others' faces ranged from bemused to surprised. Not because a cat had transformed into a woman—they'd all seen June shift before. But because they were all aware of the stormy history between Baz and June. Just now she was snuggling against Baz like a lover. Not that he minded, but they had an audience, plus she wasn't fully cognizant.

Someone cleared their throat.

Baz smoothed June's hair from her face and gave her a squeeze. "Rise and shine, Keeper."

Her lashes fluttered, and suddenly she was smiling up at him, another one of those dreamy smiles that spiked his pulse. "Hi," she said.

He smiled back. "Hell of a catnap. You took a year off my life, June Bug."

"Is someone going to fill me in?" Samantha asked, sounding agitated now.

"You're shivering," said Daniel.

"I'll kick up the heat," Vaughn said.

"I'll heat up some wassail," Katie Sue said. "Enough for everyone."

Roe was on her heels. "I'll help."

The varied voices seemed to jar June's senses. Wide-eyed, she pushed away from Baz's chest, then sprang from his lap, backing into Jett.

She apologized quickly, then focused on Samantha, cocking her head and narrowing her eyes. "Are you... *you?*"

Sam looked at her curiously. "Of course I'm me. What the—"

"I know why you haven't been able to locate Marin," June said to Baz. "He's body hopping."

Chapter 5

Warmed wassail helped to take off the chill June had feared she would never shake. Although nuked Red Bull would have been better. She couldn't remember the last time she'd felt this drained. Between lack of sleep, drawing on borrowed power three times today and getting zapped by magic, physically she was spent.

Her mind, however, was wired.

The challenge was to focus. On the crisis, not Baz. They'd bonded telepathically, and even afterward, in her unconscious state, she'd felt his presence, heard his voice, sensed his concern.

For her.

Focus.

"Just so I have everything straight," June said, tearing her gaze from Baz's, "as a suspected minion to the monster responsible for this darkness, Leo Gantry was transported by the council to an Otherworld holding cell, pending a formal investigation."

"At the request of the council, I cast a spell that should have prevented Gantry from shifting and escaping. Obviously," Baz said, "Marin intervened."

"As Keepers," Roe said, "we were notified of Gantry's absence the moment it was detected."

"Why wasn't *I* notified?" June asked. She was a Keeper, albeit a reluctant one. Yet again, she felt like an outsider. Out of touch. Uninformed.

"I called you myself," Sam said, "but you didn't answer."

Frowning, June pulled her cell phone from her pocket. Dead. "I thought I charged my phone," she said more to herself than anyone.

"Happens to all of us," Vaughn said.

June didn't believe him. Every person sitting in this parlor had a keen responsibility to their charges and fellow Others. They wouldn't forget something as important and routine as juicing their phone. She glanced at Baz and instantly knew she was right. The censure was gentle, but there.

"Whatever," Katie Sue said, glossing over the missed communication. "Less than ten minutes elapsed between Gantry's escape and the attack on the church."

"And you got there anyway," Jett said.

June rubbed an ache in her chest. How could everyone be so nice to her when she'd screwed up so badly? Her gaze floated to Sam's evergreen tree, so beautifully decorated. The menorah on the mantel, the nativity scene near the archway, the Yule log burning in the fireplace. Samantha Mycroft embraced and celebrated any and all faiths, whereas right now June herself had little to no faith in anything.

She'd never felt so bleak.

"Obviously Marin bewitched Gantry into setting the church on fire," Sam said. Always calm, always stoic Sam.

June nodded. "He seemed, for lack of a more imaginative term, possessed. I'm betting his actions and words were not his own."

"'The Devil came to me and bid me serve him,'" Baz recited.

"The exact phrase used in 1641 by one of Salem's accused citizens that sparked the witch hunts," Jett said. He met everyone's questioning expressions with confidence. "I may be a selkie and committed to the sea, but I know my history, and I love Salem and I'll do what I can to protect the innocent."

Katie Sue leaned into her longtime lover. "Is it any wonder I adore this man?"

The ache in June's chest intensified as she observed the genuine affection burning between Katie Sue and Jett, Sam and Daniel and Roe and Vaughn. All three couples had pledged their love on Christmas Eve. All three were engaged, even though "mixed marriages" between Keepers and Others were generally frowned upon.

Once upon a time, June had envisioned herself in just such a mixed marriage with Baz as her husband.

Then again, they'd been under a spell.

Then that spell had been lifted, and she'd spent the past eight years resenting that deception as well as Baz's betrayal. She'd rationalized their bewitched affair by deciding she'd confused lust for love. So why was she wondering what it would be like waking up in his arms every morning? Why was she aching for his kiss? Why in the universe was her heart twisting with romantic yearnings?

She chanced his charismatic gaze and nearly melted from the intensity of his regard. His *passionate* regard.

June squeezed her thighs together, suppressing the sensual tingle. But she knew all too well that scratching the itch would only complicate her new position as

Keeper. It wasn't as if she stood a snowball's chance of finding the same eternal bliss as her cousins.

Men like Baz didn't commit to a one and only, let alone forever.

Men like Baz, bad boys to the bone, were constantly on the prowl.

Hence him kissing the stars out of Lolita Dorring on the same day he'd gone through the breakup with June. Just thinking about it iced her heart.

"Earth to June."

She blinked at Sam. "What?"

"We were discussing the possibility of rampant paranoia."

"Anyone with an interest in local history would recognize Gantry's ravings just as we did," Roe said. "Imagine what the media could do with this."

Vaughn nodded. "Between the darkness and Gantry's rant, someone's bound to suggest that the Devil is back in Salem."

"Your rogue warlock is stoking the fire for hysteria and a twenty-first century witch hunt," Daniel said to Baz.

"Turning humans and maybe even Others against Wiccans and magicals—anyone they associate with the word 'witch.'" Baz dragged a hand over his stubbled jaw. "If we're hunted and persecuted, or even just run out of town, what do you think will happen to tourism?"

"Shouldn't you be more concerned about the welfare of your people?" Roe asked.

"Wait," Sam said, scooting to the edge of her seat. "I see where Baz is going with this. Without the witch element, tourism—and the whole economy of the town—would suffer."

"Think of the businesses that could go under," said Katie Sue. "Witch House, Nightmare Gallery, the House of the Seven Gables…"

"And that's just the tip of the iceberg," June whispered.

"Marin isn't simply determined to destroy the local coven," Baz said. "He intends to destroy Salem."

An eerie silence fell over the parlor. Even the snap and crackle of the Yule log ceased.

Sam visibly shook off a chill. "I still can't believe that monster invaded my body."

Daniel pulled her closer. "Hard to believe Marin's that powerful. Hopping from body to body to thwart detection."

"The ultimate identity theft," said Vaughn.

"He can't linger long in any one person, though," Baz said.

"Long enough to make me electrocute my own cousin," Sam snapped.

"You didn't zap me," June countered. "Marin did."

"Imagine if he snatched the body of a powerful Other," Roe said. "Like Vaughn. Imagine the damage he could inflict." She shuddered.

Vaughn squeezed her hand. "No one's snatching this body, hon."

"I'll make sure of it," Baz said, getting to his feet.

"A protection spell," June said, mind whirling. "Yes, yes. Bless them all, Baz, and be quick about it." She glanced at the clock on the mantel, then out the front window. Christmas morning. A day of birth, of miracles, yet no assurance of a rising sun. The only light came from Sam's holiday decorations, the exterior lights casting an eerie glow on the snow-covered lawn.

Heart pounding, June pushed to her feet and buttoned her coat.

"Where are you going?" Sam asked.

"Stalking in a winter wonderland."

Chapter 6

"I can't believe it!" June slammed the receiver down on the phone on her uncle's desk, feeling as if she had a lump of coal sitting in the pit of her stomach. "Not one of the local newspapers agreed to pull the story on Gantry. So what if they already went to press? Pull the plug. Call back the delivery trucks!"

"Even that wouldn't help," Baz said. "This story broke the moment bystanders whipped out their smartphones and connected to their social networks." He gestured to the plasma-screen television, one of Artemis's last purchases. "Look. It's on the morning news."

Blood boiling, June grabbed the remote and turned up the sound.

"The Devil came to me and bid me serve him!"

She cringed when the lightning bolt struck. She wasn't exactly sad that Leo Gantry had gotten smoked, but she wasn't happy that the death blow was being televised. "What is *wrong* with people? Children could be watching!"

Baz shushed her, his attention on the reporter.

June crossed her arms and stewed. She'd bolted out

of Mycroft House intending to take the monster by the horns. Her plan had been simple. Shift into cat form and prowl the whole of Salem until she locked on Marin's evil energy. She could do it. Now that she knew the warlock's psychic scent, she could track him. She was sure of it. But Baz had caught up to her on Sam's lawn, bringing her to a halt right next to that annoyingly cheerful, motion-activated, singing Santa. June had been forced to listen to Bing Crosby singing "You're All I Want for Christmas" while Baz lectured her on the danger of shifting yet again given her compromised state. She couldn't argue with his calm logic. She was exhausted and stressed and had yet to recover fully from the last transformation. She wasn't sure how she'd survived Marin's lightning bolt, except it must have been much weaker than the one he'd used on Gantry. She might not be so lucky at their next meeting.

Hence plan B. Minimizing the negative effect of the church fire and Gantry's damning quote. Unfortunately, that idea had tanked, too. The television reporter was spinning the story just as June and Baz had feared, highlighting the old fears regarding witchcraft, possession and the Devil's magic. She tied it all in with the darkness that had been enveloping Salem for the past few weeks, citing rising crime statistics and an increasing lack of goodwill toward men.

June cringed when the woman recycled ancient propaganda, speaking as though witchcraft and black magic were one and the same. Um, *no.* Apples and oranges! Spiritualism and Satanism!

"So much for fact-checking and journalistic integrity." Fuming, she thumbed the remote and silenced the sensationalistic reporter.

"Witches and Wiccans have spent centuries trying to correct that error," Baz said as he turned away from the blank screen. "Marin's not only obliterating the joyful spirit of Christmas, he's inciting social and religious intolerance."

Deep inside, June believed a good, long, *normal* dose of daylight would chase away the wicked shadows and negativity. They just had to figure out how to make that happen. But despite all those years of studying mysticism and the occult, she couldn't think of *one* similar previous case. Surely Marin couldn't be that original. Surely a similar curse had been documented *somewhere*.

June stood up so fast that her desk chair tumbled backward. "There *has* to be a counter spell to this insidious darkness," she said, while dashing for the stairs heading down to Twists & Tales. "Something in the *Universal Coven's Potion Encyclopedia* or the *Book of Spells*. Something I missed. Something we're both unaware of."

She sailed down the narrow stairwell, missing the last step completely and nearly taking a header. Heart in her throat, she caught her balance and flicked on the main light switch, bathing the bookshop in a bright golden glow, illuminating every shelf, every book.

"If the answer isn't in one of these two volumes—" she went on while opening the UCPE "—then perhaps it's mentioned in one of the other books in the shop."

June felt, rather than heard, Baz come up behind her. His charismatic aura shimmered and pulsed. She'd never been so aware of another person in her life. He moved closer and placed his hands on her shoulders—a comforting gesture offering strength and support. It would be so easy to turn into his arms. Easy and dangerous. Oh, how she wanted to tune out the curse and to tune in to Baz—his touch, his scent, his taste.

"Wanting to shift in order to search for Marin was a

noble intention, Bug. Calling every newspaper in town in hopes of squashing a toxic story was inspired."

"Except it didn't work."

"It will take you hours to scour every pertinent text in this room. You're exhausted. Let me help." He squeezed her shoulders, then stepped away and broke into a chant.

June whirled, always fascinated when Baz worked magic. In his jeans and flannel shirt, he looked more like a lumberjack than a wizard. Far more rugged and handsome than any Merlin ever portrayed on film. Her heart skipped as she noted the grace of his fingers as he beckoned book after book off the shelves. She deciphered his poetic chant—a revelation spell—in which he asked for specifics pertaining to the spell that had caused the darkness. At least fifty books now floated in midair, pages turning as though fanned by an invisible hand. He made it look so easy, yet she knew the extent of the focus required in raising power, releasing and directing energy, binding the spell. Within all those steps were more steps. He was undoubtedly in the throes of an adrenaline rush. June was in a state of wonder and admiration. Her heart warmed when he asked, as all Wiccans and noble magicals did, that the spell harm no one, ending with, "As I so will, so shall it be."

Her breath caught with the last flutter of pages. She looked from the books to Baz, her stomach sinking when he shook his head. Another dead end. Whatever hope she'd harbored died as each book magically returned to its rightful place. "I don't believe it."

"We'll figure it out, June. Have faith."

"In *what?* In you?" The man who'd broken her heart? "In magic? In miracles?" Where was the metaphysical protection when her parents met their tragic end? Or, for that matter, poor Artemis? "In *myself?*" Someone who'd managed to alienate herself from her own coven. "Do you know how hard I've studied, Baz? How much knowledge is crammed into my brain? I swore I'd never again be deceived by witchcraft, and now this. My first challenge and it threatens the entire town." Temples throbbing, she rubbed her hands over her eyes. "How can I not know the answer? Or at least have a clue as to how to defend my charges?"

He stepped forward and traced his finger over her furrowed brow. "What if the answer's not here, but here?" He indicated her heart. A heart that had slowed to a dull thud.

"I feel numb, Baz. Dead. Hopeless." She felt like the most ineffectual Keeper in the world, a disappointment to Others everywhere, as well as her family. She needed to feel something. Anything.

Instant gratification stood in front of her in all his big, bad glory.

June reached up and grabbed two fistfuls of Baz's thick hair. She pulled him down and nipped his lower lip. "Make me feel, Baz. Make me want to fight for tomorrow."

The heat in his gaze seared her senses. "You'll hate me after. You'll hate yourself."

"Maybe. Maybe not."

"Good enough."

He claimed her mouth, and she swore the earth moved and angels sang. His kiss was everything she remembered and more. Her brain grew fuzzy, as if drugged by his lips, his tongue. His hands moved over her, awakening every molecule in her exhausted body. Charged with lust, she tugged up his shirt, her palms smoothing over his ripped abs and strong back.

Their kiss became frenzied, and before she knew it he

had swooped her into his arms. "No magic," she whispered as he carried her up the stairs to her apartment.

"Not of the witch kind," he said as he laid her on the king-size bed. "Can't promise otherwise, Bug."

Chapter 7

Making love to June in the midst of a crisis was reckless and harked back to Baz's old ways. A selfish choice, yet he couldn't resist her. Them. He'd poured his heart and soul into making her feel alive. Making her feel *him* and his love. Incredible, but his feelings had never died. He'd simply pounded them into dormancy, but now her kiss—that one kiss—had reawakened his love with a vengeance.

Stripping her naked had peeled away the years, and the raw passion that had once burned between them burned again. He'd relished the feel of her bare skin, her taste, her scent. Her incredible flexibility. The way she'd mewed when he coaxed her higher and higher, savoring, pleasuring. They'd peaked together, and he swore stars exploded in his mind's eye.

Now she slept in his arms. She felt good and right curled up against him, even though so much was wrong between them.

It still rankled that she'd had so little faith in him all those years ago. Yes, he'd screwed up. But he'd explained. He'd apologized.

And she'd walked away.

He'd despised her for that. But he'd also looked inward. At who he was and who he wanted to be. He didn't want to run like June. He didn't want to forsake his heritage. He wanted to thrive in Salem and among all witches, Wiccan and magical. He wanted to follow in Esmeralda's footsteps. Regardless of June's opinion, his grandmother was a good and strong leader. She'd only ever had the coven's best interest at heart—and that included Baz and June.

Baz glanced at the illuminated digital clock on Artemis's, no, *June's* nightstand.

Seven in the morning. Official time for a normal winter sunrise. He looked to the window, anticipating dawn simply from force of habit, but all he saw was black. Stark darkness. Not even a twinkling of stars.

That didn't mean he'd lost hope. But he worried that his faith and optimism wouldn't prove strong enough to save the day, his fellow witches and Salem. The greatest power for change resided in the skeptics. That much he knew. The Scrooges. The people who'd lost all faith.

Like June.

If only she believed…

She stirred in his arms, and he cursed the ache in his chest. He didn't want to love Juniper Twist. He was the next high priest of the local magical coven. She was already that coven's Keeper. Her inability to trust witches, to trust *him,* was a thorn in his side and a kink in the natural way of things.

"You're staring at me."

His lip twitched. "How can you tell? Your eyes are closed."

"I sense you." She looked up at him then, her gaze still sweetly dazed. "Yup. Staring."

"You're beautiful."

"You say that to all the girls."

"Wrong. And you're not just any girl, Bug. You never were."

She tensed. "Then why did you kiss Lolita?"

There it was. The bonehead block between them. He'd explained before, but by damn, he would explain again. Only this time he wouldn't give up until he made June understand. He'd been too emotional the first time around. Now he was calm. Rational.

"It *would* be nice," he said, clinging to patience, "if we cleared the air once and for all."

"Yes, it would."

"My story hasn't changed."

"Great."

"But *I* have."

That caught her attention. Sheet clutched to her beautiful breasts, she shimmied back and nodded. "I'm listening."

"Are you?"

"As it happens, I'm questioning everything tonight. Today." She glanced at the clock, then out the window, sighing at the unnatural darkness. "Even my judgment. Talk to me, Baz."

Remembering how this conversation had gone in the past, he braced for disappointment. If she still thought the worst of him, so be it. *This* time he wouldn't take her lack of faith to heart. He wouldn't let it affect his self-esteem.

"I was as surprised as you to learn that my grandmother had invoked my soul mate. And just as angry." As if any man would want his grandmother meddling in his love life. "But what bothered me most was your assumption that nothing of what we'd felt for each other was real. Let me finish," he said when she started to speak. "Even after Esmeralda admitted her deed, my feelings for you remained the same. But your insistence that I was somehow defending her, that I was clinging to the idea of our *supposed* true love out of pride… Your skepticism wore at my confidence. You made me doubt myself. *Us.* Lolita had been coming on to me for weeks. I admit I found her physically attractive. As crazy as it sounds, I thought if I kissed her, I'd know if what I felt for you was real or imagined. If I wasn't in love with you, I'd be turned on enough to want more than a kiss. As it happened, the kiss fell flat and all I felt was remorse."

"That's not what I sensed when I walked in on you two."

"Are you sure you were tuned in to me?" he asked. "Lolita's a witch, too. Isn't it possible that you keyed in on her more fervent energy?"

June blinked up at him, and he sensed something he'd never sensed before on this subject. Doubt. Confusion. A window of opportunity.

He stroked her hair off her sweet face, fearing her, wanting her. "Kissing Lolita was rash and reckless. Definitely insensitive. I apologize for that. To be honest, I think part of me was lashing out at you for bailing on us so easily. You wouldn't even consider the possibility that what burned between us was genuine and not caused by that incantation. How could you have so little faith?"

She licked her lips, swallowed hard. "I just…I guess I never understood what you saw in me. I was geeky. You were cool. I was plain. You were…" Her appreciative gaze flicked over his face, his body. "Well, *you.* You could have had any girl in town—human or Other. Actually, you *did* have a lot of girls."

"Not while I was with you."

"I know. Still… When I learned about the spell, I felt

deceived. Foolish. Then when I saw you kissing Lolita I felt betrayed and even more foolish. I didn't want to deal, didn't know *how* to deal."

"So you ran away."

She met his eyes. "You could have come after me."

"I *should* have come after you. But I was hurt and young and ruled by pride."

"We were both young."

A clean slate was all he asked. "Are we good here, Juniper?"

Her luscious mouth quirked. "You called me by my given name. I guess you mean business."

"I mean to put the past to rest."

She stared up at him for a long moment. "Done."

He narrowed his eyes. "Just like that?"

"It's been eight years. Not exactly *just like that*." She smiled a little, placed her palm to his chest. "I'm good with you, Baz. Honest. But I'm still miffed about that spell. I can't help it. It tainted everything."

"What if it only pushed us together sooner than the natural march of time? What if we were meant to be together regardless? It was intended to *find* my soul mate, not create her out of nowhere."

"Soul mates?" She wrinkled her nose. "You really believe there's such a thing?"

"I believe in a lot of things."

She rolled onto her back, stared up at the ceiling.

He could see her brain churning, although he didn't know if that was good or bad.

"Do you believe in Santa Claus?" she asked.

"I believe in the idea of St. Nick. I believe in the magic of Christmas."

"Why?"

He searched his soul and answered honestly, "Just because."

"Blind faith."

"I suppose." He rolled onto his side, pushed himself up on one elbow and studied one of the most cynical women he knew. "What are you getting at?"

"That's powerful stuff, faith. Belief. Hope. This darkness has been eating away at those elements, snuffing out the magic of the winter solstice, Hanukkah, Kwanzaa and Christmas. And now, because of that fire and Gantry's evil insinuation, people will gossip and maybe even plot against Wiccans and magicals. They *should* be celebrating the spirit of giving, peace on earth, goodwill toward men." Her gaze flicked to his. "You own a construction business, right?"

"We specialize in renovations." He wondered at her train of thought. WizBang Renovations transformed houses and businesses and, for a price, Baz would charm a room. Locals of a certain mind-set appreciated metaphysical boons. Hence his company's motto: We work magic.

June shot out of bed—naked and beautiful and suddenly jazzed. "Get up. Get dressed. Hurry!"

"Where are we going?"

"To inspire goodwill."

Chapter 8

June rattled off her plan as she and Baz dressed. She felt a little guilty stealing peeks as he pulled on his clothes. Deriving so much pleasure from ogling the man's hunky body was pretty shallow considering the crisis, but, holy smokes, he was even more ripped than the last time they'd been together. Probably had to do with all the physical labor connected with WizBang Renovations. The thought of him hauling lumber and swinging a hammer was pretty darn sexy.

Don't think about the sex.

But even as he pointed out the many holes in her idea, her mind drifted to the way he'd made her body sing. He had always been a masterful lover, but over the years he'd honed his skills even more. She didn't want to think about how or with whom. Of course, he hadn't been celibate for eight years. Neither had she. Yet somehow, at this moment, none of that mattered. Maybe it had to do with the intensity of his focus. Baz made her feel as though she were the center of his universe.

Although she wouldn't feel full closure until she'd spoken with Esmeralda. And then…

Then she had no clue where things would go with Baz. If anywhere.

"You're zoning out on me, June Bug."

"What?" She stumbled on the steps as they made their way down to the bookshop.

He caught her arm, steadying her, although his touch unbalanced her in other ways.

Don't think about the sex.

"I'm sorry. You were saying?"

"What's the last thing you heard?"

"Something about insurance and building permits, and how it's Christmas Day and the city and county offices are closed."

"Aside from legalities and safety issues, you're asking me to call in my men and ask them to work—on Christmas. Wiccans and magicals may not celebrate the religious aspect of the holiday—"

"—but we do spend the day indulging in festive traditions with friends and family. Preaching to the choir, Baz." She hurried to the coat tree and nabbed her velvet coat. "The point is, this is unlike any Christmas we've ever seen. There's nothing normal about the darkness or the rising hostility. We need to obliterate the negativity and sense of doom inspired by Marin's curse. We're going to make it through this day, sun or no sun, without attacking one another. We're going to inspire goodwill and the spirit of giving by rebuilding St. Peter's!"

"I admire your conviction and goal," Baz said while helping her into her coat, "but trust me when I say what you're suggesting is impossible to achieve in a month, let alone a day. St. Peter's was badly damaged. The building needs to be inspected by a structural engineer. Chances are he'll advise tearing it down to the foundation. There are cleanup issues. Safety issues. Codes to be met. Insurance claims to be made."

It wasn't what June wanted to hear, but she trusted in Baz's expertise. "What about a temporary structure? An immediate place on grounds where the congregation can meet. Did you hear that newscaster say there was supposed to be a Christmas Day service this afternoon? If we could provide them with a place to worship tonight and until the church is rebuilt…"

"Build a temporary church." He raised a skeptical brow while shrugging into his bomber jacket. "In one day."

"Think of it like an old-fashioned barn raising. The whole community joined in and by the end of the day—" she spread her hands wide "—ta-da!"

"A whole community as opposed to one construction crew."

"Don't worry. You get your people and square the permit thing somehow with whomever, and I'll get the community. Specifically the witch community. That's the beauty of my plan," she said while whisking out the door. "Even though we're the ones Gantry set up for persecution, we'll be the ones to inspire goodwill."

"We set the example and humans will join in?"

"Exactly."

"Except they won't know they're following the lead of the persecuted. Most witches live in anonymity."

"That's not the point. Marin will know. He'll see we're not lashing out or running away. We're initiating good. The point is to make the gesture. A gesture of peace and goodwill toward men—no matter their faith—supporting, celebrating and saving the true spirit of Christmas, yes?"

He smiled at that, driving away the chill settling in June's bones as they walked to their cars.

"No offense," he said, "but as Esmeralda's grandson and the future high priest, it would go faster if I reached out to our coven."

"Except it needs to be me." Reaching out, connecting as their Keeper. It was something she should have done the minute she got back to town. She thumbed her key fob, unlocking the doors to the SUV left to her by her uncle. Pulse racing in anticipation of this challenge, she spun around and knocked into Baz. "Sorry. I almost forgot. I could really use a few baskets filled with oranges, wassail and candles. Would you mind conjuring something up for me? I wouldn't ask, but I shouldn't visit empty-handed on the holiday, and like you said, everything will be closed."

Baz grunted but stepped back and focused, stocking her backseat with baskets full of cheer. "I hope you don't expect me or any of the other witches working on this *temporary* church to invoke magic in order to get the job done by midnight."

She gave a sheepish shrug. "Nothing obvious anyway."

"Building a safe and viable place of worship in *one* day—especially on Christmas—is already going to attract a lot of attention, Bug."

"I'm counting on it."

"Humans will be present. It's against the rules to practice obvious magic in front of them. You know that."

"You don't play by the rules. Remember?"

Baz nabbed her by her scarf and reeled her in against him. "Never realized there was a bad girl lurking inside the good girl."

Her heart thudded as he dropped his forehead to hers. "Not a bad girl," she said. "A Keeper."

"Your father and Artemis would be proud."

A wave of emotion washed through her. More likely

they would be worried. What if she hesitated or panicked? What if she failed? What if the humans rooted out and turned against the witches in spite of her plan? What if Christmas was forever tainted? What if they still couldn't find a way to defeat the darkness and the sun never returned?

"Sometimes you think too much." Baz brushed a kiss over her mouth, then conjured a sprig from the air and pinned it to her lapel.

"Mistletoe?" She raised a brow. "You're inviting anyone I greet to kiss me?"

"I'm not *that* giving," he said. "Think on your studies. The Druids."

Her mind riffled through years of collected information. "The Druid priests distributed sprigs of mistletoe as a form of protection from thunder and lightning and other forms of evil." She glanced at the sprig on her lapel. "Nice thought, Baz, but they traditionally hung the mistletoe over doorways."

"Putting a spin on tradition." Baz indicated the burn mark on her coat. "Marin already struck you once."

"I was caught off guard. I know his scent now. His aura and vibrations." She fingered the small talisman of protection. Her heart swelled as she looked up at the man she was falling in love with all over again. Standing on her tiptoes, she gave him a tender kiss before parting ways. "Don't worry about me, Baz."

"Too late, Bug."

Chapter 9

By the time June reached Esmeralda Collins's house, her stomach was a knotted mess. Only a few hours into Christmas Day and the paranoia had already commenced. Driving through town, she had noted random altercations and acts of desperation, a noticeable increase from the day before. Pedestrians having words. Drivers exhibiting road rage. To her surprise several shops had opened for business. Some advertising talismans to "ward off the Devil's magic." Some hawking "solar simulators" to create artificial sunlight. To her shock and dismay, she'd even spied a few people picketing Salem's most popular attractions and protesting the local witch element—past and present. She'd anticipated intolerance to flare, but seeing it in action sickened her to the core.

And this was only the beginning.

Unless she was able to accomplish the seemingly impossible and turn the tables on Marin.

She turned off the engine, dropped her forehead to the steering wheel and took a calming breath.

Before she could reach out to her charges and then beyond to the Wiccan community, June needed to make amends with the high priestess of the magicals, Baz's grandmother, Esmeralda Collins. The woman she'd cursed to the moon and back for making her believe in a false love. She'd also accused Esmeralda of having political motives for promoting a union between a Collins and a Twist. Flashing back on her emotional outburst, June cringed. She might have been a tad overdramatic. She definitely hadn't allowed Esmeralda to get a word in edgewise.

The passenger door opened suddenly, jerking June out of her reverie. She gave a startled gasp, anticipating a hostile force. But instead of a malevolent warlock, an old woman wearing a festive hooded cloak and smelling strongly of healing and purification herbs, climbed inside.

For crying out… "Esmeralda."

"Put this monstrosity in gear and hit the gas, Juniper," Esmeralda croaked. "We've got people to see."

"But you're sick."

"I'll live. For a while longer anyway."

"Don't talk like that."

"I'm surprised you care."

"Of course I care." The woman was Baz's grandmother. She'd been a good friend of June's grandfather and, although they'd knocked heads from time to time, she'd worked closely with June's dad and uncle. Even June had felt affection for the high priestess…until she'd learned of the spell. "Did Baz tell you I was coming over?"

"He didn't have to. We're under attack. Naturally we'll want to fight back. You're our Keeper. It's your job to keep the peace between us and humans. That said, yes, my grandson called me."

Knowing his intentions were good, it was hard to be

mad. Still, did it mean he thought June was incapable of mending bridges and enlisting help on her own?

Esmeralda's gaze was strong and steady even though her body was obviously hurting. "Your plan is inspired, Juniper."

The compliment made her uncomfortable. "I was influenced by something Baz said." She turned on the engine and kicked up the heat, hoping to keep the chill out of Esmeralda's old bones. "When he first told me that you two suspected Marin, he mentioned the danger of retaliating with hostile measures. He said if we acted in anger or desperation, we'd be playing into Marin's hands and strengthening the spell."

"You know the old saying. Negativity breeds negativity."

"I'm hoping an overwhelming dose of good might act as a counter spell of sorts, buying us time to find a real solution."

"It can't hurt."

"Speaking of goodwill…" June squirmed in her seat. "I'd like to clear the air about our past quarrel."

"I don't recall us quarreling, Juniper. I recall you shouting at me and refusing to allow me to explain my actions. You were practically hysterical."

"Yes, well—"

"Would you like me to explain now?"

June nodded. She sincerely needed to make peace with this woman, and with herself. She'd been harboring resentment for eight years. Talk about a boatload of negativity…

"As you know, my grandson used to be quite the rebel. He got into more trouble than I'm sure you're aware of. Your father and Artemis were good about helping to defuse certain situations. At any rate, I worried Baz's short temper and impetuous nature would land him in hot water with human law officials or the Other council sooner rather than later. Either could taint his future as the high priest of the coven. He needed a distraction, a gentle influence. He needed to settle down. I knew his soul mate was out there. I simply invited the gods and goddesses into my circle and asked for their help. I never mentioned your name, Juniper."

June blinked. "But Talia Jamison told me she overheard you talking to her mother about how you cast a love spell on me and Baz."

"I did indeed have a conversation with Talia's mother. Basha's one of my dearest friends, but Talia either misunderstood or embellished the story. That girl's always been one for stirring things up. You should know that."

June *did* know. But at the time Talia had been so convincing, so sure of herself, whereas June had been waiting for the next bad thing to happen in her life. Talia had delivered the anticipated catastrophe.

"When Baz took a sudden shine to you," Esmeralda went on, "I assumed you were the one. I was surprised, but pleased. You were such a sweet girl, and you had an immediate positive effect on my grandson. But then you fell prey to gossip and believed the worst. Of me. Of Basel. Your lack of faith in us and in yourself was unsettling. Either you weren't Basel's soul mate or the timing was off. You were only eighteen at the time. As you railed at me, I realized how *very* young you were. Insecure and emotionally fragile. I attributed it to losing your parents not two years before and then bouncing between the homes of various relatives. Although I know for a fact the constant shifting around was unnecessary."

"I didn't want to be a burden on any one family for too long," June blurted. She'd had a horrible time adjusting to the loss of her parents. And although all of her cousins' families had been more than happy to take her in, she had felt out of place in every home. Looking back, she supposed it didn't help that she'd also been dealing with normal moody teenage issues. Baz had coaxed her out of her longtime funk, a funk she'd tried very hard to keep to herself. Their six-month relationship had been fast and torrid. It had always felt too good to be true. So it made sense, she supposed, that she'd so easily embraced the notion that their love was a bewitched farce.

"No one thought you a burden," Esmeralda said. "But I understand why you might have felt that way. Your sensitivity will serve you well as a Keeper. Insecurity, however, will not."

June swallowed, absorbing Esmeralda's thoughts and her apparent confidence in June's abilities.

"You've been away a long time, child. You've traveled abroad, immersed yourself in your studies. You came back when you were needed and, although it took you overly long, you're ready to assume your position. You have my backing." She arched a silver brow. "If you want it."

"I want it." Something shifted inside June. She couldn't name it exactly, but it was close to a feeling of invincibility. "I can beat Marin, Esmeralda. That is, *we* can beat him. I refuse to believe he's capable of successfully manipulating a witch hunt and damning Salem to eternal darkness. He can't be that powerful. We can't be that weak. Working together, we'll beat back the negativity and intolerance."

"I've already reached out to my coven," Esmeralda said, "but we'll need additional support. Let's start with Mica Templeton. She carries a lot of weight with the Wiccan faction. She's at her store. I phoned ahead."

Mica was a close friend of Sam's. Her store, Ye Olde Tyme Shoppe, was on Essex Street, not far from Mycroft House. June steered her inherited SUV in that direction. "I'm sorry I didn't pay my respects in person sooner, Esmeralda. It was rude."

"Yes, it was. But I don't hold it against you."

"Why not?"

"Because I have faith in you. In who you were born to be."

"And that would be…"

"A wise and strong Keeper."

"How can you know that?"

"How can you *not* know that? You're a Twist. It's in your blood."

Was it? June's stomach twisted as a memory flared. She loved her dad. Worshipped her dad. She still treasured his every word. Surely his assessment of her character had had merit. For certain it had influenced her mind-set.

"Spit it out, Juniper."

"Being a Keeper may be in my blood, but I might not have the stomach for it long-term."

"Who put that stupid notion in your head?"

"My dad." She took the turn from Herbert Street to Essex too quickly, causing the SUV to slide on the slushy pavement. She compensated, but her nerves jangled all the same. Esmeralda had discovered her Achilles' heel. Her dad. Or rather, her dad's doubts in her ability to fulfill her destiny.

"What did Merle say? Exactly."

June flexed her hands on the steering wheel. She would never forget his words. Ever. "I was fifteen at the time, and volunteering at a homeless shelter during winter solstice. There were so many, of all faiths, who had so little. There was an altercation between a human and an Other and I... Well, I panicked. Dad stepped in. After he addressed the situation, he hugged me close and told me it was a good thing that the role of Keeper would never fall to me. He said I was too sweet. Too kind." Her heart ached. "How is there such a thing as too kind?"

"There isn't." Esmeralda sneezed into an old-fashioned handkerchief. "Merle was a good Keeper, but he was also a chauvinistic ass." She pointed. "There's Mica's shop. Pull over."

June did as ordered, but frowned. "Are you dissing my dad?"

"I suppose I am. *Men*. They have this ingrained primal sense of dominance. Listen to your heart, Juniper." Esmeralda cut her a meaningful glance. "In all matters."

June shut off the engine, but her mind was revved. "We're here," she said.

"Yes, we are." Esmeralda unclasped her seat belt. "Let's kick some witch butt."

Chapter 10

Baz was astounded by the overwhelming response to his holiday plea. Yes, he had faith in the good people of Salem—human and Other—but this was above and beyond his wildest expectations.

After rousing his crew and putting them on standby, he'd paid a visit to Father Chopra, who was trying to comfort his parishioners on the loss of their church. The focus of the man's ministry was on community, so he was overjoyed by Baz's proposition. The priest had no illusions about raising a church in one day, but he welcomed the opportunity to bring people together in hope. His mind-set mirrored June's. A proactive response to the crisis would spark positive energy, and even a sturdy tent would fill the bill.

Baz had assured the man they could do better.

Together they'd contacted the mayor, who, as it turned out, was desperate to promote optimism and goodwill as a way of combating the effects of the unnatural and unrelenting darkness. He, too, was worried about the fate of Salem and its people. Enough so that he convinced the police and fire departments and assorted commissions to bend their rules and aid Baz and Father Chopra in their frantic quest to provide the congregation with a place to celebrate Christmas. As a group, they decided to designate a portion of Salem Common as home for the temporary house of worship, since the park was only a few short blocks from the original church.

Two hours after parting ways with June, Baz was on site along with his crew and approximately fifty city workers who'd all agreed to volunteer their time and energy.

On Christmas Day.

Engineers, electricians, architects. Subcontractors specializing in framing, roofing, drywalling and flooring.

June had been successful in her quest, as well. More Wiccans and magicals had been rolling in by the minute, every man and woman ready to attack whatever task they were assigned. In addition, she had called her Keeper cousins. They'd alerted their charges, and now skilled laborers from the Other community were also hard at work. The greatest challenge had been in getting everyone organized, but now everything was going smoothly.

Almost too smoothly.

Baz stepped away from the quickly drawn-up diagrams he'd been studying with a local architect. The grounds had been flooded with halogen power lights illuminating the work space as well as the workers. Given Marin's ability to body hop, the warlock could be anywhere, even here. Baz didn't possess June's feline sixth sense. The enemy could be standing right next to him in the form of one of his WizBang crew and he wouldn't know it. It made him twitchy.

"Can you believe this turnout?"

He turned just as June came hurrying toward him, sidestepping lumber and mounting supplies. His heart skipped at the sight of her. "You got an amazing response, Bug."

"Thanks to Esmeralda."

"She called me on my cell after you dropped her at home. She was impressed with your charm and intelligence. Said you could talk a witch without a broom into buying a Hoover."

June rolled her eyes. "As if vacuums can fly."

"Thanks for talking her into going home instead of weathering this cold."

"My greatest challenge of the morning. She's a little on the, um, determined side."

Baz grinned. "You mean stubborn."

"Yeah. Well." She rocked back on her booted heels, her cheeks flushing as she held his gaze.

Either she was chilled from the frigid wind or she sensed his need to kiss her senseless. He'd worried about her every second she'd been out of his sight. Now that she was here, an obsessive, protective impulse flared. He wasn't sure what he would do to Marin—or to anyone, for that matter—who ever caused June harm. The realization rocked his hard-fought calm. Given his powerful magical skills, he knew he could do some serious damage.

They stood inches apart—trying to look professional, he supposed. The Keeper and the future high priest of the magicals. He stuffed his hands in his pockets. She wrapped her arms around her middle. "A television crew is on its way," he said matter-of-factly. "They're keen on reporting a positive story. Imagine that."

"Mica's organizing a day-long feast for everyone working on the church," June said with the same detached tone. "They're setting up tents and tables and bringing in portable heaters. A place for workers to rest and have something to eat."

"Samantha found me a few minutes ago," Baz said, aching to pull June into his arms. "Told me she enlisted Rabbi Solomon, Father Alistair and Rabbi Jenowitz, who each enlisted their flocks. There are other clergy members on the way, as well."

"Sam knows everyone." June glanced around at the organized chaos. "Everyone's here or on their way, Baz. Every faith. It's overwhelming."

"It's inspiring."

They fell into an awkward silence. Construction was underway. The noise was deafening, the crush of people distracting.

He reached out, and when June took his hand, he silently led her through the crowded site. He targeted someplace quiet and private, barely making it into a copse of trees before pulling her into his arms and claiming her mouth in a torrid, possessive kiss.

She responded fervently, matching his passion, driving him mad.

Moments later she pushed him away to arm's length. "Wait. This is wrong. The timing is wrong. We're in the middle of a crisis."

"Right." He disentangled her hands from the back of his neck. He kissed her knuckles, then angled his head. "Every man has a weakness, Bug, and you're mine." He cursed the pang in his gut. "It scares me."

She shook her head. "Is this about us sleeping together? Are you worried I'm going to ask you to commit? I know you're not the marrying kind."

"Dammit, Juniper." Temper flaring, he released her hands and braced himself against a tree trunk. "You don't know me at all."

"It's just…" She hugged herself, looking flustered. "Us. Hooking up and talking about making a long-term commitment in one day after being estranged for eight years. Don't you think that's weird?"

He met her eyes steadily but didn't speak.

"Three Keepers all getting engaged within twenty-four hours. What are the chances? Unless…"

"Unless what?" He narrowed his eyes.

She broke his gaze, shrugged.

Oh, hell, no. "You're kidding, right? You think your cousins are bewitched? That some magical cast a Keeper love spell?"

"I didn't say that."

"You didn't have to."

"I just think it's weird."

"I get that!"

"Why are you angry?"

"Because I love you, dammit! Always have. Always will. And it's torture, quite frankly, because you don't have faith in my feelings. Hell, you don't have faith in anything." Furious, Baz straightened away from the tree. He could feel negative energy pulsing through him, skewing his judgment. He'd lost control. He'd lashed out. This was bad. "We should get back." He needed to cool off. To calm down.

He grasped June's hand and led her back toward the crowded building site. She didn't fight him. Didn't argue. Of course she didn't. Because even after reconnecting in bed, after he'd poured his genuine affection into their lovemaking, she couldn't take a leap of faith and believe that they were destined to be together. She didn't believe in soul mates. Or St. Nick. Or the magic of Christmas. He wanted to believe enough for the both of them, but all his optimism was submerged with the anger swirling inside him.

Maybe she was right to push him away. Looking toward the future, how could he spend his life married to a woman who tested his patience at every opportunity? Not to mention that the very thought of someone hurting her tempted him to do bad things in her defense. As a Keeper, she would knock heads occasionally with both humans and Others. Things could get rough. How would she feel if he lashed out in her defense? If he fell back into his old ways?

She wouldn't like it.

And neither would I.

Chapter 11

June was shell-shocked.

Baz loved her, although he didn't seem happy about it.

He'd caught her off guard with his declaration, with his anger. He'd intimated *marriage.* She was at a loss for words, and his hustling her back into the construction craziness didn't help. It was crowded and noisy, even more so than before. Christmas music blared from the Salem Common bandstand, where a group had set up and the lead singer was merrily belting out a rock version of "Joy to the World."

Baz let go of her hand and rejoined Father Chopra and the men who were constructing the frame of the temporary church.

She rubbed her palm across her forehead, trying to wrangle her thoughts and emotions.

A jolly bearded man was dressed as Santa Claus and seated on a velvet throne. Where had that come from? He was surrounded by costumed "elves"—Santa's helpers— and bags and bags of gifts. Children were waiting patiently in line.

"They're from the homeless shelter."

She started at the sound of Samantha's voice so close to her ear. "Don't sneak up on me like that."

"Who's sneaking?" Sam nudged her and smiled. "Get this. Word is spreading like crazy about this goodwill project. They're calling it the Winter Festival of Hope. One newscaster reported that a bunch of toys were destroyed in the fire. Toys that the congregation had intended for the less fortunate." She pointed to Santa and his elves. "All *those* toys? They were donated by children for children. Kids who woke up in warm houses, in their own beds, and who were treated to lots of gifts from Santa and their parents."

June's heart squeezed, and her eyes teared up. "That's amazing."

"It's just part of the magic you inspired today, cousin." Sam draped an arm around her shoulder and squeezed. "You're trembling! I know this is overwhelming, but—"

"It's not the show of selflessness, although that *is* incredible." June glanced over at Baz. He was working hard alongside his men. He looked intensely focused, and she felt a dash of regret that his focus was no longer directed at her. "I'm a little shaken up," June confessed. "Baz just…never mind."

Sam smiled. "There are worse things than being in love with Baz."

"Who says I'm in love?"

"Aren't you?"

"We've been estranged for eight years."

"And now you're not."

June swallowed a scream of frustration. Was she the only logical person on this planet? She shifted and looked at her cousin, the eldest and quite possibly wisest of her Salem cousins, in the eyes. "Don't you think it's weird that you, Katie Sue and Roe all got engaged within twenty-four hours?"

"No."

"Seriously?" June frowned. "And what if I… That would make *four* of us. In twenty-four hours. You don't think that's suspicious?"

"I think it's magical."

"That's what I'm worried about."

Now Sam frowned. "Oh, come on. You don't think… Thanks for the insult, June."

"What—"

"You don't think Daniel's actually in love with me? You think I don't know my own heart? That we're *be-witched*?"

June flushed, unsettled that she'd hurt Sam's feelings. "I didn't say that."

"But that's what you're thinking."

"I don't know what to think."

She was surrounded by merriment and goodwill. The music, the food, the gifts. The crush of people from every faith all working together to raise a church in one day.

A Christmas miracle.

Just then Roe and Katie Sue rushed up.

"Get this," Katie Sue said, wide-eyed and jazzed. "We were going around making sure all the workers had hot coffee and we got to talking to Emma Firestone."

"She's Wiccan," Roe said, "and she was telling us this ancient story. Something about how Norsemen believed the sun was a wheel of fire that would roll away from the earth and back."

June nodded. "I know the story." Just one of the many tales she'd learned in her studies. "They encouraged the return of the sun with bonfires, as well as logs that they burned in their homes. That's where we got the concept of Yule logs." She frowned in concentration. "I think I know where you're going with this. But I'm pretty sure the mayor would frown on giant bonfires in the park."

"Not that part," Katie Sue said. "The other part."

"The part where they decorated bows of evergreens with star-shaped ornaments in an effort to attract the sun back to the earth," Roe said. She waved an arm at all the surrounding snow-laden trees. "We could do that!"

At the very least it would be one more happy task pulling the townspeople together. June shrugged. "It couldn't hurt."

The two women whooped, then took off, hopped up on their counter-the-darkness mission.

"I'll help you," Sam said, running off before June could make amends for what she'd said earlier.

"Rats." She hadn't meant to diss Sam and Daniel's love. She knew their feelings were genuine. Deep down she had the same faith in the love between Roe and Vaughn, and Katie Sue and Jett. "So what's my problem with Baz?"

She turned just in time to see a statuesque woman walk up to Baz and start coming on to him. She blinked. It couldn't be, but it was.

Lolita Dorring.

June's blood burned, her heart pounded. She fisted her hands at her sides, itching to take a swing at that witch. Especially when Lolita leaned into Baz, then smirked over his shoulder at June. What the Devil?

A shiver iced down June's spine. *The Devil's magic.* That wasn't Lolita. Well, it was, but it wasn't. Marin had stolen her body. June sensed the warlock. Smelled the evil. Oh, yeah. That kind of wicked had a stench. What was he planning? What did he want?

To incite negativity. Violence. Intolerance.

Did he think that if he made June jealous she would attack Lolita? Cause a scene? Start a fight that would spread and envelop the town?

That was exactly what he wanted. For the woman who'd inspired the Winter Festival of Hope to go bat-shit crazy and sully the festivities. He wanted to feed off her hostility.

Nice try, warlock.

She was bigger than that. *Smarter* than that. Drawing on her studies and confidence, she shrugged and smiled, as if she didn't care two Christmas figs about Basel Collins. *He's all yours.* Interesting, though, that Baz's body language screamed "back off." Did he know that was Marin flirting with him and not Lolita? June didn't think so. And she couldn't tell him so with telepathy. That only worked when she was a cat. Baz had warned her about shifting under stress, and she'd already shifted too often in too short a time as it was. Dare she risk it? What if she was too weak to shift back into her human form? Ever?

Lolita—*Marin*—latched on to Baz's arm, directing him toward the trees. The warlock wouldn't zap Baz with one of his deadly lightning bolts right here in front of everyone. But in private…

Don't go into the trees! June screamed at him with her mind. *Not Lolita. Marin!*

She knew Baz couldn't hear her, but why was he following Lolita's cue when he clearly wasn't interested in her? He didn't want Lolita. Or any other woman. "He wants me! He loves me!" June shouted out loud. "And I love him! Marry me, Basel Collins! Right here. Right now."

Baz turned toward June, Lolita still clinging to his arm. The other woman looked a little dazed. Baz looked…shell-shocked.

But he was smiling.

June's heart hammered—with fear, with love. She needed to get in between Baz and Marin. If the warlock zapped anyone, let it be her.

She thought about shifting again, but she'd made herself the center of attention. She couldn't shapeshift in plain view of humans. She would have to do this as a human. As a Keeper. As Baz's soul mate. Something wonderful blossomed inside her as she moved toward the man she loved. Something powerful.

Faith.

Faith that their love was stronger than Marin's black magic. That good would conquer evil.

People parted like the Red Sea, and the music faded away. She heard whispers about true love and a Christmas wedding. "How romantic," someone said.

It *was* romantic. Even though June was ready to take a death zap from Marin in order to save Baz's life, she'd never felt more alive. "I love you, Basel Collins." She meant it with every fiber of her being.

His dark eyes danced. "I love *you,* Juniper Twist."

The air crackled. No, the *sky* crackled.

Everyone looked skyward. Except for Baz and June. They only had eyes for each other.

Lolita twitched, then went limp.

The warlock suddenly materialized beside her. Thank the universe, all the humans were focused on the sky.

"Marin," June whispered.

"I know," Baz said.

June's Keeper cousins and their lovers appeared as if out of nowhere, surrounding the powerful warlock. Only he didn't look so powerful now.

"Vengeance will be mine," he croaked.

"Not today, Marin." Esmeralda swept in, pinned

a huge sprig of mistletoe on him and smiled when he groaned in misery. She glanced at June, who was stunned to see the woman she'd dropped at home. "You thought I'd actually miss out on this show? Well done, Keeper."

June flushed with pride, her heart dancing with joy. Surrounded by friends and family and the spirit of good-will, she'd never felt more at home.

Baz passed Lolita over to Father Chopra, who was standing close, eyes wide with wonder. Fully focused on June, Baz took her hands in his. "You were saying?"

She could scarcely breathe. Something wonderful was happening—inside of her and up in the sky. "Will you marry me, Baz? I know I'm not perfect, but I'm yours. Heart and soul. If you want me."

His lips twitched. "Oh, I want you, Bug."

More crackling and flashing, and this time June couldn't help but look up at the heavens. She gasped along with everyone else when the black sky ripped open, revealing fissures of light.

Sunlight.

"We've got Marin under control," Daniel said.

"We'll be back," Sam said with a wink.

"Don't start the nuptials without us," Esmeralda added.

Every being—human and Other—of every faith let loose with a wave of "oohs" and "ahhs," along with a round of deafening applause, as life-giving sunshine broke through the last of the insidious dark. But instead of racing home to celebrate the return of the sun, every-one rushed back to work.

"Let's take advantage of the daylight!" someone yelled.

"We'll raise the church by midnight for sure," some-one else said.

Construction resumed. The music kicked up, a cheery rendition of "Winter Wonderland."

June glanced at her watch. One o'clock in the afternoon. She knew in her heart that sundown would come at a normal time. And that tomorrow morning and every morning after, Salem would enjoy hours of daylight just like the rest of the world. Basking in the sun and in Baz's love, she moved into his arms. "We did it."

He smoothed her hair out of her face, held her close. "You scared the hell out of me, taking on Marin like that. I was trying to get him away from you," he said. "Away from everyone."

"So you *did* know it was Marin."

He looked at her disbelievingly. "You thought I'd go off with Lolita?"

"No. Well, not to kiss her or anything. I had—*have*—faith in your feelings for me." She smiled up into her handsome lover's mesmerizing eyes. "We took on a powerful warlock without utilizing any supernatural skills. I wonder if that's what countered his curse?"

"You said it yourself, June Bug. Faith, belief and hope. That's powerful stuff."

"Enhanced with a double shot of love," she said. "It's pure magic."

Baz kissed her then, madly and deeply, in front of everyone. "I'm holding you to that marriage proposal, Bug."

She smiled up into his shining eyes. "As soon as your grandmother and my cousins get back."

"Happy Christmas, June."

"Merry Christmas, Baz."

Epilogue

Winters came with a vengeance to Salem, Massachusetts. Some more than most.

This last more than any.

Although centuries had passed since the infamous Salem witch trials, modern man had proved equally susceptible to mania and violence when spooked by the unknown. The terrible and perpetual darkness that had descended on the city had ravaged people of every faith, from Christian to Wiccan to Buddhist, pitting man against woman, human against Other.

Instead of the Devil, evil had come in the form of a renegade warlock. A wicked outcast intent on revenge, he'd worked heinous black magic, summoning evil thoughts and deeds, calling down never-ending darkness, inciting panic and hatred, testing beliefs, challenging love…

And yet goodness had triumphed.

Light had returned.

On Christmas Day.

Some rejoiced in the birth of a king, while others praised the rebirth of the sun.

Everyone celebrated a return to normalcy.

The mayor called the governor; the governor called the president.

The president called the experts at NASA.

Unaware of Otherworldly interference and unable to cite a scientific phenomenon, they declared the return of light a Christmas miracle.

Meanwhile, the citizens of Salem raised a church in a day and celebrated the impromptu weddings of four cousins known to the local Others as Keepers.

The spirit of giving, the power of faith and the wonder of love prevailed long after Christmas Day as Salem forged a bright future, learning yet again from past mistakes.

Maybe the Devil was in the forest, but he was not within their hearts.

* * * * *

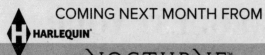

#173 DARK WOLF RUNNING • *Bloodrunners*
by Rhyannon Byrd

As a Dark Wolf, Elise Drake is one of the most powerful of her pack, and yet...she has a troubling secret. One she knows will never let her be with Wyatt Pallaton. Despite being fascinated by him, she knows her fear of him learning the truth keeps her from acting on her intense attraction to the sexy Bloodrunner. And now a new fear is consuming her—one that involves a mysterious stalker. But when she finds herself in Wyatt's tender care, she begins to consider letting her guard down...especially if it means getting closer to her protector.

#174 NIGHTMASTER • *Nightsiders*
by Susan Krinard

In order to learn the Nightsiders' plans to break the armistice between the vampire and human population, dhampir agent Trinity Ward must pose as a blood-serf, to be claimed by one of the most powerful Bloodmasters in the vampire kingdom: Ares. She is prepared to seduce Ares to become his mistress and win the privilege of accompanying him to Council meetings, where she hopes to learn the truth of the Council's plans. But as an intense attraction grows between them, they both become endangered by those who would separate and destroy them.

REQUEST YOUR FREE BOOKS!

2 FREE NOVELS FROM THE PARANORMAL ROMANCE COLLECTION PLUS 2 FREE GIFTS!

YES! Please send me 2 FREE novels from the Paranormal Romance Collection and my 2 FREE gifts (gifts are worth about $10). After receiving them, if I don't wish to receive any more books, I can return the shipping statement marked "cancel." If I don't cancel, I will receive 4 brand-new novels every month and be billed just $22.76 in the U.S. or $23.96 in Canada. That's a savings of at least 17% off the cover price of all 4 books. It's quite a bargain! Shipping and handling is just 50¢ per book in the U.S. and 75¢ per book in Canada.* I understand that accepting the 2 free books and gifts places me under no obligation to buy anything. I can always return a shipment and cancel at any time. Even if I never buy another book, the two free books and gifts are mine to keep forever.

237/337 HDN F4YC

Name	(PLEASE PRINT)	
Address		Apt. #
City	State/Prov.	Zip/Postal Code

Signature (if under 18, a parent or guardian must sign)

Mail to the Harlequin® Reader Service:
IN U.S.A.: P.O. Box 1867, Buffalo, NY 14240-1867
IN CANADA: P.O. Box 609, Fort Erie, Ontario L2A 5X3

Want to try two free books from another line?
Call 1-800-873-8635 or visit www.ReaderService.com.

* Terms and prices subject to change without notice. Prices do not include applicable taxes. Sales tax applicable in N.Y. Canadian residents will be charged applicable taxes. Offer not valid in Quebec. This offer is limited to one order per household. Not valid for current subscribers to Paranormal Romance Collection or Harlequin® Nocturne™ books. All orders subject to credit approval. Credit or debit balances in a customer's account(s) may be offset by any other outstanding balance owed by or to the customer. Please allow 4 to 6 weeks for delivery. Offer available while quantities last.

Your Privacy—The Harlequin® Reader Service is committed to protecting your privacy. Our Privacy Policy is available online at www.ReaderService.com or upon request from the Harlequin Reader Service.

We make a portion of our mailing list available to reputable third parties that offer products we believe may interest you. If you prefer that we not exchange your name with third parties, or if you wish to clarify or modify your communication preferences, please visit us at www.ReaderService.com/consumerschoice or write to us at Harlequin Reader Service Preference Service, P.O. Box 9062, Buffalo, NY 14269. Include your complete name and address.

SPECIAL EXCERPT FROM

HARLEQUIN®

NOCTURNE™

Read on for a sneak peak of

DARK WOLF RUNNING

by Rhyannon Byrd

When a deadly stalker makes Elise Drake
his prey, Bloodrunner Wyatt Pallaton will stop
at nothing to protect the scarred, beautiful
redhead...and make her his own.

With his sharp gaze locked on the most magnificent female he'd
ever set eyes on, Wyatt Pallaton did his best to choke back the
deep, aggressive growl rumbling up from his chest—and for
the most part, he succeeded. But then, *most* was a relative term.

With his large hands clenched into hard, straining fists in his
lap, Wyatt ground his jaw and tried like hell to keep it together.
But there was only so much that a man could endure. Based on
the pathetic fact that he was shaking apart inside with lust and
need and too many damn confusing emotions, he could only
assume that he'd finally reached his limit.

After months of biding his time, waiting for the stubborn
woman to acknowledge their attraction and come to him, he'd
had enough. Not surprising, he supposed, since as a primal,
aggressive male, waiting wasn't exactly one of his specialties.
Undeniably dominant in nature, the thirty-five year old Bloodrunner was accustomed to going after what he wanted with
single-minded intensity, not stopping until he had it—but
these were unusual circumstances.

And Elise Drake was a far cry from your average female.

Considering the length of time he'd been without a woman, he'd known tonight wouldn't be easy. He'd tried to stay calm, but the sight of Elise walking down the aisle in her bridesmaid gown, the flowing whisper of silver-gray silk accentuating the sumptuous perfection of her figure, had damn near done him in.

Of course, Elise Drake was hardly just any woman. Fiery and cool, strong and yet at the same time achingly vulnerable, she was a fascinating combination of opposites that had managed to turn his entire world on its head.

And no matter how bloody difficult it proved to be, he was done driving himself slowly into this maddening state of frustration. One way or another, things were about to change.

Come hell or high water, she was done running.

Will Wyatt and Elise come together in a blaze of passion, or will the past haunt them forever?

Don't miss the exciting conclusion of DARK WOLF RUNNING by Rhyannon Byrd, part of the Bloodrunners series

Available December 3, only from Harlequin® Nocturne™.

HARLEQUIN®

NOCTURNE™

Two very different worlds, each filled with lust and power…

Rumors of war are rumbling in the vampire city of Erebus. Undercover agent Trinity Ward must pose as a blood slave to unearth the truth and keep the peace between vampires and humans. Acting now as a serf to Ares—a powerful Bloodmaster—Trinity must give herself to him….

Yet one look into his striking eyes turns submission into burning desire.

NIGHTMASTER

by *NEW YORK TIMES* BESTSELLING AUTHOR

SUSAN KRINARD

**Available December 3,
only from Harlequin® Nocturne™.**

All she wants for Christmas is...

When they come home for Christmas, three military heroes have visions in their heads of things far sexier than sugarplums. But the women they love want more than just one very good night....

Pick up

A Soldier's Christmas

by *Leslie Kelly, Joanna Rock* and *Karen Foley,* available November 19 wherever you buy Harlequin Blaze books.

HARLEQUIN®

A *Romance* FOR EVERY MOOD™

Love the Harlequin book you just read?

Your opinion matters.

Review this book on your favorite
book site, review site, blog or your own
social media properties and share
your opinion with other readers!

Be sure to connect with us at:
Harlequin.com/Newsletters
Facebook.com/HarlequinBooks
Twitter.com/HarlequinBooks

HARLEQUIN®

A Romance FOR EVERY MOOD™

**Stay up-to-date on all your
romance-reading news with the
Harlequin Shopping Guide,
featuring bestselling authors, exciting new
miniseries, books to watch and more!**

The newest issue will be delivered right to you
with our compliments! There are 4 each year.

Signing up is easy.

EMAIL

ShoppingGuide@Harlequin.ca

WRITE TO US

HARLEQUIN BOOKS
Attention: Customer Service Department
P.O. Box 9057, Buffalo, NY 14269-9057

OR PHONE

1-800-873-8635 in the United States
1-888-343-9777 in Canada

Please allow 4-6 weeks for delivery of the first issue by mail.